Cathryn Todd is a retired registered nurse with over forty-years of experience of caring for older people. It wasn't until the 1990s that there was more research into caring for people with dementia, hence the author completed an MA in gerontology, and specialized in dementia care. Cathryn Todd lives in Manchester, UK, and is married with three children and two grandchildren.

To all the brilliant and caring people I have met, who work tirelessly to improve the lives of older people, and to all those we have cared for who have enriched our lives daily.
Also, my husband who gave me some peace and quiet to write, and supported me throughout.

Cathryn Todd

SHADED MEMORIES

AUSTIN MACAULEY PUBLISHERS™
LONDON * CAMBRIDGE * NEW YORK * SHARJAH

Copyright © Cathryn Todd 2021

The right of Cathryn Todd to be identified as author of this work has been asserted by the author in accordance with section 77 and 78 of the Copyright, Designs and Patents Act 1988.

All rights reserved. No part of this publication may be reproduced, stored in a retrieval system, or transmitted in any form or by any means, electronic, mechanical, photocopying, recording, or otherwise, without the prior permission of the publishers.

Any person who commits any unauthorised act in relation to this publication may be liable to criminal prosecution and civil claims for damages.

This is a work of fiction. Names, characters, businesses, places, events, locales, and incidents are either the products of the author's imagination or used in a fictitious manner. Any resemblance to actual persons, living or dead, or actual events is purely coincidental.

A CIP catalogue record for this title is available from the British Library.

ISBN 9781398400061 (Paperback)
ISBN 9781398400887 (ePub e-book)

www.austinmacauley.com

First Published 2021
Austin Macauley Publishers Ltd®
1 Canada Square
Canary Wharf
London
E14 5AA
+44 (0)20 7038 8212
+44 (0)20 3515 0352

Prologue

Mary eased herself slowly from the chair and looked around the room. She knew she had to leave this place, and she needed to get home. Slowly, Mary walked to the door. Moving around was difficult these days, she ached all over and her legs didn't respond to commands from her brain. "Must take my hand bag," she muttered. The handbag was all-important, nothing else mattered, and she could get the rest of her things later.

How she ever ended up in this place was beyond her comprehension. Oh it was clean enough and the food was passable, quite good actually and the people were not unkind. It was just that they didn't want to want to listen to her when she told them she wanted to go home. Come to think of it, they didn't listen to anything she said really. They made no effort to get to know her, probably because they were all so busy. Yes, that was it. The other problem was that Mary had a lot she wanted to say, but these days she couldn't find the words. Sometimes, she felt as though she was shouting, but the words just wouldn't come out.

Mary found her handbag; it was next to her bed where she always kept it. The handbag contained her prized possessions. In it she had her purse, door key and photograph. Also, there was her favourite pearl necklace, her comb and an embroidered handkerchief. Okay, she was ready now, ready to go home. Slowly but purposely she opened the door, and carefully she walked down the corridor to the front door, looking and listening all the time. It was further than she had thought, but she was grateful that she had made it. Mary opened the door, which to her surprise wasn't locked. She took a moment to breathe the fresh air, it was a long time since she had felt the breeze, seen the sun. She set off, anxious to get away from this place, eager to get to her own comfortable home. She knew she would be fine once she opened her own front door. She would prove them all wrong. She would be happy again.

Mary looked around hoping to see something or someone she recognised, but she could not see anything.

Mary stopped suddenly. She wished someone would help her, help her to be happy again. All Mary had to do now was to find a bus to take her to Oak hill, and then she would be fine, nearly home. She started walking but suddenly she felt dizzy, tired. It wasn't the first time this had happened. She managed to carry on walking, but her legs felt heavy. She could see the bus stop and a bench, and she managed to get there and sit down for a short rest. The bus will come soon she decided, and then she would be ready to go.

Chapter 1

Patsy

June 1997 and it was the first day in a new job for 20-year-old Patsy Bennett. Born into a single parent family, her mother had spent most of her time and her money in the local pub, added to which, she did some dodgy wheeling and dealing in the poverty-stricken part of town where they lived.

Then there were the many men that her mum took up with, none of whom stayed around very long, but her mum didn't seem to care. It didn't take long for Patsy as a young child to know that in order to have any kind of life she would have to survive on her own. Despite this, Patsy was a popular and pretty child, well liked in the area, chatty but polite with lots of friends. Thankfully, she did not get bullied, even though she regularly went to school, not only hungry but looking dishevelled in her second-hand clothes. Fortunately for her, she was not the only child living in similar circumstances; the area was rife with social problems.

Patsy was tall and slim with long blond hair, huge blue eyes and good bone structure. Education did not play a big part in Patsy's life. She left school with no qualifications. She had other things to think about and number one was surviving her home circumstances.

So, when she did leave school she had several jobs, working in a chip shop, a department store, and then a well-known supermarket. Patsy knew deep down that she needed more from a job, but she also knew she was lucky to be in work. Yes, she certainly knew that. At least she had some money at last, enough to get by. Her mum would ask her regularly to lend her money; Patsy always reluctantly gave in knowing the money would be spent on drink.

At the supermarket, she liked the customers. She had a good easy manner with them and she was as popular with them as she was with her workmates, but she always thought that there had to be more. Then reality would kick in and

Patsy would think to herself, I'm not very bright, never have been, this is probably the best I can do. There were possible prospects with the job, Patsy knew that, but in her head Patsy never saw herself progressing in any line of work.

She rented a bedsit when she was seventeen. It was dismal, but the rent was cheap and most importantly it represented freedom away from her mother's problems. The room was in an old Victorian house and divided into five beds bedsits. The other tenants were mostly older and down on their luck, all living their own lives with their own problems, and not having much time for anyone else in the house. Patsy struggled like the other tenants to pay the rent, but she was an independent and attractive woman now or so she used to tell herself so, it was worth the struggle. "Stay positive girl," she used to say to herself.

One day, Patsy was chatting to a customer as she was checking out the woman's shopping. She liked the checkout because she had contact with the customers. The young woman had a full basket full of groceries and Patsy noticed she was wearing a uniform. "Just finished work?" asked Patsy.

"Yes," said the woman, "I work in a care home looking after old people, love the job."

Patsy found herself telling the woman about how she would like a worthwhile job and the woman looked at Patsy, smiled and said,

"Well, if you really want a challenge why not try care work? It's hard graft but every day is different, oh and by the way, the pay is as terrible as the hours." And she smiled at Patsy.

"Isn't it depressing looking after old people?" asked Patsy.

"No, not at all. It can be sad sometimes when you get close to the people you care for and they are ill or they die, that's horrible, but most of the time in a good home it is a happy place and it gives you a good feeling, you know, helping people?"

Patsy thought long and hard about what that woman had said. It was crazy, she couldn't do that, but the more she thought about it, the more she knew she wanted a challenge.

"Yes, why not," she said out loud later that day, "I need the kind of job that I can get involved in, I'll give it a go." And Patsy was determined to make this work.

After numerous applications, not helped by the fact that Patsy found application forms difficult. She couldn't spell very well or so she told herself and as for what hobbies she had, well none really, no time and no money for luxuries. They all asked about hobbies, which Patsy found hard to comprehend. After all, what could hobbies possibly have to do with work?

One day, however when Patsy had almost lost hope in the notion of getting a job in care, she received an invitation for an interview at a good home with an excellent reputation. Despite her lack of experience, and her almost rough demeanour, the manager saw something promising in Patsy. Her beaming smile and the underlying intelligence, yes definitely something, and she offered Patsy a full-time job.

Patsy was so glad to have this job; she looked at it as a new beginning, better than stacking shelves in a supermarket or working in a factory. Not for me she thought, she would give this a go. After all how hard could it be looking after old people? The staff at the supermarket gave Patsy a good send off, although many of them couldn't understand her new choice of career, and even Patsy was having doubts as she walked through the door and into the nursing home.

The 3-day training course covered the basics, general health and safety and food hygiene, and how to move people safely. They were told most of the residents had dementia; some had physical disabilities as well. They were encouraged to treat people with respect and to always knock-on resident's doors before entering.

Patsy wasn't even sure what dementia was. They weren't given much information and Patsy didn't want to be the one to ask. She thought the others probably knew far more than she did. There were two other new carers on the course, Rosemary, or Rosie as she liked to be known, an outgoing dark-haired girl who was a couple of years older than Patsy, and Iris, a small quiet woman in her 30s, and Patsy soon found herself enjoying their company. They were all new and they all got on really well. Iris was married with two children and she had worked as a carer in hospital, so Patsy decided Iris must know everything.

Rosie was the youngest of six children, and like Patsy had tried numerous jobs before, but Rosie had worked as a carer in a home with a questionable reputation, so for her this was a good move. Patsy decided this job was turning out to be good, a new beginning; she had new friends and she had a career. They were all on a tea break one day and Patsy said in a low voice to Rosie and Iris,

"So do you two know all about dementia?" The other two looked blank and said they didn't but felt too stupid to admit that to anyone. Iris said she had come across many people with dementia but the condition had never been explained properly to her. "Just get on with it, I was told."

There was a brief pause and they all laughed at the realisation that not one of them had the courage to ask the question.

The layout of the home comprised of several separate areas where residents could live in smaller groups, a homelier environment was the idea. Each area had a team of care assistants and housekeeping staff, and a nurse led each team. In addition, there was one large commercial kitchen with a team run by a chef manager where all the meals were prepared. Patsy was assigned to an area, which had a pleasantly furnished communal lounge, and a small kitchen where tea, coffee and snacks could be prepared. The bedrooms were quite small; all furnished the same, a hospital bed, a wardrobe, chest of drawers, bedside table and an easy chair.

Those residents who had a close family who visited regularly had more personalised rooms, family photographs, better quality bedding, vases with fresh flowers, little touches provided by their nearest and dearest, all which made the room homelier. People who had no family or friends visiting had a sparser room with just the items provided, and hospital bedding, but nevertheless the rooms were bright and airy and all had an en-suite bathroom.

Patsy was surprised and pleased that she had survived the induction and on the fourth day, Patsy nervously went to her area wondering how the day would go. She was teamed with another carer, a girl called Jess who had worked as a carer for about a year. Jess was about the same age as Patsy, but small in stature with a short spiky haircut. Patsy was very nervous but excited at the same time to be doing the 'real work'.

Jess was quick to point out that the older people living at the home really had no idea what was going on.

"They babble on all day and wander so you have to take them back to their chairs or their rooms," she told Patsy.

Patsy asked, "Do you ever have time to talk properly to them and get to know them?"

Jess reluctantly replied,

"It's hard enough this job, cleaning them up and feeding them without trying to understand what's going on in their minds, and anyway we need our breaks and we wouldn't get them if we sat and tried talking to the old dears. We're the ones who do the work you know, not like these nurses who do a bit of paperwork. Management doesn't really know what we have to do."

Patsy knew that she didn't have any experience, but she didn't think much of Jess's approach to the job, and she wondered why someone like Jess would want to work there. The rest of her team were mainly women, with the exception of one or two men. All the carers were of varying ages. Most of them were very experienced and tolerant, and Patsy noticed how kind and caring they were towards the residents. They were also all kind to Patsy and helped her to settle in the work environment.

Rosie and Iris were assigned to different areas, but the three made sure that they would meet up at breaks and after work to check on each other. Patsy asked Iris things she didn't understand and, Iris always did her best to answer.

The work as Patsy soon discovered wasn't easy. The majority of the residents were incontinent, so there were endless processions taking people to the toilets and sometimes, because they were so busy, it was too late and incontinence pads and clothes had to be changed. Many of the residents wandered aimlessly all the time, and it was hard to get them to settle. Then at meal times, getting people to the tables was an art in itself, and encouraging people to eat was no easy task. There were people with swallowing difficulties and any liquids had to be thickened. Some of the residents ate in their own rooms, and many needed someone sitting with them at mealtimes to help them to eat their food.

Patsy was always kept busy but as she worked, she wondered more and more about these older people. What were their thoughts and what kind of lives they had led before they became ill? Patsy found herself loving all of them.

There was Albert who had owned a grocer's shop and was always giving tips about the best buys of the day. He treated everyone as though they were his customers, but when he was tired he would shout in a loud voice,

"OK, sorry, ladies and gentlemen, time for closing now."

Alice had been a dancer and spoke about her times in the chorus line at the Palladium. At some point in her life she had moved to Manchester, why and when no one seemed to know, but she still had a broad Cockney accent and often used the Cockney rhyming slang, which made everyone laugh.

Jim and Doreen were a married couple who had owned a pub in the centre of Manchester, bombed during the war and yet still standing, and they had endless stories about the characters who had frequented their establishment. Jim had dementia; Doreen had had several 'strokes' and was unable to walk.

Although Doreen did not have dementia and she didn't seem to notice Jim's forgetfulness at all. If Jim couldn't remember something, Doreen would step in with the answer and they would chat away to each other and to everyone else. They certainly both loved to chat. The couple had moved to the home because it was nearer to their four children who doted on mum and dad and visited daily. All their children had large families, and when they all visited together the home was certainly lively.

Edna was born and lived all her life in Manchester. She had given birth to ten children, some of whom lived locally and visited regularly. Sadly, Edna's husband had died some years before, but Edna talked about her children all the time, they were her life and she loved them with a passion.

Maureen, a fifty-six-year-old lady, had suffered a cerebral vascular accident, commonly known as a stroke. Maureen was exceptionally young to be in a nursing home, but there was nowhere else for her to go. Maureen was from a deprived area of Manchester and well known in her area as one of the local characters. She had lived in squalor for many years and was known for her feisty nature and the occasional fist fight when someone upset her, despite her being confined to a wheelchair. She was also known for frequently moving around the home in her wheelchair and helping herself to other people's belongings and then denying any wrongdoing vehemently.

On one occasion, she had taken credit cards, money and tools from a contractor who had been working in the home, and then despite being caught red handed by staff of stashing her ill-gotten gains in a drawer in her room, she appeared to be horrified that anyone should accuse her of being a thief. However, despite Maureen's dubious character she was well loved by staff, she was a lovable rogue. Yes, one thing Patsy did know, they were all interesting people with stories to tell.

She found herself particularly drawn towards Mary, a lovely 67-year-old attractive lady with dementia who had a warm smile and was very well spoken. A proper lady Patsy thought through and through, although, just like Maureen she did seem to be young to live in a nursing home. Most of the residents, apart from Maureen were a lot older; the average age was probably about eighty years old.

Mary hardly spoke, but then she would suddenly ask, "Where is she? Where is she?" and a concerned Patsy would respond by saying, "Who. Mary, who do you mean?" Mary would just look at her sadly and cry uncontrollably, and Patsy felt hopeless. It was a pattern and others too constantly asked about someone and their obvious grief did distress Patsy. Patsy wanted to help the distressed Mary and said so to Jess, who replied that it was a mistake to feel sorry for them,

"They talk rubbish half the time, it's just the way it is," she said in a matter-of-fact voice. Slightly irritated she continued, "Oh, and watch them, some of them will pinch you and hit you, and the language, well! So Patsy don't feel too sorry for them."

Patsy noticed people with dementia commonly used to ask, "Where are my children?" Or, "Where is my mother?"

"Part and parcel of the condition," Jess explained, "just tell them their mother has died and their children are now grownups." Jess sighed wearily and Patsy did not really understand her, but she sensed that these people were distressed, and she felt helpless because she didn't know how she could help them. Patsy tried to imagine what it was like being told what to do and being treated like a stupid person. Patsy knew she might hit or pinch someone quite easily if they treated her like that.

Chapter 2
Mary

Mary was back in her room, trying to reflect on what had happened. It was all so clear in her mind. She knew where she was going and she knew she had to get there but suddenly out of nowhere, three of them came running out of the front door shouting her name. They had taken her back to the room and offered to make her a cup of tea. She had tried to protest, to get them to leave her alone, but for some inexplicable reason the words would not leave her mouth. So she had no choice and she went with them. Now, she was back, back in that room, sitting on her chair and drinking a cup of tea, which had sugar in it. Why did they not even know that she didn't take sugar? She must have told them a hundred times, but they didn't hear her.

Mary sat in her room, as her thoughts turned to her parents and her life growing up. Her parents were very religious and very strict, but they weren't bad people, of that, Mary was sure. She wanted to explain all this to these people, to tell them about her past, show that she was a real person. Lost in thought, Mary laughed to herself as she remembered being described in one school report as a 'shy, lonely child who did quite well at school, good with figures and art and sensible. "Yes, that probably was me. Now they would describe me as a stupid old woman."

My family went to church every Sunday and the priest was a regular visitor to my home. My mother treated him like royalty, "More tea, Father? A piece of homemade cake perhaps?" I dreaded those visits. The priest always frightened me because he had a stern manner and spoke down to me; he did that with all children. I used to think that he had no time for anyone young. I didn't like religion then and I don't know. It never did anything for me; in fact it destroyed my life.

My parents were of the generation where they didn't believe in encouraging a girl to pursue an academic career, unlike my brother who went on to university, after serving in the RAF. The Second World War was a time, which affected all our lives unfortunately, but at least he could pursue an academic career. He did eventually become an eminent research scientist. *Funny,* Mary thought, *it all seems like it was yesterday.*

I attended a private convent school where the nuns concentrated on frightening us girls and preached constantly about the sins of the flesh. I was never quite sure exactly what they meant until she the latter years of school life. Sadly, I should have liked to go on and study art and design, but that wasn't to be. Instead, I was expected to take a mediocre job until I got married, and then I would spend my days staying at home looking after my own family. At that time of my life, I accepted all this, never thought to question any of it. Why didn't I question it? Mary thought, but then she was happy enough to go along with it, that was the way in those days.

Someone coming into her room interrupted Mary's thoughts and telling her it was time to get ready for bed. The evening sun was still quite bright and Mary wondered what time it was, surely it was too early, she wasn't tired, but she didn't object. Instead, she allowed herself be helped to wash and be put into her nightie and helped into bed. The woman, not unkind drew the curtains and wished her goodnight.

Mary lay in bed, thinking about her first job. It gave her some comfort to remember a time when everything felt normal, not like now. The job was at the post office, or as it was then known, the GPO.

"There's no point in you staying any longer at school," my mother had said, "May as well earn a living and one day you'll have your own family and you don't need learning for that."

I just did what I was told, Mary thought. Just like I have to do now, but I don't have to, don't want to do that now. Still wide awake, I'm back to my time at the GPO that I can remember. Women staffed the exchange during the day and men during the night. Staff had to have a good speaking voice and be of a certain height in order to reach the top sockets of the junction box. At the GPO, I was taught how to answer the calls promptly, and yet again, looking back that was also a strict regime, but we did have some fun, us girls. Mary laughed to herself when she thought of some of the customers, some of the things they used to say.

The supervisor would be in charge of five or six operators, while the chief supervisor oversaw all the staff working the shift. The chief operator was the strictest and had to be treated with the utmost respect. People would put on their 'telephone voice' when asking to be put through to a number and as the staff knew most of them, we knew that they didn't normally speak like that, which always made us giggle, especially when we met them outside work and they were speaking in their normal voices.

Mary still didn't feel like sleeping; the nights seemed endless in that place. Occasionally, someone would quietly come into her room, which Mary objected to. Why couldn't they leave her alone? Mary struggled to get comfortable, she needed her own bed and her own pillows, but she settled back into her memories, back to when she was a young girl.

Tall and willowy, thin really, and with long dark brown hair which she would put in rags after washing her hair to make it curly, as was the fashion. She had always been proud of her hair, because it was her most attractive asset. Mary knew that she still had nice hair but these days she needed help to style it, and it was not always styled just how she liked it.

I had some good friends then, and as I got older we used to get up to all sorts, going out altogether, only to the cinema or for coffee or to the pub. Mary knew her mother and father did not approve of all their antics. They were all boy mad but in a light-hearted way. It was never serious and we were all very proper. Sex wasn't on our agenda, well I certainly didn't really know much about it. I met a boy one night in the pub. I thought he was very handsome, he was on leave from the army with some friends and I was there with my friends from work. We all socialised together, had a drink and a laugh and by the end of the night, this boy had arranged to meet me on Saturday, just he and I to go to see a film, and that was it, my first proper boyfriend.

I was eighteen and he was 22, tall with reddish hair and very handsome in his uniform, and I thought he was the most handsome man I had ever met. Joe knew everything about life, well at the time I thought he did. He would talk to me about his escapades and about world affairs and I really loved him and thought that he loved me too.

My parents were not pleased with the relationship, Mary laughed to herself.

"You're far too young," my mother would say, but her words fell on deaf ears. Joe was invited to my home for tea, only the once so they could meet him. It was an uncomfortable experience for me, even harder for poor Joe. We had spam sandwiches and plain cake made from powdered eggs, the standard meal when we had guests, mainly because food was still rationed.

My parents asked him endless questions about his job prospects, and in between the questions there were long silent periods and disapproving looks from my parents. When Joe left, my father told me that I could do better, and my mother remarked that his hair was untidy considering he was in the services and then she said kindly, "Never mind love, the right one will come along."

Joe was intelligent and worldly with skills he had learned in the army so it wasn't like he had no prospects. I thought he was very respectable and handsome, I didn't care what my parents thought. We had some good times, we went to the pictures and we went dancing. He told me I was beautiful and I believed him, because he made me feel beautiful.

The door opens and another woman who Mary vaguely recognises peers through the door, "You OK, Mary? Still awake, it's late love, try and sleep."

Mary objected to being referred to as 'love' by this young woman but she nods and attempts to smile.

"Do you need the toilet Mary?" the woman asks.

Mary wonders why these strangers think it's acceptable to ask such personal questions but it seems to be common practice here. After being helped to the toilet, Mary is helped back into bed. "Night, night, don't let the bugs bite," the woman says.

I lie here and think; there is nothing here to remind me of my old life, it's all very modern, nothing like my home. I really cannot remember how I came to live here. I do recognise some of my lovely clothes but I also have other clothes in my wardrobe, clothes that I would never wear. They must belong to someone else. Apart from the clothes I carry everything dear to me in a handbag, which I keep with me at all, times.

I know I am not in the best of health but despite what they say, "Mary you can't manage, you need looking after," I know they are wrong. I could manage in my own home where I want to be. Good gracious, don't they know I have always taken care of myself? I had to learn to be independent, earn a living and take care of myself.

The people who look after me, they look like nurses, well they wear uniforms and they give me tablets, too many tablets in my opinion. What are they all for? I never used to take even an aspirin. Most of them seem to be genuinely kind people, there are a few exceptions, but they are all so busy, and they don't have the time to talk to me. If they did I might get some answers, but they don't, so I sit here day after day and I look back and remember. That's all I can do now. That and try and get back to my home.

In the office of the nursing home where Mary Reynolds lives, the staff discuss Mary's latest attempt to leave.

"I know you mean well," a nurse explains to the carers, "but Mary has vascular dementia and all she wants to do is to go home to her life as she knows it. Mary doesn't know she is ill, she can't understand why we won't let her leave. Next time, walk with her, outside if necessary until she can be persuaded to come back into the home."

The three carers listen and nod but Rachael could see that they still don't understand.

Chapter 3
Patsy

Mary played on Patsy's mind for some reason, but when Patsy asked Jess one day if Mary had any family, Jess was adamant that as far as she knew, Mary had never been married and only had one brother who very rarely visited.

"Sometimes she has a middle-aged woman who comes to see her, Annie I think she's called, but I don't think she is local and she doesn't come often. No relation I don't think."

"Mary's so much younger than the others," Patsy remarked but Jess said that she may be younger but she was still 'all mad', a remark that annoyed Patsy and she was quick to tell Jess.

"She's ill Jess, not stupid, none of these people are." Jess shrugged and told Patsy that she had a lot to learn.

So gradually Patsy settled into her new job and loved it. There was so much to absorb, turned out it wasn't easy caring for older people. However, despite the disability of dementia, along with other illnesses, Patsy discovered that older people told interesting stories, and staff and residents spent much of their day laughing and joining in the conversations whenever they had the time.

Patsy loved all these conversations she had when she was helping someone to bed or bathing them or helping them with their meals. She enjoyed these times the most because she had the time to chat to them. More and more Patsy began to realise that these people she was caring for may have an illness, but they were real people who had led interesting lives, had relationships, children, jobs, lovers. Oh yes, they all had a story even if they couldn't always explain the full story.

The nurses, who mainly gave out the medications and did dressings and coped with the endless paperwork, did not have much time for hands on care. They were always there for help and advice, but the care assistants did the bulk of the actual day-to-day care. The carers varied, most really kind and dedicated.

The older women had their own routines, but they took their responsibilities seriously and really did care. A few were either lazy or indifferent.

Because Patsy was young, she often got the running jobs, "Run and get me the nurse love, your legs are younger than mine."

"Run and get some clean sheets pet, you're quicker than me." Patsy soon learned her place in the pecking order. Jess was well meaning enough if a little brusque, but it was obvious to Patsy that this was just a job to Jess until something better turned up. Jess preferred to spend time in the laundry where she could have a quick cigarette, which she frequently did.

There were laughs though at break times when staff would discuss all manner of topics. The older staff had many a tale to tell about caring for people in the 'old days' and how strict the regime had been. Some of them had worked in geriatric wards in the hospitals, and they spoke about long hours and having to take orders all day but their devotion for the job was evident. They spoke of having only one carer and one nurse to look after thirty patients, and how they had blisters on their feet from the long shifts.

Patsy noticed that they talked about their work but said very little about the actual personalities of the people they cared for. The care was there, they weren't unkind, but they were perceived as just old people in a bed, or sat on a chair where they were put, and that was that.

The younger ones were just as dedicated, but they would be talking more about their love lives and would arrange nights out. They would probably all go to the local pub about once a month when their shifts allowed. These outings were popular and most of the staff looked forward to having a few drinks and a laugh.

There weren't many job perks, as the lady in the supermarket had said, but staff could have free meals while they were on duty. This meant that Patsy could have a hot meal and snacks, which saved her own money and time, spent shopping and cooking.

Patsy wanted to know so much more about dementia so she could help her residents more, but she knew that her education was sadly lacking. No one seemed to know much about the condition. She asked some of the nurses what they knew and how she could help the residents more.

"What do I do when Edna walks to the door trying to go and pick her children up from school?" Patsy asked one of the nurses.

"You tell her that her children are grown up now, it's called reality orientation and it brings them back to the present time, back to reality. The only way really is to tell them the truth." The nurse was adamant about that.

Patsy tried that the next time Edna went to the door, "Let me out, it's time to get my kids from school," Edna shouted, and Patsy would give the reality orientation a try,

"Come on, Edna love, your kids are all grown up now, think about it, you're 82 years old now Let's sit down."

Edna sat down for a few minutes but then made for the door again. Patsy tried telling Edna, "Your daughter was here earlier Edna, remember? She brought her kids with her," and Edna agreed and settled but 5 minutes later, Edna would go back to the door shouting, "I have to get my children from school, they want their tea."

This could go on for quite long periods, often in the late afternoon when the schoolchildren had long since gone home, but Edna would get more and more distressed. Patsy knew that this reality orientation didn't work.

It had been six months since Patsy started her job, she had settled well and learned a lot. There were so many bad stories about nursing homes but Patsy knew that in this nursing home, the residents were looked after well. There was a good team spirit; the working conditions were not bad compared to other jobs. The pay wasn't great but Patsy loved her job, she definitely loved helping people.

One shift, Patsy was working alongside one of the nurses called Rachael, and when they went for their break, Patsy mentioned that she would like to know more about dementia. Rachael was visibly impressed and told Patsy about several books and articles she knew of which might give Patsy more of an insight, although, Rachael remarked,

"It is like hitting your head against a brick wall, people have their own ideas and changing care practice is not always easy. I want to know more too but I try telling people what I've learned, and I've found that old habits die hard, the most dedicated carers think I'm mad. Most of them think that we should lock the doors and never let our residents through the door; they say they are safer and you can see the logic. The new research is harder to practice but in the end, I believe it is so worthwhile."

Patsy mentioned the reality orientation she had been told about and Rachael explained that the new thinking was not reality orientation. There were several articles written about validation therapy, most notably by one of the first, 'Naomi

Feil.' The therapy explains that it is more effective going with the person's feelings and having empathy with the person's distress. Rachael explained that to tell someone like Edna that her children, who she wanted to pick up from school were now all grown up might appear to be a kind rational explanation to us but not to Edna,

"What you have to remember Patsy is that in Edna's mind and more importantly, in Edna's time, she is a young mum who is looking after her children, and you will not persuade her otherwise. Give it a go, read and see," and with that, she went to her locker and gave Patsy a recent article.

Patsy went home that night deep in thought about what Rachael had said and it made sense. Anyway, it was worth looking into it more she decided but it wasn't going to be easy. For a start, reading didn't come naturally. She couldn't remember when she had last read a book.

"I'm just not that bright," Patsy spoke out loud, but she started to read the article anyway, and found that she could not stop reading.

The next day, Patsy went into Mary to assist her getting up and dressed and Patsy, in her breezy manner was chatting away when Mary grabbed Patsy's arm and asked, "Will you help me find her?"

Patsy hadn't got a clue what Mary meant but she did know that Mary was very distressed.

"Find who Mary?" she asked. Mary started crying and Patsy put her arm gently around Mary to comfort her, which seemed to help, but Patsy felt totally out of her depth. That incident made Patsy think about how she had handled the conversation and she knew then that her only chance of helping Mary and all the others was to knuckle down and find out more about dementia. Come on girl, she told herself; you've got to do it. Get learning!

Patsy was determined to learn as much as she could about dementia, so at the first opportunity she went to see the manager of the home. Rita Lovell was a kind jolly lady in her 50s, an attractive woman, if a bit overweight. She was a qualified nurse with years of experience and Patsy was nervous. She wasn't sure what reaction she would receive, but she started to tell Rita what she thought, why she needed to learn more, and she waited for Rita's answer.

Rita listened patiently to Patsy and then there was what seemed to Patsy to be a deafening silence, but eventually Rita leaned over and spoke kindly to Patsy.

"I know how hard it can be, trying to understand how to help in a positive way. For years, we have treated these poor people without understanding what our patients are thinking, not knowing about their lives before the illness. We're good at keeping them all physically well cared for, we know about their physical problems, but we know so little about how to help with their feelings and their frustrations. There is more research now but it's very new and not widely available to many health care professionals."

Rita thought for a minute and then continued, "Tell you what, Rachael has done some research in dementia, she's interested in the subject and I did ask her to keep me up to date so we can all improve our care. I'll have a word and get her to take you under her wing. Believe me I'm right behind you, and I shall support you in whatever way I can, I'm impressed Patsy, I knew I was right about you."

Chapter 4
Mary

The days go by so slowly; oh they do their best I suppose. We have concerts and arts and crafts, various different activities to occupy the days, but I can't move around like I used to. I walk very slowly now and they tell me I need help. They are forever telling me I have fallen several times, but that's just not true. I don't fall when I walk to the front door. I do know that I can't always do what I want to anymore, but sometimes it's so hard to remember why. What did happen to me?

The meal times are the highlight of the day. It's a chance to move to a different area and have contact with other people although we don't really talk much. I don't talk much. I don't want to talk much these days and sometimes I just stay in my room. The food is quite palatable, I'm not a fussy eater but I don't have much of an appetite anymore.

The people in uniforms talk to us, which I appreciate, and some of the other people talk, but it doesn't always make much sense. I used to love chatting to people at work, but it's funny, the words don't come easily anymore. I've lived on my own for a long time and yet I have never felt as lonely as I do now.

The door to my room opens and one of the nurses comes in. "Do you want to come down to the concert, Mary?" she asks. "It might just cheer you up a bit to listen to some music."

She means well I know, but I would rather stay here and think, think about those times in my life. I try to explain but it's hopeless. I cannot find the words, so instead I smile and manage to answer, "No, thank you, dear." And she leaves me alone.

What I would really like is to sit in the sun and get out and about but that never happens now. I never go anywhere. I used to read a lot, but nowadays I can't concentrate. The television in the lounge is always on but that doesn't interest me. All I have are my memories and sometimes they are not clear. Did I really have that life? It is so long ago and yet in many ways, I don't feel old, but I sometimes wonder how old I am? Apart from my disabilities, which I don't understand fully, my mind still feels like that off a young girl.

There is a hairdresser who comes here and as I sit in front of the mirror getting my hair done, I see a face I don't recognise, an old lady with grey hair and no makeup. I used to love getting my hair done, and I always wore makeup, not a lot but still it brightened me up and made me feel attractive. I was never known as a beauty but I took pride in my appearance, I always wore nice clothes and I was always told that I was an attractive woman.

Strange really how I can remember things that happened so long ago, although I remember it as if it was all so recent. I sit in my chair in this place and I remember my life, a life that was always busy. Now everything is so confusing, I am not able to explain exactly how I came to be in this place. I wish someone could explain it all to me.

I had a chance of getting married and possibly even a family, and I did meet other young men, but after Joe, well afterwards nothing was ever the same. I was frightened for a long time of giving my love to another man; somehow to love meant I might find myself on my own again. I became a loner, I had no friends, and I never went out.

I got a job as a receptionist, bookkeeper in a small builder's merchant. Not my choice of job, but with my check history, I couldn't afford the luxury of being choosy, however it did prove to be a useful experience and at least it took my mind off things. I was always courteous to the customers, would work long hours and before too long I became an invaluable employee, but I can't say that I was ever happy.

The owner of the yard Mr Stewart was a hardworking, unassuming man who was happily married with two sons. After a relatively short time of working for Mr Stewart, he announced to me one day that he was promoting me to office manager. Although I was flattered by the praise, it also struck me as rather funny as I was the only person aside from him in the office, and Mr Stewart was out of the office a lot looking after customers and supervising deliveries. Nevertheless, the promotion also carried a salary increase and for that I was forever grateful.

I knew that I had to continue to live at home with my parents. I also knew things would never be the same, but it would enable me to save more money and eventually become independent. I always knew that I had to leave home; we hardly spoke anymore, my parents and I. They appeared to have washed their hands of me. I was unhappy, but looking back, I was always strong and determined.

Mr Stewart was a good boss, very amiable and kind. I think he felt sorry for me and he was always asking me how I was. He appeared to be concerned, and when Mrs Stewart used to come to the office she always made a point of telling me that I was welcome at their house any time. I was appreciative of their kindness, they were nice people but of course they could never understand what had happened to me, and that my life could never be the same again. My life was only about providing a future to put right my mistakes. Of course, I would never share that thought with Mr Stewart and his lovely wife, or indeed with anyone else.

When there was overtime to be had, I was there much to Mr Stewart's delight. My predecessor from the little I knew about her had been a reluctant worker, turning up late for work and with a string of excuses to leave early or to not turn up at work on many occasions. I think the Stewarts were secretly relieved when she left.

The business was booming and there was always work to be done, and when Christmas was fast approaching, I was given a small bonus and to my amazement, another pay rise in appreciation for my hard work. I always gave my mother money for room and board, but I spent little on myself. I had one good business suit and a couple of smart blouses for work. Apart from that, I never went out and most of my money went straight into the bank.

Christmas was always a miserable time at home, no presents were exchanged any more, no family happiness. My parents expected me to attend church, which I reluctantly did to keep the peace, but I had no time for religion. I asked myself why God would want me to be punished so harshly, but there was never an answer.

By the time I was 30 years old, I had saved a considerable sum of money and I was looking for a business of my own. I found a little shop in a small village called Oak hill and my plan, well more than that; it was my dream to open it as a quality dress shop. Much to my surprise, my parents gave me the balance to buy the shop outright. I am not sure whether they felt guilty or whether they just felt sorry for me, or even that they wanted the house to themselves. I had to admit that I had been pretty miserable company for years, as had they, and there always was too little left unsaid. The Stewarts were sad to see me leave, but Mr Stewart gave me a hefty leaving bonus and wished me well.

Oak hill was a small village in those days, a very leafy and respectable area. The locals, mainly housewives or career women would have to travel into the large towns to buy their clothes so, there was a market for me to offer quality clothes at competitive prices in a friendly environment. My love of art paid off and I discovered I was able to choose classy and fashionable clothes for my discerning customers. Word soon spread and people used to come from all over to buy my fashions.

I was never pushy with the customers, always polite and friendly, but they liked the way I would spend the time with them choosing the clothes, which flattered their appearance. I certainly would never allow them to buy clothes that didn't suit them and in the main, my advice I think was appreciated.

The shop had a small one-bedroom flat above where I lived, which was my pride and joy, furnished with taste and love and always clean and tidy. At the end of every busy day, I would retire to the comfort of my flat and look for new purchases, new trends to stock my shop. I never forgot what happened, that terrible time, I thought about my secret every day but life had to go on. My goal was to earn a good living and hope beyond hope that my nightmare would be over one day.

I was always busy, probably why I didn't have time for friends, and I had come to be something of a loner. Not much of a life for a young woman some might think but I had had enough excitement, enough trauma and besides I was an entrepreneur. I had my customers to talk to. I was busy and I was happy.

Other shop owners in the village were mainly either businessmen or couples, all older than me. Some of the wives I think looked down on me when I first opened the shop because of my age. They thought my business would bring the area down, after all someone of my age must be selling this new fashion rubbish rather that quality. But, over time I earned the respect and the custom of many, if not all of the women in the area.

It was 1960 and it was a time of change for us all. A good time to be in the fashion industry, new fashions, and new designers went alongside new music, and films. It was a time of liberation alongside plenty of jobs and more money in general for the majority, after the lean times during and straight after the Second World War.

By 1966, my business was so successful; I felt that I needed to expand. The whole village was also growing. Indeed by that time we even had a Woolworth store. That arrival had caused great excitement in the village when it was built, because we all knew we were not just a small suburban village any more. Oak hill was now on the map.

Some of the locals were not too happy, they saw change as a bad thing, and they preferred the village to stay as it was, but for me it was an exciting time. I rarely went back to visit my parents, there was nothing to say really; nothing could ever be the same. My father died suddenly, and a short time afterward, only a couple of months in fact, my mother died. Despite everything, they did love each other. We had never really talked and I think they were happier when I left. We had drifted apart a long time ago; I was always an embarrassment to them, a reminder. If only we could have spoken about the incident, but that was never an option. Their estate was left to Bill and I, quite a considerable amount surprisingly, but the money meant nothing. I was comfortable materially, and I had no time for emotions. I could never forgive them.

A couple of months later, the owner of the shop next door to mine sadly died and his relatives decided to sell, that was my opportunity to jump in. I was in the right place at the right time, and thanks to my success, and my inheritance, I had the money. I had big plans for the extension to knock into next door but I needed to find a reliable builder and shop fitter to make the necessary alterations, and that was how I came to meet Eric Bradley. Eric was in his early 40s and came to me highly recommended and with an impressive portfolio. Together we planned to make the two shops into one with the stipulation that it would cause the least interruption to my business.

Eric was easy to work with, he had good practical ideas and as the work progressed with Eric and his team, the shop was looking good. We spent so much time with the shop project that we were somehow drawn towards each other and quickly became not only colleagues but also friends. He was easy to talk to and for the first time in years, I found myself laughing and enjoying being happy in a man's company.

One day, we were sitting having a cup of tea and Eric told me that he had been married very young, but that his wife had died a few years ago of cancer.

"I was devastated," he told me, "but I just threw myself into my business. We never had children, and now I live on my own and that's fine, but it can be a lonely existence sometimes."

As he spoke to me, I understood completely his grief and loneliness.

Eric wasn't particularly good looking, but he was warm and hardworking. He knew his trade and in between working we laughed a lot together. He was well known in the area, he had done work locally, although he travelled from the other side of Manchester where he lived.

Eric asked me if I would like to go out for dinner. He knew of a good local restaurant near my shop, and although I also knew of the restaurant, mainly because the owner used to come into my shop regularly to buy her clothes. I had never eaten in her establishment, well I was too busy to go out to eat, and I had no one to go with and besides I was always tired after my long days. Still, I did like Eric a lot and it would be a nice change to have somewhere to go, and someone to go with and so I readily agreed to go.

It was later that evening that we were sitting in the restaurant looking at the menu. I had a glass of wine, Eric a beer while we decided what to order. The owner made such a fuss of us, she seemed to be pleased, judging by some of her comments she made, to see this young woman, me, finally getting some sense and enjoying an evening out. The other diners, all people I knew, politely acknowledged Eric and I, but there was a fair amount of whispering and looking over at our table, much to our amusement.

We discussed some finer points about the shop and where we were up to with the build and refurbishment, and then we talked, and I mean we really talked and laughed and had a really enjoyable evening, and as he walked me back home, I think we both knew there was something special between us.

That was the start of many outings, and as the work progressed on the shop, so did our relationship, until it wasn't long before Eric didn't have to travel home to the other side of Manchester every night. He would stop over a couple of nights a week in my bed in my cosy flat and I was happy.

"Why not just move in Eric?" I asked him one evening.

"Still got my house to see to luv, and we can't have too much of a good thing." And we both laughed and that was the last we spoke of it.

We had been out to the theatre in Manchester to see a new film, "A man for all seasons." It was an Oscar winner and had great reviews. Afterwards we went into Chinatown and had a meal. It was a perfect evening and I found myself wondering why I had lived such a lonely life. It didn't matter I told myself and anyway some day we shall be together when we get married. I even thought I might be lucky enough to get pregnant.

The shop was ready, and I was delighted with the results of all the hard work. It was wonderful, very tasteful with the new fittings and pale pastel decor. There were armchairs strategically placed on the thick carpets, and several large mirrors so the clients could wander around the shop and see the clothes in the good lighting.

I arranged a grand opening, organised caterers and made sure my stock was current and tasteful. The evening was a huge success. My shop was widely known and with extra space, I had been able to introduce more lines, which were paraded expertly by the models I had hired for the opening of the extended space. Eric was by my side as always, my Eric, so reliable. He was accepted by the community now as part of my life, so no stranger looks in our direction as we mingled with the guests, his arm always around me.

My business went from strength to strength, and by the time I was forty, I could confidently call myself a wealthy woman. Eric and I had our relationship, which hadn't changed or moved forward. I was disappointed that he had never mentioned marriage possibly even more disappointed that I had never managed to get pregnant. I desperately wanted to have the chance to be a mother. That was not meant to be, I had to accept that, but I was in love with Eric and I felt my life was fuller with him. I was happy with my role in life, and time ticked along nicely.

Chapter 5
Patsy

It wasn't too long after her meeting with Rita, that Rachael approached Patsy to discuss their plan to broaden their knowledge. It turned out that Rachael had done quite a lot of research and she was excited that Patsy wanted to do the same, but Patsy was nervous. She decided to explain how she felt,

"Look, Rachael, I want to learn, very much as a matter of a fact but I'm not good at book work, never did well at school, in short, I'm not the brightest button in the box."

Rachael laughed, "Let's just take it slowly, Patsy, this is how it goes. I shall give you a book, you read it and then we meet to discuss it. OK?"

"I'll give it a try, thanks Rachael," said Patsy.

"Fine, the first book is this one," Rachael said as she handed Patsy a book, not too thick Patsy thought as she looked through it. "This book by Tom Kitwood caught my interest," Rachael said. "He's a psychologist and it's easy to read, but see what you think?" And with that Rachael walked off and left Patsy with many thoughts, the main one being, "Shall I be able to do this?"

Later that same day, Patsy sat in her bedsit with the book. One of the people in another flat was playing some music loudly which, Patsy thought was not helping her studies. Patsy tried hard to remember about the last time she had read a book and gave up. She finally settled on her bed with a packet of cheese and onion crisps and a glass of Coca Cola and with a sudden determination to do this, she started to read.

An hour and a half later she put down the book, she hadn't even heard the loud music anymore. She started to get ready for bed; after all she had an early shift the next day. When she was settled in bed sometime later, she went to switch the light off, and then she picked the book up and carried on reading.

The next day Patsy couldn't wait to speak to Rachael, and when they did finally get a few minutes to talk, Patsy was full of enthusiasm, "It is fantastic, it's easy to read even for someone like me. He talks about treating someone with dementia just as you would like someone to treat you, and he talks about 'person centred care', which is all about treating the person, not the illness."

It made total sense Rachael. "We need to find out as much as we can about the people we care for and then we can communicate with them."

"Surely it can't be that easy?" Patsy sighed.

"I don't think it is easy," said Rachael, "but it does get you thinking about the person and not the illness, and by the way, stop putting yourself down. I know a lot of very educated people who have never bothered to try and help or understand like you're trying to do."

Patsy was excited, "When I finish that book what else can I read?"

"Don't worry, I'll give you another book, must admit you have got a passion for this, I think we'll work well together," Rachael said smiling.

The next day after work, Patsy sat with the residents talking to them and asking questions about their lives. Many of the answers were vague and in different times. They talked about the war, about their young children, their jobs; it was as if they had never become old. Some of the residents did not speak at all and Patsy wondered how she could reach out to them. Patsy reflected on what Rachael had said about it not being easy, but Patsy was determined to find a way, and she was convinced that learning as much as she could about dementia and the people she looked after was the key.

It was late afternoon, Edna was standing by the door ready to go to school for her children and getting very distressed because she couldn't open the door. Patsy gently put her arm around Edna and said to her, "Edna, you are upset, aren't you? Let's go and get some tea and have a chat." Edna nodded and reached for Patsy's hand and miraculously, in that moment Edna forgot her distress. Patsy sat with Edna while she had her cup of tea and Edna told her very calmly about each one of her children. Patsy was gratified that the validation technique she had learned about had been successful with Edna. Edna was certainly much less distressed than Patsy had seen her previously. She was also aware that there would be times when it would not be so successful, but she was convinced that she had learned something valuable.

Patsy left work and set off for home and then suddenly remembered she was supposed to meet some of the girls in the pub. Patsy desperately wanted to get home to read her book, but she also didn't want to let her workmates down, so just after eight pm, she walked into the local. There were about eight girls there all out for a good night and the chatter flowed easily. Patsy loved these nights out normally and she knew her search for knowledge would have to wait until the next day, so she settled down to an evening of drink and laughs. Several men in the pub kept looking over at the girls, which led to giggling and whispering about who they fancied the most, but Patsy knew she didn't have time for men, she had more important things to do.

Rosie and Iris were both on the night out, Iris didn't stay long, she had her husband and two kids to go home to but before she left she said how great she thought it was that Patsy was trying hard to understand dementia,

"I really admire you Patsy," she said. "I've struggled to know how to care for people with dementia for years. Nothing was ever explained to me the way you have, it will make our job so much easier and I finally feel we are getting somewhere."

After Iris had left, Rosie took Patsy to one side,

"Look Patsy, I've seen this flat advertised, how about us sharing? It's not a bad size and we can have some fun, besides it gets you out of that crummy bedsit?"

"Sounds great" Patsy said, "When can we go and see it?"

The two girls met after work the next day, the flat was a five-minute walk from the home and had a living room, a small kitchen and a bedroom. The bathroom was shared with another of the flats but that didn't bother the girls. "Won't you miss your family, Rosie?" Patsy asked.

"Of course, but we are a bit overcrowded at home and it's high time I spread my wings, and besides you can come home with me and meet the crowd. My mum makes a great Sunday dinner."

The rent was manageable for both of them and for Patsy the thought of having someone to share with and to have more room, and it was handy for work, too many pluses to turn down. So much so that when Patsy returned home to her bedsit, she looked around at the dingy room and couldn't wait to move on.

The move proved to be a bit chaotic with their different shift patterns, but one Saturday morning when they both had to be at work for two pm, they finally made the move into their flat. Rosie's mum had sent several bits and pieces, cooking utensils, bedding, a couple of slightly faded pictures and a vase complete with plastic flowers. The girls didn't mind. They were delighted. The flat was furnished, albeit sparsely but it didn't matter, they both decided it was a palace to them. After quickly putting all their things away in some order, and with plenty of giggling, they rushed off to work for their shift.

"I've got us a bottle of wine for later," said Rosie so we can celebrate the new flat.

They soon settled into the flat; it was luxury to Patsy, and because they worked different hours, Patsy had plenty of time for her reading, but now she could relax with a book on the old but comfy sofa in the living room. The two girls painted the walls and gradually they bought bits and pieces for their new home to make it more comfortable, a coffee table, lamps, pictures, it was an exciting and a happy time for both of them.

Patsy and Rachael met regularly. Rachael had a limited amount of books, and she suggested to Patsy that they could both visit the library, and the even better news was that Rita, their manager had offered them access to the computer. Patsy was horrified at the thought, "I can hardly write a full sentence let alone use a computer, and I wouldn't know where to start."

Rachael gave her a sympathetic look, "Will you stop decrying yourself Patsy Bennett? You are one of the brightest people I know. Look, I'll soon have you competent in computers and we can access so much knowledge from the Internet."

"I'll give it a go," said Patsy unconvincingly.

One Saturday and Patsy was deep in conversation with Rachael when Rosie breezed into the staff room, and quietly asked if she could join the study group.

"I want to know more too, I've seen Patsy with these books and I can't wait to learn how we can all learn to do our jobs better." Both Rachael and Patsy looked at Rosie and then at each other.

"Why don't you join us, it'll be great?" said Patsy and she put her arm around Rosie.

Rachael was more sceptical, "I don't know," she said, "You know you'll have to be totally committed and put the hours in?"

"She can do it," Patsy said as she rushed to the defence of her friend.

Rosie looked dejected but then said, "No Patsy, Rachael is right. I haven't got your commitment, I've seen you studying when you're tired, when you could be going out, and it's not me. I like my social life but I have every faith in you, and all this learning stuff will help us all do our job better. You go for it ladies, oh and I'll do more washing up and clean the flat more often as my contribution."

Patsy and Rachael smiled,

"You've got a good friend there Patsy." Rachael sounded very serious.

"Oh come on you two," said Rosie, "you'll both have me in tears in a minute."

The studying progressed albeit slowly. The different shifts they both worked made it a difficult for them to meet up as often as they would have liked, but they both studied on their own. Other staff at the home were supportive, they too felt that any knowledge would help them to do their job better.

Patsy made the decision to visit the local library and try to find some relevant books herself. On her first visit, to say she was nervous was an understatement. Patsy had never set foot in a library before, but she was determined, she had to do this, and she wanted to do it on her own.

The woman on the desk looked at Patsy over her bifocals and smiled. "Can I help you?" she asked. Patsy was so nervous she could hardly speak.

"Um yes please, if you don't mind I'm looking for anything to do with dementia, any books that is?"

The librarian thought for a minute, "We have a limited number of books about dementia, not much call for it you see? But we do have computers you can access. There are probably articles and book listings, and I can certainly order the books in for you. I can have a look what we have got though."

Patsy panicked, she didn't want to admit that she hadn't the first idea about how to use a computer, but then she realised that honesty was the only course open to her.

"I'm sorry," she said, "my name is Patsy Bennett and I started work as a care assistant a short while ago in a home, and many of our residents have Dementia. I am desperate to learn more about the disease so I can look after them better, but I wouldn't know where to start with computers, wouldn't even know how to switch the thing on." Patsy knew her face had gone bright red and she also knew her voice had let her down as she was almost stammering.

The woman never faltered. "My name is Sonia Faulkner," the woman said smiling, "I do know how to use a computer and I am more than happy to help you learn."

Sonia proved to be a competent, patient teacher and after an hour or so Patsy felt a little more confident, "You did really well," said Sonia. "Don't worry you'll soon get the hang of it." And Patsy knew she would, well eventually. Sonia had found several articles, which she printed off, and also books, which she said, she would order in. They scheduled more sessions, and Patsy said she had been promised access to the home's computer with her colleague Rachael, who would also help her, so after thanking Sonia profusely, Patsy left the library with valuable reading material and a spring in her step.

Rachael and Rosie were duly impressed with Patsy's account of her visit to the library, and with the information she had obtained. They all had a shift to work but during their meal break, Patsy and Rachael had a quick look through the articles and arranged to meet at a later date to discuss them fully.

"And now you're computer literate," Rachael said laughing, "I'll have a word with Rita to see when we can use the computer here."

"Ha! Ha! Hardly computer literate, but at least I do now know how to switch the thing on," Patsy said, but she was smiling because she felt so pleased with herself. It was a start, and best of all she was happy.

The more Patsy read, the more she felt she was beginning to understand. The psychologists and sociologists who wrote about dementia reinforced the need to empathise with the feelings of someone with dementia, rather than try to bring them back to the present time. There were many other types of dementia and Patsy read more and more as he had finally finished for the day, she had a list of questions for Rachael, after all Rachael was a qualified nurse who had studied illness. She would be able to explain in easy terminology until Patsy could understand. Rachael was only too happy to answer Patsy's questions.

Rita was excited too. At their meetings Rachael and Patsy would share their findings.

"I can't believe I didn't know any of this and here's me professing to be all knowledgeable in my job. I need to start reading and quick, but look, how can we move forward and put some of this into practice?" Rita was excited at the prospect.

Rachael was quick to jump in, "Well, Patsy, and I thought we could start with finding out more about the lives of our residents, lives they had long before they were ill and came to live here, we know so little about them."

"I wholeheartedly agree with you Rachael," Rita said sympathetically. "But we are all so busy trying to do our jobs, how do we find the time to find out about the past lives of every resident?"

Patsy had been listening quietly to her two colleagues, she had so much respect for them both and she was a little worried about offering an opinion, but she had ideas and eventually she said,

"How about we ask the relatives to write a life history? I've read that it can be very beneficial. Ask the relatives and friends to tell us as much about the lives of their loved ones as they know. I'm sure most would be happy to do that if we explain to them why we need that information."

"Good idea, Patsy," said Rita, "I'm all for that, but what about the people who don't have visitors? We are lucky there aren't many in that situation here but still, they probably need our help even more?"

"I don't mind trying to find out more about those residents. I can work in my own time." And for some inexplicable reason, Patsy knew that she would start with Mary, find out more about Mary's life and the secret she was so reluctant to share with anyone.

It was agreed that they would start to accumulate more information about their residents, and Patsy wasted no time in looking into Mary's file, only to find very little information, other than a medical history. She did have a contact number for Bill, Mary's brother so she summoned the courage to telephone him.

Bill was surprised to hear from someone from the home, and he sounded very worried when he asked, "Is Mary OK?"

"Yes, sorry it's nothing like that, she's well," and Patsy heard the relieved sigh. "No," Patsy continued, "I am a care assistant at the home and I have been learning more about how to communicate proactively with people with dementia. We are contacting relatives to find out as much as we can about their lives, then we can talk to people about things in the past, does that make sense?"

There was a long pause and Patsy was regretting this phone call, she'd handled it all wrong, how could she be so stupid?

But then Bill said, "Yes, I will help in any way I can. Perhaps I can meet with you at the home and we can talk, and I can see my sister? I need to see my sister."

They arranged a date and time and Patsy felt that after all maybe she hadn't handled the conversation so badly. Patsy told Rita about contacting Bill, she was worried in case she had gone too far, this was all so new for Patsy, but Rita approved,

"I don't know him well, he doesn't visit often but he appears to be a decent man who cares about his sister."

Bill Reynolds arrived at the home to meet Patsy a few days later, and after both introducing themselves and exchanging the usual pleasantries, Bill gave Patsy a folder,

"I've written down as much as I know about Mary. She was a lovely kid and a lovely young woman, quiet you know, very attractive. Then she had a very successful business, a dress shop for many years." Bill was talking very fast; Patsy could tell this was difficult for him.

"Thank you so much for the file, Mr Reynolds, we are hoping that if we can find out more about Mary's life, we can help her more," and she knew that Bill understood what they were trying to do.

He leaned over to Patsy. "Please, call me Bill. I've been to see Mary, she is so distant, I don't think she knew who I was, and I do want to help in any way I can. We lost touch you know, I lived in the States for many years, my work took me away, but then I suppose Mary and I lost touch a long time ago. She didn't want to keep in contact and I, well, I didn't know how to put things right. I got married; I have two sons and grandchildren who live in the States. I have had a full life which Mary was not part of. I was divorced, my wife got tired of living abroad, she never really took to it." Bill put his head down.

Patsy let Bill talk but she was confused at some of the things he said. She wondered what had caused a rift between Mary and him. Bill spoke quickly, too quickly as though he wanted to get all the guilt he was feeling off his chest. Patsy sat quietly and listened.

Bill Reynolds sat at the edge of his chair looking uncomfortable. Patsy didn't want to push him so she asked about what kind of foods Mary liked, did Mary like music, and if so what kind of music? Bill finally relaxed a little and answered her questions,

"Although you must know I have had so little contact with my sister for so many years, I'm not sure I'm giving you the right answers. My recollections are of when Mary was a young woman."

"I know you worked abroad, but Mary says very little, however she does ask for someone, a woman or girl quite frequently, someone called Susan?" Patsy had the feeling she was on dangerous ground asking this but it was necessary, this could be the key to helping Mary.

There was a long pause and Bill said quietly, "It's difficult to talk about it you know, but something happened to Mary, when she was a young woman, something which affected the whole family but none more that Mary. I didn't help because I felt unable to support her, I feel so bad about that and I think about it often. It's all so different these days, but back then, my parents were so upset, it destroyed them, I had to think of them and yet I also wanted to help my sister.

Oh how I wish it had never happened," and he buried his face with his hands and cried.

At this point, Patsy felt that she was distinctly out of her depth. She was wishing she had never started this, never phoned Bill Reynolds, but she had gone too far now so she smiled at Bill and softly said,

"Look, Bill, shall we leave it there and perhaps, if you think of anything else, you could contact us?"

Bill stood up to leave and then suddenly he turned to Patsy, "I have more to tell you, but not now. I'm not ready, but I do believe you want to help Mary and so do I. Why did I not do more for her? That poor girl, my little sister Mary," and Bill sobbed and sobbed and Patsy put her arms around him and said nothing. Words were not necessary.

The meeting with Bill had a profound effect on Patsy. She realised how inexperienced she was. "What right have I to interfere in peoples' lives?" she asked herself, "I'm out of my depth here, but I need to help Mary."

With no immediate answers, Patsy felt for the first time that maybe she should stop and leave all this to the experts. She walked back to the flat with a heavy heart. Rosie was already home and over a hastily put together meal and a lager, Patsy poured her troubles out to Rosie.

"Look, Patsy, you are doing a brilliant job. Everyone is behind you and look at the difference in so many of the residents. They are visibly happier, more alert, more content, and you have only just got started. You can't give up now." Rosie was banging on the table by now which made Patsy laugh.

"You do look funny though Rosie," and the two girls cracked open another lager.

"Patsy, you need some fun," Rosie said, "You need to enjoy yourself. You never stop working and studying, which is great, but you also need to act your age, so I am arranging a night out." Patsy smiled; she knew just how lucky she was to have such a good friend.

Chapter 6
Mary

It was the summer of 1976, a gloriously hot summer, and I didn't have much time to enjoy it as the shop was as busy as ever. Everyone, it seemed wanted cool summer dresses and my stock had having to be forever replenished. Sunday was the only time I could take a day off, but quite often Eric would be working. He's worse than me, I thought. He would work seven days a week.

On these Sundays, I had a real wish for a garden. The shop had a yard at the back where I had put pots of flowers and a small table and chairs so I could sit and read a book in the sun, but it could never be the same as a lush garden.

I wanted to buy a bungalow with a nice garden and there were some within walking distance of the village. I'd seen them and really liked them and it wasn't as though I didn't have the money. When I had mentioned it to Eric, he wasn't so keen on the idea. "What do you want with a bungalow?" he asked. "You would miss your flat and you have enough to do here without the upkeep of another home. No Mary, if you really want a house you should invest in a property in Spain. Everyone is doing it nowadays and I have a friend who is involved in building luxury apartments over there. He can get you a really good deal, and you can make a fortune letting it out to holidaymakers. That's what you should do Mary, I'm telling you."

What Eric didn't seem to understand was that I had no wish for an apartment in Spain? I had never had a holiday, and I didn't want a property I would never see. I had never been to Spain, never wanted to, no I wanted a bungalow, but I didn't argue the point with Eric. I'd noticed that he had become more distant lately and although I still loved him, I felt that we were drifting apart. He still only stayed at my flat once or twice a week, sometimes not even that. My instinct told me money was far more important to him than it was to me. Eric was always investing his money in something or other and he wanted me to do the same. He would constantly be telling me to invest in this or invest in that,

"I'm making money from these investments, so could you."

Well maybe, I thought but I was a bit too cautious. I liked to see where my money went; after all I had worked hard to be where I was. The thought of being on my own again was far worse than arguing with Eric and I told myself, yes he had his faults but so did I. For this reason, I never mentioned the bungalow again, but I did walk down the tree lined road looking at the neat gardens and wishing I lived there with my Eric. Then, as always common sense stepped in, and as I walked, my thoughts went back again to that terrible time I could never forget. Somehow, if I couldn't buy the bungalow it was not so bad, it paled in significance with the memory of losing someone so precious.

Some weeks later I was working in the shop. It was Saturday afternoon and very busy. I had an assistant to help me, a lady of a similar age to me called Ada who was very stylish and good with the customers. Ada didn't need a job, her husband had a very good job, although I'm not sure what he did, something to do with banking, but he did work away from home quite a bit.

They lived in a large house in Oak hill, her children were grown up and had all left home. When she applied for the job, she said she needed something to do with her time, and as she had always been interested in fashion, this was the ideal job. Ada had proved herself to be invaluable, she could come in at a moment's notice and not only that, she was always buying something, never bothering to look at the price tag before she bought. She did however appreciate the staff discount I gave her.

It was a typically busy afternoon, and a lady I hadn't seen before came into the shop. She was in her late forties and cheaply dressed, not typical of our usual clientele. All the clothes were now distinctly upmarket high street, which my regular customers wanted. Ada was assisting her, picking out some lovely pieces for her to try but the lady obviously wasn't interested in anything, "No, no, not me, wrong colour, not my style," was all I could overhear.

Ada came over to me after some time looking worried and said the lady had asked several questions about me. "Was I married? Did I have children? Did I live on the premises?" It was all very odd and disconcerting even though Ada had been very discreet with her answers.

I approached the lady and introduced myself, knowing that somehow she knew, or she had heard something about me,

"My assistant tells me you have been asking questions about me," I said, "May I ask why?"

She looked embarrassed and a little flustered as she answered,

"I am sorry, my name is Rosalyn Burgess and I know it sounds odd but I felt I had to come and tell you something." She paused and looked even more embarrassed.

"You see, I have an elderly aunt who lives near the village and she is ill at the moment so I'm staying with her, and quite often I come to the village to shop. Well, a few times I have seen you with a man, a man I know well, and you look very?" She paused again for what felt like an eternity, then she said, "You look very together."

I took a step back, I was confused but somehow I knew that this woman had bad news for me, "Shall we go upstairs to my flat, we can talk more privately, Rosalyn did you say you were called?"

Ada, bless her, instinctively knew something was wrong and she waved me upstairs,

"You go," she said. "Everything is under control here," and with that, I led Rosalyn to my sitting room upstairs.

I insisted that she had tea; anything to delay what she was about to tell me. I just knew it wasn't good, but maybe I was being pessimistic, after all, how bad could it be? Rosalyn sat with her cup in her hand, she was obviously nervous. I smiled at her reassuringly and asked her what she had come to tell me. She leaned forward and in a low voice she asked me if I had known the man she had seen me with for very long.

"Oh yes, a number of years," I said. "We're a couple," and I felt proud to be able to say that.

Rosalyn was hesitant, but eventually she nervously said, "That man, Ronnie Birchall, he lived with me, for several years, oh he had his own place but he stayed with me two or three nights a week. The problem is, I have to tell you this. Don't trust him, you can't trust him. I had my suspicions for a while. I think he had other women, other women he was conning out of their money.

"He had quite a lot of my money over the years. I didn't always look so poor, so shabby you know. My husband left me comfortably off when he passed away, but when I met Ronnie, he persuaded me to invest in various different projects. I was a fool, I trusted him, loved him and I gave him the money and never saw it again. I told him to leave me alone in the end. It was a bitter parting and then,

I saw him with you and alarm bells were ringing in case he was after money from you." By this time, Rosalyn was speaking and crying at the same time and it took me all my time to keep up with her.

I let her speak without interrupting; after all she wasn't talking about Eric. She'd mistaken him for someone called Ronnie, oh the relief, but still I felt very sorry for Rosalyn, she'd obviously had got herself in a bad relationship. I touched Rosalyn's hand gently and softly said,

"Rosalyn, I can't tell you how sorry I am for you, it's terrible to meet someone who does that to you, but you said his name was Ronnie. The man I'm with is called Eric, Eric Bradley."

Rosalyn became very agitated. She stood up and leaned over Mary and shouted, "I'm telling you, Ronnie is Eric, or whatever he calls himself. I bet his real name is something completely different, but now I know for sure that he is just no good, just a con man. Whatever you want to believe I'm warning you to be careful, be very careful Mary," and with that she walked out of Mary's flat.

"Poor woman," said Mary out loud, but there was a nagging doubt in her mind as she walked back into the shop.

"Are you OK Mary?" asked Ada, "I've been busy but worried about you at the same time."

"No, I'm fine, thanks, Ada. She had some deluded idea that Eric is some con man she knows, this man has taken a lot of money from her, but really, as though it could be my Eric? I feel so sorry for her but I think she may be either mistaken or perhaps even mentally ill, the poor woman."

Mary did not see Eric for a few days after that incident, which wasn't particularly unusual as he worked hard and he liked to go back to his own place quite regularly.

"Need my own space sometimes love," he would say and although Mary always felt a little sad about this, she accepted it.

She didn't see any more of Rosalyn either, it was almost as though their meeting had never happened. Mary decided not to mention it to Eric; after all it couldn't be him, could it?

Mary's thoughts were suddenly interrupted.

"Here's a nice cup of tea Mary and would you like some lemon drizzle cake?" Mary wasn't sure what was happening. She was in that room again with old people and that nice young girl was offering her tea and cake. *I wish I could remember her name, such a lovely kind girl,* thought Mary.

"Sorry, Mary, did I wake you? You were having a lovely nap there. It's me, Patsy. I've just come on duty, here till 10pm tonight, so I can help you into bed later. Just let me know when you're ready."

Patsy carried on talking, telling Mary about her flat and her books and about learning how to use the computer. It was so reassuring for someone to talk to her like a normal person, and she was so young, like I was she thought.

Suddenly, Mary grabbed Patsy's hand and said, "Be careful, and take care of the ones you love."

"What happened, Mary, can you tell me so I can try and help?" Patsy spoke gently, she was kneeling in front of Mary so they could have eye contact, but Mary just sat, sipping her tea and said nothing.

Patsy could see tears in Mary's eyes and she decided to leave the conversation, hoping another opportunity would come along.

Chapter 7

Patsy felt her life had changed completely; she had her job, her friends, her new home and her studies. Everyday, she read and learned something new. Her discussions with Rachael and her computer studies with Sonia had opened up a new life of learning, something Patsy had never thought she could achieve and she loved it. Patsy now firmly believed that she could possibly make a difference to the lives of the people she cared for. She and Rachael met regularly with Rita, their home manager to discuss their progress.

A large number of residents now had personal life history's, written by their friends and relatives. Small details were included, what foods did they like Did they like music, reading, watching TV? Did they like to go out a lot before they were ill and if they did, where did they go? If they didn't go out and socialise, what did they like to do? What occupations did they have? Important memories in their lives, now all documented, memories about partners, children, jobs, all of which could be talked about with the individual resident as often as possible.

Rachael wanted to organise outings, small groups at a time with every resident having one carer with them, in order to maximise some quality time.

"Oh, sounds wonderful," said Rita, "But we haven't got the funding to manage the home and outings."

"Perhaps we could start out with going to the shops or the park, small trips that we can manage." Patsy suggested.

So, that was the plan, and before long, staff and residents were seen much more in the locality, in local shops and parks, talking to the people they were caring for, not just pushing wheelchairs. Local people got used to seeing them and many stopped to chat, some even volunteered to help. Staff asked their residents about what they liked to buy, what were there memories about their outings, who did they go with? All the time reminding them about their life experiences, just talking, talking and most importantly, listening.

Most of the staff were very enthusiastic about the idea and many came in to work in their own time to take one of the residents out. They could see how the older people started to become much more alert and enjoyed seeing people and being part of the world again. They laughed and smiled and staff found it all so worthwhile. Staff went out in work time as well, the other staff were happy to cover the home for short periods, and Rita allocated overtime shifts to staff when she was able to budget for the extra wages.

Patsy asked Mary if she would like to go to a dress shop and perhaps buy something.

"Oh, no dear, my walking is not good and you are so busy, and what do I need a new dress for?" was the reply from Mary.

"Well," said Patsy jokingly, "For a start, you can ride in that top of the range wheelchair you've got, with me pushing you along, and I really want to take you out Mary. You know all about dress shops so you can weigh up that posh shop to see if it meets your standards, and if it does, you can spoil yourself and buy a new dress. When did you last spoil yourself Mary? Not for a while I bet, and then you can wear your new clothes if you want to when we go out again, because we shall go out again if you enjoy yourself. Is that OK?"

Patsy was speaking very fast hoping that Mary would agree to go. Mary couldn't think of an answer, and because she had never known such kindness here or heard anyone speak so fast or with so much enthusiasm, she laughed and agreed to go. So on Patsy's next day off, she turned up at the home bright and early to take Mary to the dress shop. The staff on duty that day had made sure that Mary was smartly dressed with her hair done to Mary's taste. Mary had chosen her outfit, and staff had put some makeup on for her, she looked lovely.

Just before they set out Mary asked Patsy for her handbag. She opened the bag and started searching for something. Patsy asked Mary if she could help and Mary asked if she would check that she had a clean handkerchief. As Patsy searched the bag, she suddenly realised that the handbag had very little in it, nothing personal. Patsy felt sad and said nothing but she reassured Mary that she had a hanky in her bag.

It was June and a lovely sunny day, not too warm but very pleasant. Mary hadn't been out for such a long time, and as Patsy pushed her along in her wheelchair, talking all the while to Mary, Patsy could see how interested Mary became of her surroundings. The houses and shops, the people passing fascinated Mary, the tree lined streets. It was like living again, she felt almost happy.

"Here it is Mary, the posh shop. Was your shop anything like this?" Patsy asked as they pulled up outside. Mary looked in the window and saw all the dresses, shoes and handbags,

"Um, not a bad window, quite stylish. I would have put in a bit more colour, but not bad," she said.

Patsy opened the door saying in a low voice, "Let's go inside then, but only if you do all the talking, it's a bit out of my league," and Mary giggled.

Mary soon came into her own once inside the shop. She guided Patsy around the displays of clothes, picked up handbags, scarves, felt the quality of the clothes, and she felt at home, this was a world she could deal with it.

A tall middle-aged lady approached them and spoke to Patsy in a very strange accent which was a mixture of the Queens English and strong Mancunian.

"May one be of assistance modem?" she said, looking at them judgmentally. Patsy was taken aback; this well dressed apparently upper-class woman immediately intimidated her. Patsy thought she spoke a little like someone from the royal family, well slightly.

Mary however took everything in her stride, she knew this type of pushy overbearing sales assistant, and she had spent her working life determined not to be like that,

"Yes dear, I am buying today, I'd like to look at some dresses, preferably blue and I want a good material."

The assistant stepped back as though she had never heard or expected anyone old, and in a wheelchair speaking so assertively, and she had to admit, this old lady had poise and breeding. Yes, she thought, she had money to spend, and with the promise of a handsome commission, she rushed off to find something that this lady would like and hopefully buy.

Patsy looked on in horror as this scene played out. On the one hand, she was so proud seeing Mary so comfortable and so vocal, and on the other hand, she couldn't comprehend the initial ignorance of the sales assistant. *Did I use to be like that?* Patsy thought. *Before I did this job?*

After quite some time and several outfits later, Mary chose which dresses she wanted to buy. A solicitor handled Mary's finances and Patsy had arranged for monies to be available to Mary for her shopping trip.

The sales assistant had become much more amenable as time passed. She couldn't do enough to help, and she was even nice to Patsy, who knew only too well that this woman was about to make quite a bit of commission on the sale. As the assistant would say to her friends later,

"She lived in a home you know but such a well-bred lady, definitely a lady she was, I thought they were all a bit demented in those homes. Just goes to show."

As they left the shop, Patsy knew that the woman would never forget Mary and she smiled to herself thinking that they were on the right track. To take people back to their memories and allow them to once again to be part of a normal life, and to influence the people who met them. Mary and Patsy went to a little cafe and had a cup of tea and a cake, both admitting to each other that they had enjoyed the outing. Patsy had never set foot in anywhere as upmarket as that shop, she normally bought from catalogues or went to the market stalls to buy her clothes, although she had been in 'New Look' a couple of times.

As they sat drinking their tea, Mary was chatting away about her dress shop and how much she had loved it. Patsy had never heard Mary talk so much, she was so quiet normally, it was wonderful to hear her so happy. Suddenly, Mary grabbed Patsy's hand,

"Oh my dear," she suddenly said, "please help me find Susan?"

Patsy was unsure what to say, Mary was crying, so upset, "Oh Mary, I'm so sorry, surely it can't be that bad?"

Mary looked straight at Patsy, "Oh but it is dear, I said goodbye to Susan and never saw her again, but I know you will find her, you shall help me."

Patsy was so shocked she couldn't speak for a few seconds. Who was Susan? She knew at that moment that she had to find Susan, the missing link to the memory that was haunting Mary, and the irony was that a trip to the dress shop, a simple outing had been the encouragement needed for Mary to finally talk, how simple it all was. Patsy reflected and realised it wasn't simple at all. It was the reading, the studying, the planning, the teamwork, all of it had to be in place to make this happen.

"I promise you, Mary, I will do my best to help you find Susan, but it may not be possible, you know that?" Mary smiled and drank her tea, and didn't mention the subject again that day.

They went back to the home, both women lost in thought. Patsy took Mary to her room for a rest and carefully put the newly purchased clothes in the wardrobe, while Mary drifted into a peaceful sleep.

Later, Patsy sought out Rebecca and the two of them discussed the events and Mary's revelation. "We don't even know who Susan is," said Rebecca.

"Oh I know, but I can try," Patsy said unconvincingly.

"I think you should talk to Bill," said Rebecca, "If he knows Mary has told you about Susan, he may know who she is and what happened. I'll talk to him with you if you like?"

Patsy phoned Bill and asked him to speak to Rebecca and herself when he next visited. Bill agreed straight away, to be fair she had developed a good relationship now with Bill.

Bill recognised how hard Patsy was working to help the residents. He was more than interested in helping anyway he could, well apart from telling anyone about that part of Mary's life. No, he had already made up his mind; it was best to 'let sleeping dogs lie'.

Bill was true to his word and visited Mary the next day. He immediately noticed there was something different about her, but what was it? Mary was dressed in one of her new outfits. She looked so well Bill couldn't decide, was it more serene, more settled perhaps? Mary smiled when he went into her room and there was a look of recognition on her face.

Bill commented on how nice she looked, and she smiled and said, "I went back to the dress shop."

"Mary, that's wonderful, you went out and treated yourself? Did you go with Patsy?" asked Bill. Mary smiled, she looked so different, and Bill couldn't put a finger on it. She was content, he hadn't seen her so content for a long time.

Much later Bill, Patsy and Rebecca were in a small sitting room with some tea and biscuits,

"Mary looks wonderful, happy even," said Bill.

"Mary went out with Patsy yesterday," said Rebecca, "They bought Mary some clothes from a nice dress shop, and then went for tea to a cafe."

"You should have seen her, Bill," Patsy said excitedly, "Mary ran rings around the snooty sales woman, put her in her place all right, and then she chose her clothes, it was fantastic."

Bill was caught up in the enthusiasm, "I am so grateful for everything you are doing here, I feel as if I'm getting part of my little sister back."

Patsy knew she had to tread carefully, "While we were out Bill, Mary told me, all she wants to find someone called Susan?"

There was an awkward silence, Bill had tears in his eyes, and Patsy thought they had overstepped the mark, thrusting this on him. She looked over at Rebecca, who calmly leaned over to Bill,

"Sorry, Bill, it was Mary who asked Patsy to help find Susan. Is there anything you can tell us which may help?"

Bill looked at Patsy and Rebecca and he knew that now, was the right time to break the silence, "I remember it was a terrible time in all our lives. Our parents were strict Catholics, and when Mary told them she was pregnant, it brought such shame to their lives. They were respectable people, went to church every day, God fearing, I suppose you would say. They were older when they had us, actually I think the whole episode killed them both really, they never got over it. They sent Mary away. I was at university, just started actually after serving in the RAF, so I don't know that much. All I know is that our family was never the same.

"Mary wanted to keep the baby, her chap went off, and our parents insisted the baby was adopted into a good catholic home. It was awful. When I'd go home the atmosphere was unbearable, I couldn't wait to leave. Mary never forgave mum and dad and they never forgave her for the shame. None of us ever spoke about it; no one knew what to say. Mary looked to me for support but I felt sad for them all, and I supported Mum and dad's decision in the end. Whether it was right, I've asked myself a hundred times since then, but I do know that because of all this mess, I lost my little sister."

Bill felt suddenly as though a weight had been lifted. He looked at Rachael and Patsy to read their reaction, but all he saw was kindness and understanding.

Chapter 8

Something was different. Did I tell someone finally about Susan? I remember I was in my shop, or was it a cafe? I don't know but there was that nice young girl and I think I told her. How strange when I have never spoken about my Susan, not a word to anyone. Why did I tell her? I know her, that nice girl, she visits me here I think, no she helps me, but I feel better though, for telling someone. I have kept it all to myself for so long. I have a good feeling that she will find my Susan. I just know she will.

I remember that time so well, the love of my life, Joe. We only made love once or twice. It seemed right at the time, although I was hardly sexually experienced, in fact I wasn't really sure what was happening. Oh, I had heard the talk from friends about sex but I certainly wasn't prepared, but I wanted to be with Joe. Joe's leave was nearly over so I was convinced I needed to show him how much I loved him before he left. I didn't really need to worry, he would be out of the services soon and he would ask me to marry him. I was so convinced we would be happy.

I was so naive, as many of us were then. When I had my first period at school, I was about 14 or 15 years old and I had no idea what was happening. The nuns didn't give us any information about our bodies and neither did my parents. So when I met Joe, I was so worldly ignorant, and when we made love and two months later I hadn't had a period and felt sick in the mornings, it was a friend at work who suggested I might be pregnant.

"No," I said. "It's not possible." I mean we had only made love twice, how could I be pregnant? Turned out, I was very much pregnant.

My friend came with me to the doctor, I couldn't ask my mother, and there, at the surgery it was confirmed. The doctor I felt was judging me, he looked at me disapprovingly and his manner was stern,

"You had better go home and tell your parents. You shall be dammed for this young lady, a child out of wedlock." With that he pushed my friend and I out of the consulting room and slammed the door.

I wrote to Joe first, I wasn't unduly worried. I knew we would get married and I wouldn't be dammed and the nasty priest would give us his blessing, but he wrote back and said he said he was too young to be a father. He said he wasn't ready for marriage and we didn't really know each other. He wished me the best in such a formal way and that was it, no sorrow, no concern, I couldn't believe he could be so callous. I had no choice other than to tell my parents.

It was the hardest thing, telling them. There was a hushed silence as I spoke the words. Strangely, I was not ashamed, I was a little frightened at the thought of having a baby, but I was overjoyed at the same time.

I was stupid I suppose. I thought that my parents would get over the shock and embrace the thought of having a grandchild. How wrong could I be? My mother refused to speak to me apart from saying,

"The shame, what will people think?"

And my father ranted on and on about what a sinner I was and that God would never forgive me.

I went to bed that night and cried and cried, but the one thing I did know was that I would have this baby and love it whatever he or she did in the future, I would never judge a child of mine, the way I had been judged.

The next day, I was met downstairs by my parents telling me I was going away to stay with a distant aunt in the south of England. When the baby was born, it would be adopted and we would never speak about this again. I pleaded with them but it was no use, they told me to go and pack, to ring my boss and tell him I had to go away. I turned to Bill for support, wrote to him, but he said it would be for the best and then I could get on with my life. I was horrified; no one could ever understand what I was going through. The irony was that if I had been married to Joe, they might all be celebrating, happy for me even.

My aunt, who I really didn't know, I think I met her a couple of times when I was little, anyway she lived in a small seaside town in Somerset. My parents saw me onto the train and left before the train moved. I had never been away by myself before, never travelled and I had no idea where or who I was going to.

Aunt Theresa was actually very good to me. She greeted me at the station and after a short bus ride; we arrived at a pretty little house near the beach. Although she told me she didn't really approve of the situation I was in, she welcomed me into her home, took me to my room, a very comfortable large bedroom where she had put a vase of fresh flowers and left me fluffy towels on the bed.

Theresa had lost her husband in World War One and had no children of her own. She was related to my father, his youngest sister but they were not close. Neither Theresa nor my father had ever elaborated as to why. Theresa did resemble my father, she was tall and thin with long hair she wore in a bun. She always wore long dresses and coats, she was I suppose a little eccentric. She told me that she had no time for religion, reckoned it caused a lot of trouble in the world,

"As for that brother of mine, getting pregnant out of wedlock would be a mortal sin. He embraces his religion, as does your mother."

I spent my days going for long walks on the beach, helping my aunt around the house, reading and thinking about my baby. My aunt accompanied me to antenatal appointments and took great care in making sure that I ate as well as rationing would allow.

To be fair to Theresa, she said very little about my pregnancy, she didn't ask questions and it didn't bother her when my bump started to show and we went into town and met people she knew in the area. She would calmly introduce me as her niece who was having a baby, and for that she had my eternal admiration.

Theresa, it turned out had few friends, although she appeared to be well respected in the community. Her husband had been a teacher in a prestigious school in the town before the war and he had left her fairly well provided for. Aunt Theresa said that she always regretted not having any children.

When the time came, I went into labour. My aunt accompanied me and I was admitted into a small maternity home. The labour was difficult and the staff were clinical and unsympathetic and, openly demonstrated their disapproval. Theresa visited me and was angry at the way I was treated,

"It's nothing to be ashamed of Mary, they have the problem not you."

Susan finally came into the world on 30th September 1946 and as I held her I knew that she was the best thing that had ever happened to me, and I didn't want to let her go. Theresa had been in the waiting room and as kindly as she could told me that it was my parents' instructions that Susan had to be adopted into a Catholic home with a new mother and father,

"After all, Mary," she said, "There is no way you can look after a baby. You're young, Mary, with your whole life ahead, you have plenty of time for other babies."

And that was that. Despite my arguments and pleading, it became obvious that Susan and I would be parted. The cruellest part in many ways that I had Susan for six weeks, changing, feeding, cuddling her, she was so beautiful. She had a mass of red hair and blue eyes and I'm sure she knew that I was her mummy.

The day arrived when I had to hand her over to the social worker, I have never cried as much before or since as I did on that terrible day. They refused to tell me where my little girl was going or anything about her adoptive parents. I don't know what I would have done without my aunt. She took me back to her house and comforted me as much as she could, and she looked after me until I was well enough to go home. Very little was said about what had happened, Theresa told me what was done was done and said we would not speak of it again.

I wanted to scream and shout and tell her how wrong she was, how cruel my parents were and how devastated I was that Joe, Joe, the love of my life had deserted me, but I never said anything. After all, my aunt had been so kind and it wasn't her fault. She had stepped in to help and to abide by my parents' wishes, although I often think that she too secretly hoped that I could keep the baby.

Theresa accompanied me to the station and we said our good byes as I climbed onto the train home. I wished I could stay with Theresa.

I did write to her sometime later to thank her, she had been wonderful and so kind but I never contacted her again much to my shame. Theresa was just a reminder of the loss of my child. I feel sorry now because I owed her so much.

When I got home and it was as though nothing had changed. My parents never asked me anything other than to enquire how Theresa was, and life went on. There was an awkward silence in the house; it didn't feel like home anymore.

I tried to talk to my brother Bill but he just said, "Look Mary, this has nearly broken Mum and Dad, just leave it, it's all for the best, really it is." And that was that.

I was broken too. I had lost my baby; did no one understand how I felt? I vowed that one day I would find Susan and I told myself that when I had enough money, I would move heaven and earth to find her and we would be together.

I needed a fresh start, I didn't contact any of my old friends, well, and they didn't contact me. It was as if I had committed some terrible deed, I felt like a bad person. The priest didn't help, he came to the house soon after I came home, and he went on and on about how I had hurt my parents, after all they had done for me and I was lucky that they had allowed me to return home. I say home, but it never felt like home after that. I felt like a stranger with a story to tell that no one wanted to hear. I couldn't wait to get out on my own and make a life for myself. I cried for weeks, but no one seemed to notice my distress, and one day I decided I had to move on with life.

The job at the builder's yard kept me busy and although I smiled and chatted to the customers, I was desperately unhappy. Oh I had lots of offers from young men wanting to arrange a date, but that was not for me.

So that became my life for a while, working and saving, not socialising outside work and not spending money, and always thinking about Susan. I used to go and look at baby clothes in the shops, and baby toys and I would imagine being a mum and looking after her every day, loving her and planning a good life for both of us. Without money to support my child and no means of finding her, it all looked pretty hopeless. My parents appeared not to notice how insular and unhappy I was. We were all polite with one another but they remained distant. I tried so hard to find out where my baby had gone but it was impossible.

Funny how I told that young girl after all this time, she reminds me of me in some way, not sure why? She's rough around the edges but she has a good heart, she is honest and I know somehow that she won't hurt me as so many have in the past. She has the ambition that I had, the need to escape. How I yearned to escape and have a life. Yes, I have a good feeling about her and I just know that she will help me to find Susan.

Chapter 9

Patsy, Rachael, Rita and Bill were all sat in Rita's office discussing Mary's disclosure about her lost baby, Susan.

Rita was apprehensive. "Look if we do decide to trace the child, how do we go about it? Children who are adopted can find their parents these days, but I don't think it's easy for women who give their children up for them to try and find them. We don't know Susan's name now, she might be called by another name, and it was so long ago. Susan must be about 50 now, and even if by some miracle we do find her, she might not want anything to do with Mary."

There was a silence in the room as they all thought about what Rita had said. They all had the same concerns about a possible or more likely an impossible reunion.

"There are psychologists who are of the opinion that any unresolved issues suffered by someone does tend to adversely affect the cognitive impairment of people with dementia, and certainly to see Mary's obvious distress this makes me believe it to be true. After all, people without dementia who have suffered are able to talk about it if they wish, but with dementia, it is hard to express feelings or find the words," Rachael said this with conviction, and Patsy nodded in agreement and said,

"If we could find Susan and it worked out then perhaps she would finally find peace"

"We should discuss this with Mary's doctor, we can't just proceed without a medical opinion," said Rita and again there was a silence while everyone thought deeply about whether this idea was feasible, or could it do more damage to Mary?

Bill had been listening intently to the discussion, he broke the silence by saying, "I think the first thing is to try to find Susan. I was wrong when I didn't reach out and help Mary, so wrong. I'm happy to pay a private investigator; after all I have felt nothing but guilt since it happened. If it achieves nothing else, I need some resolution to this as well as Mary. Should we do find Susan, and if she agrees to a meeting, then we can consult the doctor, but at least we could reassure Mary that Susan is well and happy, hopefully that is."

Rita was of the opinion that they should still consult Dr Morris.

"Just to update her and see what she thinks."

They agreed that this was probably the best solution and Bill said that he would find a reputable company of investigators and be guided on their advice as to how easy or difficult the task to find this child could be.

Bill also offered to fund more outings for all the residents. He was tearful as he said, "I am so impressed with everything you are doing here, I'm not short of money and I can't think of a better way to spend it."

The three women were stunned and excited by the kindness and commitment. Patsy turned to Bill and smiled at him. "Can I give you a hug?" Bill laughed and the two of them embraced each other, while Rachel and Rita waited their turn to give Bill a hug as well.

The feelings of hopelessness were gone for the moment. The hard work was all worth it; it was going to make a difference at last. They all shared a feeling of hope for the future. As Bill was leaving, Patsy asked him if he knew who Annie was,

"Jess told me she has visited Mary, I wondered if she was a relative?" But Bill had never heard of Annie.

The outings were now much more frequent, ordinary things, just trips to restaurants, pubs, local beauty spots, shopping, all normal things that ordinary people do on a daily basis. Alice went to the theatre with a carer to see a show and couldn't stop talking about it.

Albert went to a local grocer's shop where the owner made a big fuss of him, and they shared stories about what items sold well nowadays, and about the impact on small businesses that the large supermarkets now. Albert spoke about some of the things his regular customers said, and added,

"If the children came in with no money, I never charged them." But the shop owner said if he didn't charge customers, children or not, his shop would not survive.

Albert thought for a second, shook his head and said, "No, I couldn't see the children go without their tea."

Jim and Doreen went to several pubs, it turned out that they were both very partial to a few drinks. Jim liked his real ale and Doreen liked a port and lemon, well more like a few ports and lemons. Patsy was worried the drink might not be such a good idea and interfere with their medication, but Rachael assured her that the benefits of a day out now and again was worth the risk and would benefit their general health and wellbeing.

Although the outings were still a very new part of life, the benefits were there to be seen. Staff noticed that the residents were much calmer and happier generally. Jess, the carer who Patsy had first met when she started her job at the home really took to the outing's idea, and even came in on her days off to take people out.

"I never knew old people could be so much fun," she remarked to Patsy one day, "When we went to the pub the other day at lunchtime, we all had such a good time, never stopped laughing at some of the tales. Jim had the whole pub in stitches with some of his stories."

Patsy thought Mary was much calmer too, she didn't cry so much, she chatted more and when Patsy went on duty, Mary smiled warmly and said, "Oh it's you dear, I'm so glad you're here." Relatives were so impressed with the project, they noticed their loved ones were much more responsive when they visited. One of Jim's sons told everyone excitedly,

"Dad was actually telling me that he had been to the pub, 'The Old House at Home', he knew the name, and mum was so delighted that they had been out together. They haven't been out like that for years, only with family and then with a lot of persuasion."

Bill meanwhile had wasted no time in contacting a reputable agency that assured him that they had done this type of work before, although it wasn't easy and may take some time. Previous investigations they had undertaken had been largely successful. They also warned him that in their experience, subsequent meetings with long lost people didn't always work out too well, but Bill knew that he would worry about that if and when they found Susan.

Mary continued to improve, smiling and much more talkative, still forgetful of course in the present time but she did appear happy to see Patsy, and she cried tears of joy now when Bill visited. Bill felt comfortable to visit regularly without those dark feelings of guilt. There were sad moments too for Mary, she would cry and talk about her Susan and chastise herself for not doing more to find her beloved daughter. Patsy would try to talk about other things to take Mary's mind from grieving, and although Mary was a very private and undemonstrative person, she would welcome a hug from Patsy,

"My Susan would have given me lots of hugs, I should love to hug her again," and Mary would smile and drift into her own world.

So, life went on in the home, everyone was more positive and the ideas for events continued. An Irish night, a Caribbean night, birthday parties, the list was endless, and the response from everyone was very positive. There was always something going on, the home was alive and vibrant. Visitors commented on how much happier the whole home had become. It was infectious.

Patsy was busy; almost too busy some would say. Her job had become her life. Besides organising trips out and gathering information for the life histories, Patsy was studying more and more, hungry for knowledge. Rachael and Rita were very involved and Sonia, the librarian who had become a close friend to Patsy was always on the lookout for new article or books for Patsy.

Life was hectic with little time for relaxation, but when she could, Patsy would go to Rosie's parents' home where there was always a welcome, a good meal and lots of laughter. The house always seemed to be full, Rosie's brothers and sisters, their partners and children, always someone visiting the house.

These visits had become a joyous escape for Patsy; she was so unfamiliar with happy family life. She visited her own mother rarely and she was always relieved to leave after the visit. Patsy's mother was currently living with a man who Patsy considered a scruffy lay about. He had never worked but prided himself with his countless exploits off breaking into other people's' houses to take what he could. Patsy didn't like him, and he didn't like her, but then again that was the common emotion Patsy had with mum's many men friends. Patsy always had the feeling that her mother was happy when Patsy finally left the house,

"I get lonely Patsy, and you never understood that. I need a man around." Her mum was always saying that.

It was such a relief to walk into a clean and homely environment created by Rosie's mum and dad, and it was on one such visit that Patsy met a friend of one of Rosie's older brothers. Patsy and Rosie arrived at the house one Sunday afternoon to be greeted with the sound of laughter and the aroma of Sunday lunch waiting to be served. Rosie's dad was sat in his favourite chair attempting to read his paper, while Rosie's eldest sister Gemma was telling her two young boys to stop tearing around the room, settle down and to give granddad some peace and quiet.

Through the window, Patsy could see Andy with Gemma's husband Paul and another man with them who she did not recognise, all having a noisy game of football. For some reason Patsy could not take her eyes of this tall dark-haired young man who she didn't know, but she couldn't help feeling an attractiveness about him which she was drawn to.

Rosie came into the room, "There you are," she said to Patsy. "Mum said dinner will be ready in half an hour. Oh look at that lot trying to kick a ball, they're like little kids."

"Not seen him before?" Patsy tried hard to sound slightly uninterested, but she was dying to know all about this handsome stranger.

"Oh, that's Ed, friend of Andy's, they play football together on the local team, and yes Patsy he is fit isn't he? Don't pretend to me that you hadn't noticed?"

Rosie was laughing as she answered and Patsy saw the funny side, her best friend knew her too well.

"OK," said Patsy, "First, well yes he is quite good looking, but second I have far too much to do to be interested in some guy."

Rosie smiled, "Oh right, then we shall say no more, but you sit next to him at dinner. Come on you, help me to set the table." She led the way, still laughing.

The guys came back into the house ready for the meal. There was a noisy discussion about whether a certain football manager should be sacked, or whether he still might be the best for his team. Rosie's dad had plenty to say about that, newspaper forgotten. Rosie's mum called them into the dining room for the meal and Rosie made a big point of introducing Patsy to Ed, and as Rosie had promised Patsy found she sitting next to Ed at the table.

Patsy was so embarrassed and Ed looked a little perplexed, but as they all enjoyed a fantastic Sunday lunch, Ed proved to be charming and funny, relating tales of the football team that he and Andrew played for. Patsy was dying to ask him more questions about himself, but although Ed was very polite and filled her wine glass more than once, he hadn't shown much interest in her.

Long after the meal and a lovely evening, Rosie and Patsy reluctantly knew that it was time to go home to their flat, they both had shifts the following day and by this time it was getting late. After saying their goodbyes, the girls were heading for the door when Ed ran after them and said he would walk part of the way with them. Patsy hadn't managed to find out more about him, and anyway she had already decided that he wasn't interested in her.

As they walked together, Rosie did most of the talking to Ed, "So, where do you live again Ed? I'm sure Andy told me you don't come from around here originally."

Ed smiled, "I live near the football club, that's how I got involved, always loved the game and it's great therapy after working all week. Came to Manchester when I went to university, but home is down in Devon." He stopped. "Ladies, this is where you go that way and I go this way, lovely to meet you Patsy, see you soon Rosie." And off he went.

"See, he fancies you," said Rosie and she linked Patsy's arm.

"Oh yes," said Patsy. "He hardly looked or spoke to me the whole afternoon. Shame though, he is so, so…nice, just my luck."

Rosie sighed and said, "Silly girl, he hardly stopped looking at you. My bet is he'll be asking our Andrew or me for your number in the not-too-distant future. Listen to auntie Rosie, I know these things."

Patsy started laughing and both girls went home after a perfect day.

Chapter 10

I kept thinking about the meeting I had with Rosalyn, but then I would put the incident to the back of my mind, problem was, it kept coming back to me.

I even had dreams, well more nightmares really where Eric would leave me penniless and spend the money on a host of different women. When I did actually see Eric, I found it easy to dismiss all these bad thoughts about him. After all, Eric was as kind and loving as he had always been. He never let me down, unless he was busy with work, and of course and I understood there were occasions when he needed his own space. "Silly," Mary said out loud, "I like my own space sometimes and I am always busy, but why or why can't I get that woman out of my head?"

I thought about looking through Eric's pockets when he was asleep, even following him,

Well where did he live? When she thought about it she had never been to his home.

Maybe if I speak again with Rosalyn? But there again, the woman, nice as she was, well she was unbalanced wasn't she? Eric did love her; she knew it with all her heart.

Rosalyn was mistaken. She had to be. That man, Ronnie must look like Eric. Perhaps Eric has a brother called Ronnie, there has to be a rational explanation. I'm a successful business woman, I'm sensible to the point where I am boring in some peoples' eyes. There is no way I would be taken in by a confidence trickster.

Eric came to pick her up that evening, they were going out to one of their favourite restaurants in Manchester. As he usually did, Eric arrived looking very smart and carrying flowers and chocolates for Mary,

"For my wonderful girl," he said as he kissed her and gave her the gift, "you always look a million dollars. My Mary, my true love." Mary lost all her doubts because she knew Eric did really love her, love her as no one had before.

Mary had taken care to look especially nice that evening. She always took care of herself, regular hair appointments, nice nails, expensive creams and perfumes and of course, beautiful quality clothes. Mary knew that tonight she wanted to look good, no, she needed to look good tonight; she needed to look special, just in case there were other women. Of course weren't. She was imagining again. She had told herself yet again that she was stupid; of course she knew she was the only one, but it could do no harm to make a special effort. Mary had chosen a cream silk dress, which she wore with a pale green jacket and cream court shoes. Mary felt good, but still a little unsure.

They took a taxi into Manchester city centre. Eric was telling Mary about the various jobs he was doing, the houses, businesses he worked in and the people he met while he was working. He always had funny stories to tell about some of his customers. Mary had once remarked that she wondered what he said about her, and Eric had laughed and said she was different, a good customer and the woman he loved.

As they entered the restaurant, Eric asked for a table in a corner, he always did that because he said that he didn't like to be where other diners could watch them. *A very private man, my Eric*, Mary thought to herself and smiled broadly at Eric. They studied the menu, Eric ordered some wine, and when they had ordered Mary tentatively said to Eric, "You know, you've never told me about your family. Have you any brothers and sisters, any nieces and nephews?"

Eric did not flinch, "Only child love, that's why I'm used to being on my own, but you have a brother don't you?"

Mary was disappointed Eric hadn't said more, "I have an older brother, yes, but I don't see much of him. He works abroad a lot of the time and we aren't that close any more."

The evening went well as it always did, the food was wonderful and there was a welcoming ambience in the restaurant. Mary would have liked a table near the window; she liked to watch the people walking by. Manchester was busy and vibrant at that time of night and Mary liked to imagine where they were all going. Mary accepted that Eric was a private person and really she didn't mind the table in the corner. She was a lucky lady, out for dinner with the man she loved, but she did wonder why he couldn't confide in her more about his life and his family. She was beginning to realise that she really did not know much about Eric.

After desert they were finishing their wine, in no hurry to rush off and Eric reached into his pocket and produced a colour brochure of some properties for sale in Spain,

"I wish you would reconsider about investing in one of these beauties Mary, you could make some serious money, here take another look," and Eric pressed the brochure into Mary's hand.

Mary was taken by surprise. She thought that this discussion had been put to bed once and for all. There was no way she wanted to buy a property in Spain and she thought Eric understood that.

"Eric darling," she said, "I already told you I want to buy somewhere in this country, near to the shop, that's if I ever decide to move. The flat suits me at the moment."

Mary didn't mention that she had looked at those bungalows in Oak hill again, and in her heart, she had visions of her and Eric settling down in one of those when they were married. Eric looked disappointed but said he understood even if he thought she was making a big mistake, "Just look at the brochure Mary. For me." And Eric smiled his charming smile.

On the way home with Eric in the taxi, the mood was subdued and Eric said he would drop Mary off, as he had an early start the next day. "Can't you stay tonight, Eric?" Mary asked, "You don't stay with me as often as you used to."

Mary had thought that Eric would be staying and she had put clean sheets on the bed and put flowers on the window ledge in her bedroom. She needed the reassurance that Eric was who he said he was and that he genuinely loved her.

Eric was adamant he had to go home. "Come on love, I stay at least twice a week and you know how busy I am. I've told you before, but there are plenty of other nights we can be together," and Eric looked into her eyes and smiled lovingly.

Later, as Mary climbed into the clean sheets and switched off the bedside lamp, she couldn't help reflecting on the evening. As much as she loved Eric, she couldn't help thinking again that she knew very little about him. He was always reluctant to talk about his life, he never really answered her questions and why did he not want to make a commitment?

Then there was this obsession with her buying this place in Spain. Why did he push her to do this when she had told him she didn't want to? Why didn't he buy it if it was so good, he had money? Mary chastised herself, deciding she was being too judgmental, after all he was only thinking of her like he always did, and when he saw the bungalow he would love it as she did. Her thoughts persisted. Who was this man; did she really believe all he told her? Mary hated herself but she did have doubts about Eric.

Mary did not sleep very well that night. Thoughts were going round and round in her head. Eventually, she gave up on sleep and got up and made some tea. Sitting in the tranquil flat above the shop, Mary decided she would have to find out more about the real Eric. She desperately hoped that she was wrong, she felt guilty at even having these thoughts, but she had to know. She was unsure how could she find out. Mary didn't really have anyone she could confide in.

Since she had lost Susan, she had shut herself away from people. Yes, she knew her neighbours, her customers, she could talk to anyone, but she had never allowed anyone other than Eric to get close, just in case they ever found out what she had done. She hadn't even told Eric about Susan, in case he judged her. "I'm going to tell Ada I'm having the day off today," she said to herself. "I need to think about what I am going to do and how."

Chapter 11

Patsy was on another trip to the dress shop with Mary, where the 'stuck up' sales assistant worked, but Patsy no longer felt intimidated and that was thanks to Mary. Mary could run rings around this woman and even the sales assistant was actually becoming quite friendly.

They were in the shop and Mary was choosing a beautiful yellow cashmere sweater. She kept asking Patsy if she had anything in her wardrobe that would go with it, and Patsy was able to tell her she had several skirts and trousers that would look great with the sweater. Patsy smiled, she was thinking that Mary had so many clothes she had something to go with everything, but these trips meant so much to Mary and she had the money. Why should she not spend some on herself?

The shop assistant asked Patsy about the home, and Patsy was only too happy to tell her all about the different activities that were organised and the woman said,

"I could ask the owner about having a fashion show at the home if you like, what do you think Miss Reynolds about helping pick out some clothes you think people would like?"

Mary was delighted, and actually so was Patsy. This woman who had treated them both with contempt on their first visit to the shop was now treating Mary with real respect. The shop assistant introduced herself as Fiona and said the owner, Louise Jessop would be in later,

"And this is just a hobby for her, loads of money you know. She pops in daily but I do all the work."

Patsy thought Fiona was probably the jealous type but she still felt they had made progress, Fiona's attitude was different, warmer, and a fan show at the home could be wonderful.

Patsy and Mary left the shop; Mary had the cashmere sweater, alongside her handbag on her knee as Patsy pushed the wheelchair along the road to their usual little cafe.

"I wonder if Susan would like this," Mary said pointing to her purchase. "I imagine she likes clothes like I do."

Patsy answered kindly, "Susan could be anywhere Mary, and she may even live abroad. Bill is doing everything he can to try and find her, but we have to be realistic, hard as it is. It was such a long time ago."

Mary smiled and said, "Oh I know you and Bill will find her dear, you will." She patted her bag that held her new sweater.

When they got back to the home, Bill had arrived for a visit. Mary was pleased to see him and whereas normally she was tired after an outing, she was anxious to talk to him and show him her latest purchase. Patsy and other staff could hear a lot of laughter coming from Mary's room. When Bill came out of the room, he was smiling broadly,

"She's so vibrant and happy," Bill said to Patsy, "I can't believe it, and she's tickled pink about some fashion show."

Patsy stepped back. "She remembered! Oh that's great. The shop might be arranging a fashion show and have asked Mary to be involved, but I'm amazed that she has remembered, normally she would have forgotten all about that."

Bill and Patsy walked into Rita's office, Rita was deep in conversation but Bill was so excited he couldn't wait to relate the afternoon events. Both Rita and Rachael were delighted and said they hoped that the fashion show would take place.

"Any luck with the private investigator Bill?" Rita asked.

"Well, they keep in contact with me, but they have warned me it isn't easy. If Susan wanted to contact Mary, that is relatively simple, but as we know, not so for a mother wanting to find a child, and of course Susan is now in her 50s. I keep hoping she will be found, and it all ends happily, but I do have my doubts."

They were all deep in thought after the success of the afternoon.

"I did speak to Mary this afternoon while we were out." Patsy said. "I tried to explain how difficult it was to find Susan, but that Bill had engaged the private investigators to try. She is so convinced Susan will be found. Whatever else Mary does not always remember, she never forgets her baby. What if we can't find her?" Tears were in Patsy's eyes, she so wanted Mary to find Susan and for a happy ending once and for all. Rachael put her arm around Patsy,

"The bond between a mother and child is a special bond Patsy. Even though Mary was separated from her baby too soon, that bond will always remain."

Patsy looked subdued, she was trying hard to understand but she couldn't help wondering if there was ever a bond between her and her mum. Maybe there was once? Patsy shrugged off the negative feelings and went home that evening to study. It had become her passion and she was, for the first time in her life believing that she was capable of achieving something worthwhile in her life.

She soon lost track of the time. Rosie was out at the pub with her new date, a really nice guy, but Rosie had made it clear that she didn't want to be tied down just yet; there was a whole lot of living to do first. Although the two girls had become firm friends, Patsy knew that Rosie didn't understand her need to succeed, but then Rosie had a secure background and a family who would always support her whatever she chose to do with her life. Patsy wished she had that emotional security, but she was grateful that Rosie's family had welcomed her so warmly into their family circle.

Patsy was deep in thought, lost in her own world when the doorbell rang. Not expecting any visitors, Patsy went to answer the door and there was Ed, looking mildly sheepish and carrying a bottle of wine,

"Sorry to bother you Patsy, I was in the pub and met Rosie, she said you were on your own, wondered if you fancied sharing this?" And he held up the bottle of wine.

Patsy was taken back, she felt like a mess, hair not combed, no makeup, she wondered what Ed must have thought, "I'm sorry, Ed, for the way I look, I got lost in my studies, been at it since I finished work." Patsy could feel her face going red, why had she not made some sort of effort to tidy herself up before she started studying?

"You look perfectly lovely to me. Hey, I bet you've not eaten. Why don't we pop over to that Indian restaurant round the corner? You look like you need a break, and you must be hungry, I know I am?"

Patsy smiled back at him, he looked as gorgeous as ever and lost in her studies, she had forgotten to eat. She thought he was joking though when he had told her she looked lovely.

"Oh I'm sorry Ed, I would love a curry, come in and have a glass of wine while I make myself respectable."

Ed followed Patsy into the flat and said how much he liked it, and after pouring them both a drink, Patsy went into the bathroom for a quick shower and change of clothes. Ed was chattering away to her while she got ready, shouting through the door, and when she did emerge from the bathroom she looked and felt much better. The conversation flowed easily between them, and by the time they had walked the short distance to the restaurant, Patsy was totally at ease and happy in Ed's company.

Ed told Patsy about his antics while he was at university. It was his first time away from home and he wanted somewhere far away from Devon where there was plenty of nightlife coupled with good tuition. He loved Manchester and said that for some inexplicable reason he was drawn to the city.

"I think in your circumstances I may have chosen London, I've always wanted to go and see the sights, but never had the chance really," Patsy said pensively.

"I know," Ed answered, all the time looking into Patsy's eyes which did unnerve her a little.

"I did think about London, I have been many times, don't know why I chose Manchester. It was an excellent course on offer and well, must have watched too many episodes of Coronation Street, because I love the accent."

They were both laughing by now; Patsy was thinking that she had never met anyone so charismatic, so honest, and so handsome. They suddenly noticed that they were the only people left in the restaurant, it was very late on a weeknight and they both had work the following day. Ed had told Patsy he worked on a local newspaper covering stories about events in the area. "Pretty mundane sometimes, but there shall come a day when I write the big stories, maybe go into television, that's the plan." Patsy was in no doubt that it would happen.

Rosie came home and wanted to know all about the night. "Wasn't sure he could drag you away from the books, but I thought I would suggest it anyway. He was dying to see you I could tell." Patsy said they had had a wonderful evening. "You know what Rosie? I'm glad you suggested he came to see me, I do like him, a lot." That evening proved to be the first of many for Patsy and Ed.

Chapter 12

Eric telephoned the day after their outing to town and said how much he had enjoyed being with her. He said he had to go to Birmingham for a few days on business to meet with his mate Peter, the friend who was offering all his business investment opportunities.

"You need to think about those Spanish properties I told you about Mary, can't go wrong and you would love it in Spain. Just think, the two of us lying by the pool, the complex has a lovely big pool, and you need to buy now while the price is right. These opportunities don't grow on trees love and I am the man to guide you. We'll have a chat about it when I get back; I know you will see sense in the end. Have to go now love, big kisses."

Mary put the phone down with a sinking feeling in her stomach. "See sense, lovely big pool, the two of us," Eric's words played on Mary's mind. None of it made any sense. Eric had never even hinted at any commitment and yet he wanted her to part with her dream, her bungalow money, something was not right.

Then again she told herself, he loved her and he was offering her a chance to make money, and perhaps she would like Spain. Just for a moment, she imagined maybe she could even open a shop there. Mary smiled at the thought of becoming a proper entrepreneur, and life in the sun, a string of shops. Maybe she should learn Spanish. She sighed and knew deep down that all she wanted was the bungalow and her shop in Oak hill, and what's more she was having more doubts about Eric's motives.

Mary waited for a quiet moment in the shop, her stock and her professionalism had spread to neighbouring areas and people flocked in. The shop was always busy and that was how Mary liked it. Mary had become quite close to Ada, she liked the way she handled customers and she had a definite sense of style. More than that, Mary trusted her, she felt she could talk to her, not about personal things of course, but if she had business elsewhere, she had no concerns about leaving Ada to run the shop. In fact, Mary was considering employing another assistant to ease the workload.

With a lull in the shop, Mary approached Ada with the idea of employing someone else. Ada was delighted,

"It would help Mary," Ada almost sighed with relief. "After all most of the time we are rushed off our feet, I'm exhausted when I get home. Don't misunderstand me, I love working here but I am in no doubt we need another pair of hands."

Mary smiled, "That's settled then. I shall contact the employment exchange, maybe even offer a post to someone young with flair and ideas."

Ada looked pleased and started to unpack a new consignment of clothes, which had arrived the day before.

"Ada," Mary said. She had thought long and hard about confiding in Ada, but confide in someone she must, "Do you remember that woman, Rosalyn who was asking all those questions." She paused, "You wouldn't by chance know where she is living would you?" Ada looked puzzled,

"Are you thinking of offering her the job? Honestly Mary, nice woman but she had no dress sense, I can't see her fitting in here"

Ada was pulling faces and tutting as she spoke which brought a smile to Mary's face. No she couldn't see Rosalyn in the shop either. What a couple of snobs they were, calling the poor woman because she wore cheap dowdy clothes. Mary felt ashamed. There but for the grace she thought but she answered Ada hesitantly,

"No, Ada, but I do need to talk to her about that man she thought was Eric. You see, Eric wants me to invest my money in a property in Spain, and Rosalyn did say that this man, whoever he is took all her money with propositions of a similar kind. Of course I know in my heart that it can't be Eric she took up with, but there are a few loose ends I need to talk to her about." For some strange reason, Mary felt so much better about finally saying this.

Ada looked seriously at Mary, "Yes I can understand that Mary, after all you work hard for your money. I have never had to earn a living like you. I am lucky to have found my soul mate who earns a good salary, but I respect everything you do and, also how good you are to me. I do know the butcher, Mr Denton quite well, bought the meat from him for years. He knows everyone, I'm sure he knows where the aunt lives. Do you want me to ask him? I could say she left something in the shop and we want to return it. Nothing odd about that."

Mary knew Mr Denton too, but she did not want to start asking questions. She was known as a private person, and she did not want other shop owners thinking that she gossiped about her customers. She told Ada how she felt, "Do you think I'm being silly Ada?" Mary felt silly but still deep down she wanted another chance to talk to Rosalyn, just to satisfy herself that her Eric was who he claimed to be.

"No Mary, I don't, I'll pop in at lunchtime," and Ada patted Mary gently on her hand. For some inexplicable reason, Mary found herself wishing it were time for Ada to go to lunch.

When Ada finally returned from her lunch break, Mary could hardly wait to hear what Ada had found out, if anything, but the shop was so full of customers, the two women were busy all afternoon. When the last customer left and Mary finally put the closed sign on the door, Ada was eager to tell Mary what Mr Denton had to say, "Bought a couple of pork chops, and then we were chatting generally, nice man. Anyway I told him how Rosalyn had left her purchase in the shop and she hadn't been back for it. He knew Rosalyn was looking after her aunt and he told me she lives in the village, not far away. Here's the address," and she handed Mary a piece of paper with the address written on it. Ada looked pleased with herself; her detective mission had paid off. Mary thanked her, still not sure about speaking to Rosalyn, the woman might be deluded and making this entire story up. Ada put her coat on. "Good luck Mary, see you tomorrow," and she left the shop.

Mary went upstairs to her flat and made a cup of tea, all the while preparing herself for a meeting with Rosalyn. Feeling refreshed after the tea, she left the shop and made her way to the address she had been given. The house was a large detached house with a spacious front garden close to the village. By the time Mary walked up to the front door, her heart was beating heavily and she questioned herself for even doing this.

Mary rang the bell, and after what seemed an age, an older lady answered the door. Mary introduced herself and asked if it was possible to speak to Rosalyn.

"She's just popped out dear, but do come in and wait, she won't be long. I shall be glad of the company, I don't get out much, problems with my knees you know, can't get about like I used to." Mary followed the woman into a comfortable living room, which was tastefully furnished.

"I'm Mrs Johnson, Rosalyn's aunt," the lady said, "Do sit down dear. I've passed your shop many times and the window always looks lovely. I don't buy many clothes these days you know, I don't socialise like I used to when my dear husband was alive. Glad Rosalyn had the sense to shop with you though, she doesn't have much of a life nowadays, not since that man robbed her of most of her money. When I think of how she used to live, lovely house, holidays, nice clothes, her husband was only young when he passed away, must be turning in his grave, and she is so good to me."

Mary instantly liked this lady but couldn't help thinking Mrs Johnson was a little too trusting, telling a stranger all this.

"Of course when I go, I have left everything of mine to Rosalyn in my will, it was always my wish since she was a small child. My husband and I were never blessed with children, and she has always been so good with both of us."

Mary was feeling more at ease, the house and Mrs Johnson were so welcoming and Rosalyn was certainly truthful about her aunt needing help. Talking to Rosalyn's aunt gave her a better understanding about Rosalyn. She felt doubly guilty of judging her for wearing cheap clothes; this poor woman had had her life turned upside down because of a con man. Of course the man wasn't Eric. Rosalyn had got that so wrong, but why did she think Eric was that man?

Mary heard a key in the door and Rosalyn came into the room, obviously surprised to see Mary sat with her aunt. Mary apologised, "I'm sorry to turn up like this, I need to talk to you and your aunt was kind enough to invite me in until you returned."

"It's fine, don't worry," said Rosalyn, "In fact I'm glad you came to see me, I don't mean to interfere, you must think I'm mad. I only wanted to stop him doing what he did to me."

Rosalyn turned to her aunt, "He's turned up again, that Ronnie or whatever he really is called, he's trying to get money from this lady. Or if he's not already trying, mark my words, he soon will be. Mary doesn't believe he can be the same man." Rosalyn was visibly upset and Mary felt nauseous, why was she doing this?

Mrs Johnson was silent for a long time, she was looking kindly at Mary and then she spoke, "My dear, if Rosalyn says it is that man Ronnie, and then believe her, he is Ronnie, the same man that you now know."

Mary said very little, well what could she possibly say? Rosalyn insisted on making tea, Mary desperately wanted to leave, but as they sat drinking tea and eating homemade cake, Mary had to admit that she liked Rosalyn and her aunt and what's more, she was now definitely changing her mind about Eric.

Chapter 13

Patsy felt so lucky, she had a good job with a promising future, friends and now she had met Ed, all because she had spoken to the woman in the supermarket and made the decision to change her job. Her old life as an unloved and unwanted child, a difficult childhood and no job prospects was gone but not forgotten. Still, she could get on with her life now.

Every day brought happiness and as she walked to work that day, she had a skip in her step. She thought about her work, the residents, she loved them all. Patsy wondered why her thoughts were mostly about Mary and her baby. What was it like to love a child so much? Despite all the different episodes in Mary's life, many of which were still a mystery, and now her illness, she had never forgotten about Susan.

The fact that she had lost her baby was stopping any chance of peace in Mary's life; Patsy was in no doubt about it. She thought about Susan and wondered what kind of a life she had had. Was she happy? Did she even know she was adopted? Would Mary ever meet Susan and how would that meeting impact on their lives? She realised that she was like Mary in many ways, the need to resolve issues, which had always made her unfulfilled and sometimes unhappy.

When Patsy arrived at work for her shift, one of the staff told her there was a meeting that day regarding some new training on offer. The meeting was to take place later that day and there was much discussion amongst the staff about what kind of training it was.

"We have learned quite a bit about dementia recently from Rachael and yourself." Jackie, a portly middle-aged carer remarked, "I have to admit that I wasn't too keen on the idea at first, learning new stuff at my age, but I've really enjoyed the talks and it has helped me in my job, taught me to question everything I thought. I just hope this other training is as good."

Iris, as always was quick to expand Patsy's skills, "Well I felt the same 'Jacks' but listen, I, like you had looked after dementia patients for years and didn't have a clue because no one ever seemed to know. I am so proud of our Patsy and what she has already achieved." Jackie nodded approvingly.

Patsy was embarrassed, she wasn't used to receiving complements and she was as eager as everyone else to know what would transpire from the meeting. At 2pm, Rita couldn't believe how many of her staff had turned up, many were on their days off, but this was becoming the pattern at the home, enthusiastic, motivated staff.

Rita explained that the home was embarking on a training programme for NVQ, National Vocational Qualification in health and social care. This programme was fairly new, but carers had a chance to further their career with a recognised qualification. Rita introduced Val who was an NVQ assessor, affiliated to the local college of further education and Val explained more about the course.

It was basically work based and consisted of assessing the work carers do on a daily basis.

"So we're not asking you to do anything you don't already do every day," Val explained, "I shall be asking some of your senior staff to become assessors so that eventually the home can become an accredited training centre."

One of the younger nurses Kate said that she would like to train as an assessor; she thought that the training would be an asset to the home.

There were lots of questions about how long it would take to qualify, and some staff were worried about having to write things down on paper. Val explained that Rita seconded the staff who undertook the training would have support and that.

"The training at level two is designed to work at your pace, but I will be pushing you along to complete the course," Val said smiling, "It is not compulsory but we hope some of you at least will take the challenge. I'll leave it with you and hopefully Rita will have some candidates ready to sign up by next week."

The meeting ended and as generally happens, the main meeting took place in the staff room amongst the staff. Some were definitely determined to sign up while others felt that it wasn't for them, mainly because of the paperwork involved.

Sadly, many of the very best carers had a bad experience with education at school, and this experience had prevented them from undertaking any academic studies. Patsy too was apprehensive, she wasn't sure if she could actually achieve a qualification, despite the amount of studying she was already doing.

Patsy mentioned her worries to Rachael the following day and Rachael pointed her finger at Patsy and sounded annoyed,

"For goodness' sake, Patsy, you of all people must do it. Think what a stepping-stone it would give you. Val said that if you pass level two and then level three, you can train to be a nurse, and then you could pursue your dementia training and make a real difference to so many people. I'm cross with you now, no question, you go for it."

Patsy stepped back, she had never seen Rachael so annoyed but on reflection it was the right course of action since Patsy knew that she needed a push to do this. Patsy made her way to Rita's office and told Rita she wanted to sign up for the course. Rita was delighted. "Good for you dear, good decision."

Later that day, Patsy and Ed were having a drink in what had become their local pub. They were sat at a corner table and Patsy was telling Ed all about the NVQ course,

"I know I signed up for it but I don't know if I want to put myself through more studying Ed. After all I seem to spend all my spare time studying about dementia, and I am putting in extra hours at work organising events and speaking with relatives about life histories. But, I do know what I want to do with my life now; I want to work with people with dementia and to help relatives and other staff to care for them in the best way. I just hope I can achieve my goal."

Ed sat back on his chair and thought for a moment, "It is so great that you know where you're going in life Patsy, but what you have to ask yourself is, what is the best way to get there? You need recognised qualifications to start you on the road to get to where you want to be. In my opinion, Rachael is spot on in that if you get NVQ, train as a nurse, you could well be on the right path. You need to decide my love, only you can make the choice."

Patsy was listening to everything Ed had to say. She respected his opinion but the words 'my love' were the words she liked the best. She smiled at Ed, she was falling in love with this guy and he loved her, she was sure of it but Ed was clever, Ed was going places. Why would he love her?

Patsy earnestly turned to Ed. "Ed, you have the brains, it's easy for you, you have a degree and a good job, we both know you are going places. Why waste your time with me?"

Ed laughed out loud, "Because Patsy, I know that you can achieve anything you want to, you're clever and you're determined, and did I mention that I fancy you like mad?"

Patsy could feel herself blushing, but she felt warm and wanted probably for the first time in her life, and she knew she had to take a step and complete this NVQ course. She wanted Ed to be proud of her.

The following day, Bill came to the home to tell them he had some news from his private investigator, "Susan was adopted by a couple called Edward and Elizabeth Harper from Somerset. They had changed Susan's name to Jennifer and now the agency is looking to find out if Jennifer got married. Hopefully, they will find her, they are pretty confident."

Patsy, Rita and Rachael were delighted, although all of them had reservations about whether a meeting between Mary and Jennifer would ever happen and even if it did happen how it would go. After the initial excitement about the news, all of them, including Bill were silent for a while.

Rita broke the silence. "Let's take one step at a time and hope we can have a happy ending," she said and they all silently nodded in agreement, each one wondering if they were doing the right thing.

"I think now is the time to discuss this with Patsy's consultant, after all, we are doing this with the best motives but let's face it, a meeting with Susan may be detrimental to Mary's wellbeing." It was unanimously agreed that was the correct course of action.

Patsy called in at the library on her way home. Sonia had some new books for her, which she was eager to read. Sonia was a great support to her and Patsy reflected on how lucky she was to have the support of her friends, and work colleagues as well as Sonia. After chatting to Sonia for a while, Patsy went into the local shop on her way home to pick up some food for tea, she was planning on having a quiet night in with her books. Later, the two girls sat in their cosy flat chatting over a cup of tea.

"Mum wants you and Ed over for lunch on Sunday if you're both free?" Rosie had a mouthful of digestive biscuit as she was speaking,

"Well, you two are very together these days, it is serious, isn't it, Pats?"

Patsy couldn't help laughing, she was as eager to talk about Ed as Rosie was about knowing,

"I do like him," she said, "well, more really, I think I love him, Rosie, but it's early days and I don't know that much about him. I mean, I know nothing about his family, and I dread to think what he'll think if and when he meets my mother."

Rosie dunked another biscuit into her tea. "I wouldn't worry about that Patsy, from what I've seen of Ed, he loves you to pieces, and you hardly see your mum anyway."

"Does Andy know anything about Ed's family?" Patsy asked, "I mean they might think I'm not good enough, with my background and well, he is clever and he has a degree and everything. We've never talked about our families even. Like I said it is early days, might not come to anything."

Rosie snorted. "Come off it, Patsy Bennett, you two are so right for each other, and one day you will have a degree, of that I'm sure, as if that matters for goodness sake, and his family will love you. Andy said something once about Ed not having a mum, I don't remember the details but ask him daft head."

Rosie got up and said she had to get ready for her hot date and, as she left the room she shouted, "I'll tell Mum to expect you both on Sunday."

Patsy started reading. The subject was institutional abuse, and the author was saying that many hospitals and care homes were managed more for staff convenience rather than their patients' wellbeing. Patients were offered little choice on basic needs such as diet, leisure activities, times to get up and to go to bed. There were too many institutions that saw nothing wrong in patients wearing clothes that belonged to others; the same applied to toiletries and even hairbrushes. Patsy was incensed, and she decided that her goal had to be to change these practices once and for all. She was so thankful that these practices had always been frowned upon in her place of work.

Patsy remembered when she had first started working at the home, she was asked to accompany a resident to a hospital appointment. While they waited to be seen by a doctor, Patsy had noticed another carer with an old lady who looked unkempt, had ill-fitting clothes, uncombed hair, stockings half-mast.

This lady was very confused and looked bewildered by her surroundings, Patsy was annoyed at her treatment, how could this lady be taken out in such a state? The carer spent all the waiting time with her back to the lady and chatting on her phone. Patsy on the other hand gave her resident plenty of reassurance; offered her tea and chatted to the lady she was with.

Before she left the outpatient department, Patsy had asked the carer where she worked. The carer told Patsy and added,

"It's a bind having to bring them out, and this one," and she pointed to the old lady, "This one is away with the fairies. At least you can talk to your lady."

Patsy nodded, she was annoyed but she didn't have the knowledge to argue at the time. It would be so different now. When Patsy returned to the home, she told Rita about the incident and Rita wasted no time in making a complaint to the appropriate inspection authority.

Chapter 14

Mary had advertised for an extra assistant in the shop, much to the relief of Ada. loved her work, and she was becoming very fond of Mary, but the job, which had started out as a bit of a hobby had become near enough a full-time job. Still, Ada was concerned about this thing with Eric. Ada thought he was quite a nice man, but now what with this Rosalyn saying that Eric wasn't the man he appeared to be? Ada didn't want Mary to be hurt.

The job vacancy advertised with the employment exchange brought several prospective employees, and Mary asked Ada if she would help her go through the applications and assist her with the interviews. Ada was more than happy to agree.

The applicants varied in both age and experience. Some, like Ada had a love of fashion and money to service that love but liked the idea of working in a high-class dress shop. Others had experience of shop work and really needed the income, but they had young children and so were limited in the number of hours they could work. There was one young girl in her early twenties who was a possible, she had just graduated from art school, and she was going on to gain a further qualification.

One Wednesday afternoon, half day closing for most retail businesses, including Mary's shop, Ada and Mary conducted the interviews. They were both surprised at the high calibre of the candidates, but the young graduate, Annie Wilson stood out more than the others.

Ada had a few reservations because she felt Annie was young and would not stay long, but Mary was very enthusiastic,

"Just what the business needs Ada, young, with an artistic flair, the windows will look wonderful and she can choose some fashion lines for the younger market."

Ada considered and finally agreed that Annie could be an asset, and she was secretly looking forward to working fewer hours, and so Annie was offered a part-time post.

The interviews had proved to be quite tiring for both Mary and Ada, so later that afternoon, Mary went for a walk, a walk which she took on many occasions down the road where the coveted bungalows were situated. One bungalow was for sale and it was ideal, Mary loved it straight away. The building was well maintained, as they all were, but this one had a lovely garden full of plants and flowers. Mary could imagine herself pottering about in the garden, well after she learned how to garden. A new venture, gardening, and with that thought Mary decided she would enquire about the bungalow at the estate agents and perhaps arrange a viewing.

It wasn't that simple though, Mary thought to herself. Much as Mary wanted more than anything to buy this bungalow, more than anything to live a quiet life on this beautiful tree lined road with her garden, there was Eric. Eric who she still loved more than anything and who wanted her to buy a property in Spain. Still, she now had a nagging doubt in her mind about Eric. She stopped walking and told herself once again not to be stupid.

Mary paced up and down the road, Spain or bungalow? She kept saying to herself, what was she to do? She was so engrossed in her thoughts that she did not notice the man coming out of the bungalow for sale, walking towards her.

"Are you lost madam?" he asked Mary.

Mary was taken aback and wasn't quite sure how to answer. After all she must look strange pacing up and down the road, this very respectable road.

"Oh I am sorry, my name is Mary Reynolds. I own the dress shop in the village and I noticed the bungalow was for sale, and I was thinking of buying a property on this road." Mary felt really silly; she was acting like a teenager, not a mature businesswoman. The man smiled,

"You looked distressed, are you OK? I know all about the dress shop, my wife tells me all the time about your shop; in fact she buys most of her clothes from you. I'm Arthur Stanhope by the way, would you like to come in for some tea? You'll know my wife Isabel."

Mary hesitated, she did know Mrs Stanhope and she had no idea that she lived on her road in her bungalow, but if she went in, she knew she would love it inside as well. After a long pause, Mary knew she had to see inside so she said quickly, "Oh, thank you, I should love to come in if it's no trouble."

Mr Stanhope ushered Mary into the spacious hall and called his wife, "Isabel, you'll never guess who is here?" Mrs Stanhope appeared from one of the rooms and shook Mary's hand while telling Mary how much she loved the shop.

The couple guided Mary around the bungalow. There was a large airy lounge, a spacious well-planned kitchen/ diner, two double bedrooms and bathroom with a separate lavatory, and Mary loved it all. She could imagine furnishing the whole place, how wonderful it would be. Then, the Stanhope's lead the way into the back garden, which mirrored the front garden with an array of trees and flowers, and there was even a garage.

Mrs Stanhope insisted on serving tea and homemade cake in the lounge and Mary suddenly felt totally at home,

"May I ask where you are moving to?" Mary could not believe that they want to leave such a beautiful home.

Mrs Stanhope laughed, "Well, not far actually. Our daughter has a large house here in Oak hill and she and her husband have built us a new bungalow in the grounds, she wants to keep an eye on us you know, says we are getting old," and she and her husband laughed at such a thought.

There followed a discussion on price and Mary told them that she would be a cash buyer and had no property to sell, and the Stanhope's said they would negotiate a fair price accordingly.

"We have been happy here haven't we dear?" Arthur said as he looked lovingly at his wife, who agreed.

"Very happy, and we have nice neighbours, and it is only a ten-minute walk to the village as you know, so handy for everything. We shall miss it, but it will be nice to be nearer to our daughter and her family."

By the time Mary had left the bungalow with a promise of contacting the agent, she had very mixed feelings. She was excited to have nearly bought her bungalow, but she didn't know how she was going to break the news to Eric. As she slowly walked back to her shop, Mary reflected on her life. Here she was contemplating buying a bungalow, she had a successful business and money in the bank, and she had done all this on her own. She could have kept Susan and given her daughter a good life. Why did she not face her parents and tell them that she was keeping the baby? All because of religion and so-called respectability, no wonder she had no time for religion, certainly not since giving up Susan. She had been judged so young, but she was a respectable woman, not a bad person, of that she was sure.

Mary examined her feelings for Eric. As much as she loved him, they wanted different things. She wanted a stable relationship and a comfortable home, and of course her precious shop. He wanted, well what did he want? Mary wasn't sure, but worse than that, she didn't trust him, not like she had.

As Mary opened the door to her flat, her phone was ringing. It was Eric asking her if she wanted to go out for a drink at a country pub that evening. Mary didn't know what to say. She knew that she wasn't ready to tell him about the bungalow, so instead she told him she had been very busy and she was tired.

"I'm going to have an early night Eric, I hope you don't mind but I need a rest."

She thought Eric seemed disappointed but she wasn't sure about that any more. Mary knew she had to find out more about Eric once and for all, the trouble was she was not sure how she could do that, but there had to be a way?

Chapter 15

Rita, Rachael, Bill, Patsy and Mary's consultant, Dr Morris sat in Rita's office discussing at length whether they were taking the right course of action in pursuing the search for Susan, or Jennifer as she was now called. Dr Morris listened to the whole story and she kept nodding but saying very little. She thought for what seemed like ages and then in her quiet slow voice, which typified her, she said that she thought that they should proceed as planned,

"We can review this if and when you locate Jennifer, and truthfully, this is untried territory as far as I am concerned but, in my opinion, if Mary and Jennifer could develop a relationship or even to just meet, I think it would be beneficial to Mary. I think it is worth the risk."

Dr Morris went on to praise the home for the innovative approach they were practicing, and said that she had noticed how much more alert and happier her patients there had become,

"I wish more homes were having the same success. People, including medical and nursing staff are not looking hard enough for any potential improvement. It's not, I believe that they don't want to help, there just isn't the right education and too many outdated practices. Looking after old people is I'm afraid still considered to be not very glamorous by many in our profession."

Patsy couldn't resist saying in a very loud voice, "Well it bloody well will be glamorous by the time we've finished doing all the things we want to do."

They all laughed and Patsy felt stupid. She was a care assistant and she felt that it wasn't her place to voice her opinion so vehemently. However, no one appeared to take offence, and in fact they agreed with her and said so.

"Old people are just young people who became older, so why should they not be treated by skilled people who show them respect? I get really annoyed," Rita was speaking unusually loudly. Patsy rarely saw Rita getting so annoyed.

As they all left the meeting, the discussion with Mary's doctor had eased everyone's mind to some extent, although they were all still worried if they were doing the right thing. The test would come if Jennifer was found and whether or not she agreed to meet her birth mother.

Patsy went back to her work, and Bill went to see Mary. Brother and sister had managed to re-kindle a relationship, despite the years before which had caused so much heartache for them both, but this was now forgotten and both Mary and Bill had become brother and sister again. Patsy could hear Mary laughing, Bill did most of the talking, telling her about his life and his work, and he brought photographs and played her music or read to her. The time they spent together seemed to be good for both of them.

Later that evening, Patsy and Ed were sat in Patsy's flat with Rosie, sharing some wine and a take-out Indian curry. Ed said in a sarcastic tone that he had had an interesting day reporting on a local council meeting. "Riveting stuff," he said, "but all in a day's work. They are talking about closing libraries now, it's sad."

Patsy was horrified, the library and Sonia had helped her so much with her studies and she looked forward to her visits to the library. The thought of the library, her library closing filled her with dismay.

The sombre mood continued with Patsy explaining about the meeting with Mary's doctor,

"If it all worked out and Mary could meet her daughter, it could give Mary some peace at last. From all the research I've read, if things from the past can be resolved then it can only be beneficial to anyone. If a person has dementia, someone who can't express their feelings like you or I can, then a resolution can make a real positive difference to their quality of life."

"Susan or Jennifer as I should call her will be pushing fifty now won't she? Ed asked. She probably has her own family and I wonder how she would react to Mary's illness, it would put a lot of people off. I mean she may think she could end up as Mary's career. Even so, I should love to write a story about it if it was to be a happy ending. I've heard so much about Mary, I feel like I know her myself, I'd love to meet her."

Rosie jumped in, "Next time you and Mary go out for tea, meet up with Ed and he can say hello to Mary. I think she'd love to meet your boyfriend Patsy."

Rosie was smiling cheekily when she spoke, and Patsy didn't think it was such a bad idea, but she was embarrassed that Rosie called Ed her boyfriend. Ed didn't seem to mind. However, Mary needed to meet more people, socialise more, and they did now have a close relationship, so she might be glad to meet a friend of hers.

Rosie said that she was going to have a bath, leaving Ed and Patsy on their own, and it wasn't long before the two were kissing. They hadn't slept together although both of them were tired of holding back, but it wasn't easy when you were sharing a one-bedroom flat. They discussed their dilemma. Ed shared a house with two others but at least he had his own room. Patsy had never been to Ed's place, for some reason he always came to hers, but he said he would ask the guys to go out for the evening,

"We have an agreement between us when we need a bit of space. Stay with me Patsy, and I shall bring you breakfast in bed, well at least coffee and cornflakes, and if you're lucky, I'll throw in a piece of toast."

Patsy laughed and said that she couldn't wait. "For the toast of course," she added. They planned to meet at Ed's place the following night, and with that Ed reluctantly said his goodbyes with a final long kiss.

Rosie returned after her bath. "Ed gone has he?" she said, "I can go out you know, or even stay at mum's if you two need some privacy. I don't want to stand in the path of true love."

Patsy was touched by her friend's kindness,

"Thanks, Rosie, but I am staying at Ed's, at least he has his own room so it makes sense. I do love him and it feels right."

Rosie smiled at her friend, "I'm happy for you Patsy, you deserve some happiness. Can I be a bridesmaid but I must insist I want a nice dress?"

Patsy picked up a cushion and threw it at Rosie. "We'll see," she said and the two girls giggled.

The following evening Patsy made the short journey to Ed's house, situated in a tree-lined road so typical of Roxbury. The house was a well-maintained spacious terraced property with a small front garden and on street parking, and as Patsy was walking up the path she couldn't help feeling nervous.

Patsy had been thinking all day about seeing Ed. It was the first time she had been to his place, and she wondered what his housemates were like and whether or not they would be there, or whether Ed had managed to persuade them to disappear for a few hours. Patsy hoped they were out, she was ready to commit to Ed and she certainly didn't want any interruptions. Ed was not her first lover, she had had relationships before but Ed was different, he was the one, of that she was sure. She had never felt so in love before.

Ed greeted her with a hug. "The guys are out until later so we've got the place to ourselves, and I've bought some food from the deli. I hope it's OK, feel a bit nervous actually." Ed was speaking very quickly which made Patsy laugh.

"I'm sure the food will be lovely and I feel nervous too, although I don't know why," she said.

Ed gave her a tour of the downstairs and they settled in the kitchen with a glass of wine. Patsy noticed the table, set really nicely with candles and flowers.

"I was going to cook but I'm not very good at anything other than beans on toast so I hope you like the food, it's all cold so no risk of burning," Ed looked even more nervous, Patsy had never seen him like this before.

"It's all perfect," she said. "I love cold food, but beans on toast are great as well."

The dinner was indeed perfect. Ed had spent money on the finest products, which he had bought from an upmarket deli in the village, and both Patsy and Ed relaxed over the good food and wine and the easy conversation.

They talked about their lives and their families. Patsy spoke about her problems she had with her mother and Ed was sympathetic, but at the same time non-judgmental.

Ed told Patsy that his mum had died in a road traffic accident two years before. Patsy was shocked because she hadn't expected that. Ed confided that he had always been very close to his mum; he was away at university when it happened,

"It was a terrible time Patsy for all of us. She was wonderful and to be taken from us so suddenly. Mum was driving home from town, the roads were icy and a lorry driver lost control and ploughed into her car. They said she would have died instantly. I rushed home, can't even remember that journey, I just knew I had to get home."

Patsy put her arm around him and they sat in silence for a few minutes.

Ed said he had an older sister, Ruby; she was a designer and lived with her partner and their baby girl in the village where they had grown up. Ed's dad lived on his own in their home in Devon, but according to Ed, his father was not short of female admirers, and he had started to socialise more these days. He talked at length about growing up in a happy home. Ed's mum had been an art teacher at the local grammar school and his dad was a solicitor. Patsy was so sad that Ed had lost his mum in such a way.

Patsy said that she was worried his dad would think that she wasn't good enough for him, "Me and my background, so different from how you describe yours."

Ed looked into Patsy's eyes. "My dad will love you silly, and my mum would have loved you too, but most importantly, I love you." And that was that.

They were soon in Ed's bedroom making love, and they both knew it was a perfect end to a perfect evening. The next morning Ed true to his promise served cornflakes, coffee and toast (with beans) to Patsy in bed, and Patsy had never felt happier than she did at that moment.

Chapter 16

It was April 1982 and Annie Wilson started work in Mary's shop. She arrived for work in a striped mid length wool dress, black court shoes, her hair in a neat ponytail and perfect makeup. Mary thought how pretty she was and was absolutely sure that they had made the right decision in offering her the job.

Annie proved to be very enthusiastic, a quick learner and good with the clients. Most of Mary's customers were older ladies, and Mary was eager to encourage a younger clientele as well. Clients had mentioned to Mary before about how their daughters couldn't find suitable clothes in the village and had to travel to Stockport or Manchester.

Oak hill was expanding at an alarming rate, and there were other dress shops, still none with the style and service like Mary's shop. There had been trendy boutiques in the village in the past, catering for young people, but none had lasted long. The owners were young without business experience, in Mary's opinion. Mary had often reflected that they had no 'staying power' and gave up too quickly.

Mary had never considered any of them a threat because although the labels were supposed to be by designers, most of the clothes were cheaply made with high prices. She wasn't worried about the latest shops that were opening either, she had a loyal clientele and she only sold quality.

Annie fitted in well. Mary would hear Ada laughing with Annie while they were having their breaks. Ada had daughters of a similar age and she could relate well to young people. Annie offered to dress the windows and the results were stunning. Nearly everyone who came in the shop remarked how they couldn't resist buying something, which was in the display. Mary was looking at some new stock, and as always she asked Ada's opinion, and she asked Annie to have a look too. Annie couldn't wait to look,

"Beautiful clothes Mary, how about this, oh and this?" and Annie excitedly chose some pieces ideal for Mary's prospective younger clientele.

Ada was taken aback, "Lovely dear, for the younger woman, but that's not who we cater for."

"But that's just it, Ada," Mary said, "It's just what we need to encourage the young ones. The village is expanding so much all the time. The older women have daughters, and there are quite a few young married career ladies living here now, and we do have competition."

So Annie chose some trendy clothes and with Mary's blessing displayed the new range in the shop windows, and before long, an added young clientele were shopping with Mary.

On her own one evening, Mary decided it was time to tell Eric about the bungalow. Arthur and Isabel Stanhope were anxious to sell, and they had had several conversations about when the sale could take place. Their bungalow in the grounds of their daughter's house was all but completed, so telling Eric was not an option, Mary felt she had to do it, although she didn't want to.

Their relationship was much the same on the surface, but underneath Mary felt differently, suspicious even. Eric took her out regularly to nice places and stayed over in her flat one or two nights a week. He still kept talking about the Spanish property and had suggested that Mary get herself a passport,

"Of course, the apartments are not quite ready yet, but if you had a passport we can view together. The sun will do you good and all my friend needs at the moment is a deposit, but they are selling fast my love so we need to get a move on."

They were sat in a local restaurant having a superb meal when Mary finally broke the news about the bungalow to him,

"It's everything I want Eric, you will love it, we could make a real home, oh and wait until you see the garden."

Eric was quiet for a moment and said quietly, "I can see you have made up your mind Mary," he paused again maintaining his composure, "I see that now, but, oh come on love you must have loads of money put away? That business is worth a fortune and you don't spend anything really. Yes, that's what we'll do, you can have the bungalow and the Spanish place."

Mary was lost for words, what was he up to? But she kept calm and smiled lovingly at Eric. However, in that moment Mary was having further grave doubts about Eric. If she bought the apartment in Spain, deep down she knew that Eric would never commit fully to their relationship; she had been a fool to ever think that he would.

Mary was deep in thought in the shop the next day, so much so that Ada was worried about her. "Are you alright Mary, you are very quiet this morning?" She tentatively asked.

"Yes, thank you Ada," Mary answered then added, "It's Eric, I must admit I am worried Ada. I told him about the bungalow and he suggested I buy the bungalow and the place in Spain, oh and he wants me to get a passport as soon as. What would you surmise from that?"

Ada was careful, she knew how much Eric meant to Mary, "Well, how about getting a passport and going to Spain to investigate these properties by you, without Eric? It may set your mind at rest, at least you would know just what properties he was talking about."

Mary thought for a moment. It did make sense but she would need to know where the properties were, and the name of the developer, still that shouldn't be hard. After all Eric was always eager to talk about these apartments. The other problem was that Mary had never been abroad before, she wasn't sure she could undertake such a journey on her own.

Mary relayed her thoughts to Ada and after thinking for a moment Ada said,

"I could come with you, but with you away I would be needed in the shop. What about Rosalyn? She seems anxious to prove to you that Eric is up to no good. If the properties are wonderful and value for money, that would put paid to her ideas."

It seemed ridiculous to Mary to ask Rosalyn, but on the other hand, Ada did have a point. She would need to pay for Rosalyn, not a problem, but Rosalyn may not want to leave her aunt or even accompany Mary on a trip, however there was no one else to ask. Mary suddenly realised that she had virtually no friends, she had never had time for them, she only had Eric and she had no intention of going with him. No, this trip was an investigation.

Suddenly she had an idea, "Ada, if I close the shop for a long weekend, would you come with me? I'll pay all the expenses of course. You've travelled widely and you know the area and well, I hardly know Rosalyn, I wouldn't feel comfortable."

Ada was flattered, "Close the shop! Mary you are worried, but of course I'll come and I shall pay for myself, it'll be an adventure. Now no argument."

And so a decision was made. Ada said she would make the arrangements when Mary had her passport.

Mary filled in her application for a passport at the post office, much to the amazement of the postmistress, "You never go away Mary, can't believe it, but it will do you and Eric the world of good to get away. Where are you going?"

Mary didn't say that Eric wasn't going, this was a secret trip, but she answered, "Oh I'm not sure yet, wait till I get my passport."

Mary left the post office certain she was doing the right thing, but she felt like a criminal about having to lie to Belinda, the postmistress. In fact, Mary was certain she was becoming a good liar, and she realised that the lies would have to continue until Mary found out just who Eric was.

After she left the post office, Mary decided to visit Rosalyn. She liked the woman and felt sorry for her and she felt that she owed it to tell Rosalyn about her proposed trip to Spain.

Rosalyn answered the door and took Mary into the living room where Mrs Johnson was sitting watching TV, and greeted Mary warmly,

"Hello dear, Rosalyn turn this TV down will you? We have a guest." Mrs Johnson turned to Mary, "Can't seem to get the hang of these new TVs, too many buttons."

Rosalyn turned the TV down and offered Mary tea. "Have a glass of sherry dear," Mrs Johnson said to Mary, and because Mary needed some 'Dutch' courage she said that she would love a glass of sherry. The small talk continued for a while and Mary enquired how Mrs Johnson was, and she was pleased to hear that she was doing much better.

Taking a deep breath Mary said, "I came here to tell you that I am going to Spain to see this apartment that Eric is so keen for me to buy. I felt it only right that you should know that I listened to what you told me, and the more I think about it things don't add up, you may be right about him. This trip should shed more light on what, if anything he is up to."

Rosalyn looked relieved, and Mrs Johnson said that she was pleased Mary had decided to investigate the man further, "Don't let him rob you too dear, keep your wits about you. I only wish I was younger, I'd soon sort him out."

Mary filled them in on the details and said that she was nervous about the trip but excited at the same time. After saying her goodbyes, Mary, accompanied by Rosalyn went to the front door,

"Thank you for telling me, Mary, good luck and if you ever need any help, don't hesitate to ask me." Mary left, glad that she had confided in Rosalyn.

Chapter 17

Patsy was finding it hard work keeping up with her own studies and working on her NVQ. The latter she found surprisingly easy. It was mainly reporting on day-to-day tasks, and Patsy found writing reports was not a chore any more like it used to be. Still, it was hard work but she knew that she needed to gain some qualifications and NVQ was a good way to start.

On her next trip to the library, she asked Sonia about the prospect of the library closing. Sonia was obviously worried, she had worked there for years and she loved her job and knew all the regulars,

"Mrs Remington likes her mysteries, and Mrs Whitehead loves a good romance. Then I have quite a few who are studying for various things, like you Patsy and I enjoy researching material for them. We have the children's corner where I read stories once a week to the little ones. I will miss it and I won't be the only one."

"You certainly won't, Sonia," said Patsy with a heavy heart, "I don't know what I'll do without you."

They both sat in silence for a while thinking about the effect on book lovers if the library were to close.

"We should have a demonstration, Sonia," Patsy suddenly said. "That library is too important to too many people to close, lots of people will support us."

Sonia thought it was a great idea and they started to plan.

When Patsy next went to work, Rachael told her that Jim, Doreen's husband was very ill with a bad chest infection. Doreen was beside herself with worry and the family spent long hours at Jim's bedside. Dr Morris and her team were treating Jim, and together with Doreen and the family they thought it best if Jim didn't go into hospital. Instead, he should remain at the home where they could monitor his condition carefully.

Patsy was upset and she went into see to Jim and Doreen. Doreen said how comfortable her husband looked and reminisced about their long life together, all the while gently touching Jim's face and looking lovingly at her soul mate.

Patsy reflected that an impending death was always upsetting. She had seen a few residents pass away in the time she had worked there and it never got any easier. Patsy gave Doreen a hug and sat with her for a short time. One of the downfalls of the job was that there was always work to do and not enough time to sit and talk to the residents.

In times of sadness, time had to be made but it was still limited. Patsy thought to herself how valuable the trips were because it did allow at least some quality time with residents, how wonderful it would be to have more quality time to spend with grieving relatives, they needed support too.

Fortunately, the family arrived to be with their mum and dad and shortly after 6 pm. Jim passed away peacefully with his family around him. Later that evening, Patsy was helping Mary to get ready for bed. Patsy was on duty until 10pm and many, but not all of the residents liked to go to bed fairly early. Mary suddenly said,

"The nice man and his wife, how is he?"

Patsy was shocked, Mary had little contact with the other residents, and remarkably Mary had remembered that Jim was ill. She was unsure of how to answer, but she didn't want to lie to her friend.

"Jim died earlier this evening, Mary, but all his family were with him, he died peacefully."

Mary stared straight ahead and said, "Good, I'm glad he wasn't on his own," and no more was said.

Patsy left Mary's room after helping her to bed and making sure she was settled with everything she needed. The staff on duty were talking about Jim and Doreen, and how sad it all was. Looking after older people for a long time had to take its toll on carers. Most of them felt that they had lost a friend too, and there was no doubt that Jim would be missed. The consolation for everyone was to help their patients to die with dignity and crucially in no pain or distress. This had been successfully achieved and there was comfort for everyone in that. Jim had been taken to a chapel of rest at the undertakers and her family was comforting Doreen.

Patsy told everyone about the conversation she had had with Mary, "I couldn't believe that she remembered that Jim was ill, I wonder how she knew."

Many of the staff present said that it was common knowledge in the home. Residents had been chatting to Jim's relatives and they knew how distressed Doreen was.

"She must have heard people talking. It's amazing how Mary has improved so much recently, more than we could have hoped for," Rachael said. "She is more interested in everything, and she looks so much happier these days."

"Mary's like me," said Jess, "more interested and much happier. I used to think looking after older people was the worse job ever; in fact I was ready to leave. Now, it's great, old people are real people, I love my job. I don't know why I could never see that before."

Patsy reflected on Jess's words and answered, "Real people yes they are, and we're moving in the right direction but we still have a way to go."

The weekly meeting with Val, the NVQ assessor went well. Val was exceptionally pleased with Patsy's progress,

"At this rate you shall finish NVQ 2 in a few weeks, and then, if you want to you can move on to NVQ 3. Any idea what you plan to do in the future Patsy?"

"I think I want to go into nursing," answered Patsy, "I really want to make a difference somehow to people with dementia. That is the goal."

Val nodded, "Rita was telling me about that, all the new projects you've been a part of introducing and how successful they've been. Whatever you decide Patsy, I'm sure that you will do well."

Patsy was chatting to Ed later about her day. They were in Ed's car on their way to a country pub for an evening out,

"I want you to be proud of me Ed, but mostly I want to be proud of myself."

Ed was quick to reply,

"I'll always be proud of you Patsy, don't ever doubt that. I love you idiot and I always will. I told my dad all about you and he can't wait to meet you. Can you get any time off and we'll go down to Devon? I've not seen dad for a while and I want you to see where I grew up, I think you will love it."

Patsy was excited and nervous about going to Devon but she promised to try and get some time off work. She needed a break anyway; life was hectic at the moment,

"I'll ask Rita, see what I can do. In the meantime I should like you to meet Mary, will you do that for me?"

"Can't wait," said Ed, after all I feel like I know her anyway. You arrange it and I'll be there. I wonder if Mary would like a trip to Oak hill, look where the shop was, see her bungalow, what do you think?

Patsy looked lovingly at Ed; tears were in her eyes, "Oh Ed what a kind and wonderful thought. So you do listen to me. Mary would love that, and so would I." Patsy kissed him and knew that she loved this man for sure.

Patsy wasted no time in asking Rita if it would be OK to take Mary to Oak hill and Rita thought it was a great idea.

"I'll go on one of my days off so it doesn't interfere with work and we can take our time," Patsy said, "I'll find out when Ed can get a day off and let you know."

Patsy didn't mention to Mary about going to Oak hill for two reasons. Firstly she didn't want Mary to worry or get over excited, and secondly, she wasn't sure Mary would remember she was going out.

On the planned day, Patsy arrived at the home and asked Mary if she wanted a trip out. Mary was delighted, she didn't asked where they were going, and just going was good enough.

They chose Mary's outfit together as they usually did. Patsy would pull different outfits out of the wardrobe and Mary chose which one she would wear. Next came the shoes, handbag, coat and jewellery, all colour coordinated, and finally the hair and a touch of makeup. Mary wasn't keen on too much makeup but she did like her lipstick, which again had to blend well with her outfit.

Patsy knew it was time to mention Ed, "I hope you don't mind Mary but a friend of mine is taking us in his car. He is actually a very good friend of mine, I feel sure you will like him."

Patsy was a bit worried Mary might object to going out with Ed, she was after all a very private person. Mary smiled and nodded, and Patsy struggled to read Mary's feelings, but at least Mary raised no objections.

When Mary and Patsy were ready, they went to the reception area where Ed was chatting to Rita. Ed came over to Mary and took hold of her hand,

"Hello, Mary, I'm Ed, your chauffeur for the day, I hope you don't mind me tagging along."

Mary smiled, "Not at all young man, it's been a while since I've been in a car, oh and my legs aren't very good these days."

Ed was quick to reply, "No problem, Mary, I can always carry you." Mary laughed and they went outside to the car.

Wheelchair loaded they set off for Oak hill, Mary in the front seat and Patsy in the back explaining where they were going,

"We thought you might like to go to Oak hill, Mary. We can look for your old shop if you like and you can show Ed and I the sights."

Mary was smiling broadly, no words, just smiles. Approaching Oak hill high street, Mary excitedly said, "I lived here," and she shuffled nearer to the window to get a better view.

"Can you remember where your shop was Mary?" Ed asked, but from Mary's silence, he could tell she wasn't sure.

"So busy now, it was never so busy when I had my shop," Mary exclaimed while looking around the street for something familiar. "Can't see the shop. It's not far from the post office." Mary was now getting upset.

Needing to diffuse the situation Ed said, "Let's all get some lunch." Ed pulled up outside an impressive looking restaurant. Patsy was relieved, Mary needed some quiet time, and this was all too overwhelming. Patsy was beginning to think this was a bad idea, bringing Mary back.

As they got settled at a pleasant table and Patsy went through the menus with Mary, Ed asked the waiter if he knew Oak hill well. The young waiter said he had grown up in Oak hill,

"I've always lived here, my parents moved here when they got married."

Patsy smiled at the waiter, "There used to be a dress shop owned by this lady here until the 1980s, but it's changed so much here we can't seem to locate exactly where it was."

The waiter thought for a minute and then said, "Tell you what, and let me phone my mum, she'll know."

Ed thanked the young man and they all got on with deciding what they were going to order. Mary was very definite about what she wanted to eat,

"I'll have chargrilled chicken, dauphinois potatoes and green beans." She handed the menu back to Patsy. Patsy was delighted, Mary hadn't needed her help with the menu, she was like a different person when she was on an outing. Ed smiled; he was relieved the trip had taken a turn for the better.

When the waiter returned with their drinks he was smiling, "My mum said there were several dress shops, but the most famous was owned by a lady called Mary Reynolds. She said she bought all her clothes there and she was sad when it closed. It's actually two doors away, still a very nice dress shop according to mum."

Ed thanked the waiter and explained to Mary that her shop was close and it was still a dress shop. Mary looked pleased and Patsy promised they would go and look after the meal.

They all enjoyed their lunch. Ed told Mary all about his job at the newspaper, and about his time growing up in Devon. "I'm hoping to take Patsy home very soon," Ed added. Patsy nodded and smiled.

"I went to that part of the world once, well Somerset," said Mary sadly, "lovely down there, the beach and the sea, but not a happy time unfortunately, it was a very long time ago, but I remember it well."

Patsy wondered if the memory had anything to do with losing Susan, but decided it was not a good idea to ask. Ed insisted on paying the bill saying, "It's a delight to finally meet you Mary, and it's not often I get the chance to take two lovely ladies out for the day." Mary, always polite thanked him for a lovely lunch.

As they were leaving the restaurant, a middle-aged lady came over to them and warmly greeted Mary, "Mary, you probably don't remember me, but I used to come to your shop all the time. My son works here and he told me you were here, so I had to come and see you. I heard you weren't well but actually you look wonderful."

Mary looked back at the woman who obviously did recognise her. "Tailored trousers suits, dark colours, of course I remember you, I knew all my customers. So nice to see you again and so good of you to come in and see me. Now, let's have a look at my shop, see what it has become now."

Chapter 18

The passport arrived and Mary set her plan into action. The next time Mary saw Eric, at her flat, she told him she had been thinking about the place in Spain and she had decided that he was right, it would be nice to spend some time in the sun, and it would be a good idea to invest in a property there,

"I'm so excited, Eric, I'm sorry I was so negative about the idea. I want to know all about it, where is it? Can I see the plans again? Who is the developer, have you known him long?"

Eric laughed; he was obviously delighted with her change of heart. He joked as he always did and said,

"Well, as it happens young lady I just happen to have the plans with me." With that he sat her at the table and spread an impressive plan of the development on the table.

There was no stopping Eric once he got going, "The development is just outside Malaga, and Mary you will fall in love with it. Beautiful apartments and the grounds are expensively landscaped around the pool. We can sit on our balcony with a nice glass of wine in the evenings and wait until you try all the different restaurants. I for one would have no problem retiring and moving to Spain with you." Eric was not stopping for breath.

"Now my friend the developer, Peter Summers he is very good at what he does, he's done several of these developments and believe me, they sell like hot cakes."

Mary sat close to the table, looking at all the plans and listening intently to Eric, all the while noting the exact location of the property. If this was real it so wonderful she might even buy an apartment. However she had a feeling somewhere inside of her, a doubt that she couldn't explain.

When Eric had finally finished and got up to leave, Mary suddenly said, "Eric when I get back, I'll get that passport and we shall go to Spain and have a look, how exciting that will be."

Eric looked confused, "Get back from where, Mary?"

Calmly Mary said she thought she had told him about her shopping trip to London. "I need new furniture for the bungalow and since I can't find what I'm looking for here, I thought perhaps a shopping expedition to London would be the answer. I've not yet decided when I am going, I'll have to close the shop for a few days, but I'll let you know." Mary couldn't look at Eric, it was another lie, but still she knew what she was doing was for all for the right reasons.

As Eric was leaving, he turned to Mary and kissed her. "Go and have your shopping trip Mary, and I'll look forward to showing you our home in the sun."

Strange Mary thought that he hadn't been shocked that she was closing the shop. She never closed the shop. He either didn't know her or didn't care.

Ada had booked the airline tickets and the hotel. From where Mary had explained where the development was, Ada knew that it was only a short distance from where she had booked the hotel. They would only be away for four days; long enough to see what she needed to see thought Mary. The plan was to leave on Sunday morning and would be back on Wednesday. Annie said that she was happy to be in the shop Tuesday and Wednesday, but Ada was worried that she wouldn't be able to cope. Mary knew that she would.

The day before they were due to leave, Mary telephoned Eric and told him she would be back on Wednesday. She also had a quiet word with Annie and told her that if Eric asked any questions, she was in London, shopping, "That's if you don't mind, dear, I mean telling an untruth." Annie had laughed and said that Mary's secret was safe with her,

"Just try and find some time to enjoy yourself," she told Mary.

Sunday arrived and Ada arrived in a taxi to pick Mary up. Mary had struggled to pack her case, after all she had never been abroad, and Ada had warned her that the weather would be hot, weather Mary was definitely not used to. When they got to the airport, Mary was amazed at the numbers of people in the terminal,

"Are all these people going somewhere Ada? Oh what a silly question, forget I asked." Mary had never felt so out of her comfort zone.

Thanks to Ada's expert guidance they passed through check in and security quite quickly and were soon in the departure lounge having coffee.

"I do hope I am wrong about Eric," said Mary.

Ada replied, "Well, Mary, hopefully we'll soon know."

When it was time boarding the aircraft, Mary was decidedly nervous, but she followed Ada onto the plane and they settled into their seats. Taxiing down to the runway, Mary did admit to Ada that she was a little worried, and Ada had reassured her that she would be fine, and during take-off, Ada constantly spoke to Mary, saying that they would soon be up in the clouds.

Despite her nerves, Mary had to admit that she enjoyed the whole experience. The drink and the snack they had, the friendly crew, and the best part was looking out of the window and seeing all the houses and roads which looked so minute from the air. Mary realised that she had led a sheltered life, too busy to allow herself enjoyment or a holiday. She was going to enjoy this trip after all despite what she would discover, and she sat back in her seat and relaxed.

The journey was a lot quicker than Mary had envisaged. Spain had always seemed to be far away, but before she knew it they had landed, collected their luggage and were in a taxi on their way to the hotel. The weather was sunny and Mary looked out and enjoyed the sights along the way. She noticed it wasn't as green as her homeland, but the views of the sea and the sun compensated.

They checked into a beautiful hotel, it was expensive but Mary didn't mind, after all, she had never travelled before. Ada had thoughtfully booked two adjoining rooms, both with a balcony, which overlooked a swimming pool and the sea. The two women unpacked and went out to look around. Mary liked everything, the pavement cafes, the beach, the sea, the smart shops and of course the sun. Ada asked Mary if she wanted to see the apartments, and after careful thought, Mary suggested they leave the visit until the following morning.

"In that case," said Ada, "let's find somewhere to have a nice dinner."

Later that evening as Mary lay in the king-size bed; she looked back on the day and thought just how lovely it all had been. Ada had turned out to be an ideal travel companion, a good friend Mary thought. Her friend had chosen everything with good taste and she had been thoughtful and good company. That night, Mary had the best sleep she had had in years.

The following morning, Mary was up early, showered and dressed and enjoying coffee on the balcony. It was a beautiful day, and even early in the day there were people going down to the huge swimming pool, and in the distance she could see boats sailing in the glistening sea. Ada telephoned Mary's room and soon afterwards they were both enjoying breakfast on the terrace. Ada said she had made some enquiries, and the address Eric had given for the development was on the coast road outside Malaga, a short taxi ride away.

Mary was apprehensive during the journey, wondering what she would find when they got there. She hoped above all that the apartments would be everything Eric had promised, this was the man she had fallen in love with, the man she wanted to share the rest of her life with. Despite the suspicions she now had, she found it difficult to believe that he was only after her money. The taxi stopped next to a large expanse of land and told them that this was the place. Mary surveyed the terrain and the obvious lack of apartment complexes.

"Are they building here do you know?" Ada asked the driver. His English was not that good, and it was hard to comprehend exactly what he said, but they did understand him enough to know that the land was unsuitable to build on. The two women were horrified and Ada suggested that they go back to the hotel, but Mary insisted they have a closer look so they asked the driver to wait for them, and they both got out of the taxi and walked over to the land. No notices about apartments, no machinery, not a hint of ground preparation, in fact there was nothing there. Both women were lost for words, Ada because she knew how upsetting this discovery was for Mary, and Mary because she knew now in her heart of hearts that Rosalyn was right about Eric.

As they were walking back to the taxi, a man walking his dog asked them if they were lost. Ada showed him the plans Mary had been given and explained that Mary had been asked to purchase an apartment there. The man was English and told them that he had lived in Spain since his retirement.

He shook his head saying, "Another one, you're not the first my dear. This is just wasteland and there never has and never will be any apartments built here. This road is due to be widened and that land will be part of that project. You are about the tenth or eleventh person who has come looking for an imaginary apartment. There are some unscrupulous people who trick people in the UK to part with their money. They want to believe in a dream, but at least you had the sense to come and look. There are plenty of lovely developments in the area, if you haven't lost all your money go and have a look at those."

Mary nodded and thanked him. Ada and Mary returned to the hotel, Mary was unsure of what to do next. She felt like going straight home and said so to Ada. They sat in the hotel bar; they both needed a drink. In a quiet corner of the bar, they spoke at length about what had just happened. Mary was in total shock, but Ada said to her, "Mary, we did think that this could happen, at least you know now and you've not handed over any money. Let's face it, it could have been a lot worse. Do you really want to go home? I say, we're here now, let's enjoy ourselves."

Mary thought for a moment, and realised Ada was quite right. She did know now and why not enjoy the time here, after all she didn't know when or if she would get a chance to travel and relax again, she needed a break, "I think that's an excellent idea Ada, what about a walk down to the beach?"

The time passed too quickly, they saw the sights, they had some lovely meals, they shopped, and in Mary's eyes it was all so wonderful. They also saw some lovely apartments, some for sale and cheaper than the one she was going to buy. Mary talked to Ada about her relationship with Eric and said that she didn't know what she would do now and Ada advised her to do nothing until she had a chance to think about it.

"Perhaps even talk it over with Rosalyn, after all she came out of that relationship with nothing, and we don't know how many other women he has conned, or indeed planning to in the future."

"Wise words," said Mary, "I shall talk to Rosalyn when we get back."

Mary was sitting on the plane going home, she had achieved what she set out to do, to see the so-called development. The trip had been traumatic and yet, she had enjoyed the experience and she knew at least that she had found a good friend in Ada.

Chapter 19

Patsy, Ed and Mary left the restaurant; Ed had given the young waiter a large tip, saying as he placed the money in the hand of the waiter,

"Thank you for contacting your mum, it made the day for Mary to meet her again."

Mary's old shop was indeed still a dress shop and Mary critically looked in the windows,

"Um," was all she said.

"Do you want to go inside, Mary?" Patsy asked, but Mary declined the offer,

"Not the same anymore, no class dear, not my shop anymore," and she waved them on. They had a walk down the high street, Ed making jokes about his wheelchair driving skills. Mary would occasionally say 'changed' or 'not the same' as they passed various buildings, and both Patsy and Ed were getting worried again that this had been a huge mistake. They offered to take Mary to see her bungalow but she wasn't interested, which worried them even more.

Ed dropped Mary and Patsy back at the home and arranged to meet Patsy later. As he helped Mary from the car she took his hand and said,

"Thank you, dear, it was nice of you to take me back, memories you know, it is not my shop anymore, I know that now. Oh and make sure that look after this young lady," Patsy smiled at Ed.

"I think she approves of you," Patsy whispered to Ed, and he nodded and laughed. Patsy asked Mary if she would like to have a rest and she said she would like that, and after Patsy had helped Mary into bed, and brought her a cup of tea, she told Mary she was going home.

Patsy and Ed were in what had become their favourite Indian restaurant later that evening, Ed said how much he hand enjoyed meeting Mary,

"You talk so much about her so I felt that I already knew her. She seems lost somehow, but there is hidden warmth about her. It's such a pity we never knew her before her illness. By the way, any news about her daughter?"

"No, not yet," said Patsy, "but if the agency manages to find her, that's when the hard work begins. I keep hoping we are doing the right thing."

Ed thought for a moment and then said, "Imagine what it was like for her to have to give her baby away. I bet she has thought about Susan every day since, and I also think it's so sad that she has kept that secret all these years. Mary trusted you Patsy, she trusted you so much that she told you her secret. For what it's worth, I think if the daughter is found, you will get her through it in the best way, but then that's exactly why I love you, Patsy Bennett."

Patsy blushed. She loved him too. She paused, and then explained that the agency was closer to finding Susan and that after Susan was adopted she had her name changed to Jennifer.

Ed said it all sounded promising and then told Patsy he had arranged with his dad for them both to spend a few days in Devon, "Can you get the time off next week do you think? I want to show you great beaches, country pubs, magnificent cliff walks, oh and I want to show off my girl."

To say Patsy was worried about meeting Ed's dad would have been an understatement, but then again, she had never really been anywhere outside Manchester, and she would be with Ed,

"I'll check with Rita tomorrow but if I am going on holiday, I want to finish my NVQ and hand it in, so my love, I am going back to my flat to do just that."

Patsy got up to leave, although it was getting harder by the minute to leave Ed.

"OK bossy," Ed was laughing, "but I insist on walking you home."

Patsy handed in her last assignment for her NVQ the following day, and asked Rita about some annual leave for the following week, "I realise it's short notice and I totally understand if you can't give it me, but Ed wants me to meet his dad in Devon."

Rita immediately answered, "You need a break Patsy, you have been working so hard, so yes, have the time off and enjoy yourself and relax, and I've got a feeling I shall have to buy a hat soon for the wedding."

Patsy thanked her and said a wedding was a bit premature; Rita gave her a knowing smile.

On her last day at work before the holiday, Patsy sat with all the residents and told them that she was going to Devon. Patsy had done some research about the county and she asked the residents if anyone had ever been there? Patsy was careful to not mention about Mary saying she had visited near there many years ago, there was a sadness when Mary had told them and it wouldn't be fair to expect Mary to elaborate unless she was ready.

Doreen said she had been to Blackpool many times, but never down south. "Never fancied it really, they all talk funny."

Albert, however, said he and his dear wife went to Devon every year for their holidays,

"I closed the shop for two weeks every year to give my wife a holiday. We loved Paignton and Torquay, but it used to take us two days to drive there. Course they didn't have motorways like now. We liked the cream teas best." And everybody laughed.

"Can you remember where you used to stay Albert?" Patsy asked, but Albert struggled to remember. After a long pause he smiled and said, "You ask my dear wife, she'll know."

Patsy didn't remind Albert that his wife had died some years before, so instead she asked, "What do you think the weather will be like at this time of year?" Albert said with certainty that the sun always shines in Devon.

Bella interrupted and called Albert a 'stupid old bugger' and then said,

"I never needed to go away on holiday, I had my home and my husband. I liked where I lived, anyway. Will one of you girls take me out for a 'ciggy'? I'm gasping for me woodbine."

Everyone saw the side fortunately and Jess took Bella out, so they could both have a cigarette.

Mary was sitting quietly throughout the conversation, but she was smiling at some of the comments, which was a reassuring sign for Patsy, who had explained to Mary beforehand what they would be discussing and if she wanted to join the group. The fact that Mary had agreed was indeed a breakthrough. Mary was usually reluctant to join in anything, much preferring the one-to-one conversations and trips out. Mary didn't say anything, but Patsy could sense that Mary had enjoyed the conversation.

Ed picked Patsy up in his car the next day, all ready for the visit to his childhood home.

Ed was excited, "Can't wait for the family to meet you, and Devon is beautiful." Ed was obviously looking forward to the trip. Patsy, on the other hand was really nervous and wondering if she had done the right thing by agreeing to go. They had only known each other a short time and from everything she had heard about Ed's family, they were so very different from hers. This definitely was a big mistake; she would show herself up big time. Ed's father and sister would despise her; they would think she was after Ed for his family money.

On the other hand, she thought, she was in love with Ed and he with her, and they wanted to spend their lives together, so she must be brave and show them that she was an intelligent, loving girl, not a gold digger. So, she put her bag in the back of the car, smiled and said to Ed,

"Let's see Devon then shall we?" and off they went.

As they drove onto the motorway, Patsy had to admit that this was an adventure for her. She had never been out of Manchester, and as they drove through the Cheshire countryside and then the Staffordshire scenery, she was mesmerised by the beautiful views. Living in the city all her life, she never imagined that there was stunning countryside so close.

By the time they reached the M5, Patsy started to relax. She and Ed were talking all the time. Ed was pointing out different points of interest and telling her more about his childhood and his family,

"My mum was so lovely, I wish you could have met her. She would have loved you, and she would be so interested in what you are doing. It was such a shock when she was killed, took us all a long time to get over it, we're still not over it really. I wish I hadn't been away when it happened, I wish every day that I could have spent more time with her. A tragic accident that shattered our happy family."

Patsy listened in silence, she knew that Ed needed to talk and she felt privileged that he was choosing to tell her. When he fell silent, she gently touched his arm and she told him she was there for him. They drove in silence for a while, and then Patsy told Ed about her conversation with the residents about Devon and he said that Albert was spot on, when he said the weather in Devon was always sunny,

"Well, that is unless it's snowing of course."

Approaching Bristol, Ed said that if Patsy didn't mind, they would leave the motorway,

"The scenery is so much nicer off the motorway and I thought that we could find a nice country pub and have some lunch."

Patsy didn't mind at all, she was enjoying it all, it was all wonderful, and she had noticed that the further south they drove, the warmer the weather became.

The journey took them through quaint country lanes until they stopped at an old-world pub set back from the road. The pub had a pleasant garden with wooden chairs and tables and Ed suggested that they sat outside for their meal. Patsy couldn't have been happier.

Ed went inside the pub to get the drinks and some menus, and Patsy sat in the sun feeling less apprehensive about meeting Ed's family. A couple sat nearby were chatting to one another and Patsy smiled at the West Country accent. Doreen was right, they did sound funny. When Ed returned with a large glass of white wine for Patsy and a small beer for himself, Patsy told him that she felt as though they were in a different country which Ed found highly amusing,

"Wait until you get to Devon, you won't understand a word anyone says. The accent is very hard to understand you know," but when Patsy looked worried, Ed squeezed her hand and told her he was only kidding.

"Don't do that to me, Ed," Patsy said, "I'm scared enough about meeting your dad without those kinds of comments."

"Sorry," Ed looked pensive, "Honestly my love you will be fine. I bet within a couple of hours you will feel completely at home. Now what shall we have to eat?"

Chapter 20

Mary was glad to get home after her trip. She felt rested in one way, strange really she thought because despite everything I discovered, I had a good time. She made a cup of tea, checked on the shop and decided to unpack. Annie had left her a message saying she hoped Ada and Mary had enjoyed themselves and said business had been good and she had managed very well. When all her clothes were unpacked, Mary poured herself a sherry and sat planning her next move.

She decided that she would complete on the bungalow and move in as soon as she could. She also decided to speak to Rosalyn and update her on her findings. She resolved to make sure that Eric Bradley or whatever his name was needed to be taught a lesson.

The next morning Mary found herself busy in the shop. Customers were intrigued as to where she had been; many remarked that they had never known her to leave the shop before. Mary stuck to the planned story about being on a buying trip looking for new fashion ideas and picking up some soft furnishings for her new home. As soon as she could, Mary telephoned her solicitor and the estate agent and instructed them both that she was ready to complete the purchase of the bungalow as soon as possible.

Mary then telephoned Rosalyn and asked her if they could meet for dinner that evening, "I have so much to tell you Rosalyn," Mary said. "I thought we could meet at the new bistro, you know the one next to the newsagent? My treat, and no arguments. Is 7pm alright with you?" Rosalyn said she couldn't wait to hear all about the trip. She said that she was happy to meet at the bistro but that she would pay for her own dinner, however Mary wouldn't take no for an answer and she eventually thanked Mary for her kind offer.

The last call Mary reluctantly made was to Eric,

"Just letting you know I'm home after a very productive trip."

Eric responded by telling Mary how much he had missed her. "Hope you didn't go spending all your money," he joked and Mary laughed,

"Eric I don't know how much money you think I have, but believe me I am an ordinary working woman, not an heiress. Listen, we'll catch up later in the week and I shall tell you exactly what I bought." The call ended with Eric telling Mary again how much he loved her. Mary sighed as she put the phone down and thought what a stupid woman she was to ever have fallen for his lies, but he would pay, oh yes, he would pay.

While she was getting ready for the evening with Rosalyn, Mary thought about her bungalow, hopefully she would move in soon, get rid of Eric and forget about love. It's not for me, love, she decided reluctantly, but she still believed Susan would find her someday. She would concentrate on that thought, and that made her feel better.

Roslyn was pleased to see Mary and Mary noticed straight away that Rosalyn was looking much more relaxed, happier even. She was wearing a smart black skirt suit and black court shoes which Mary was happy to tell her, "You are looking smart this evening Rosalyn, like a new woman."

Rosalyn blushed. "Thank you, Mary, actually I do feel better these days. I am supposed to be looking after my aunt, but somehow it is the other way around. She insisted on giving me some money for this outfit, not the quality of your clothes but I do like it. I'm eating better and my aunt's house is so comfortable. On top of all that, I can't feel miserable for long in my aunt's company."

Mary laughed. "She is quite some lady, you're lucky to have her. Oh and if you come into my shop, I promise to give you a good discount."

The two women ordered their meal and Mary told Rosalyn about her trip to Spain and the fact that there were no luxury apartments where Eric had said they were. Rosalyn certainly wasn't surprised, but Mary was grateful that Rosalyn didn't mention that she was right about Eric. "It was just as well I didn't give him any money, and the bonus was that I so enjoyed the trip," Mary told Rosalyn.

Mary was surprised at how comfortable she was in Rosalyn's company and she was very grateful that Rosalyn had taken the time to warn her. She felt so sorry that she had misjudged this woman.

"I want him to pay for what he has done to us Rosalyn," Mary said angrily.

"I wonder how many other women he has tried to take money from?" Rosalyn said sadly, and both women sat silently for a moment thinking about that.

They ate their meal quietly and after their plates had been cleared, Mary suddenly said,

"Look, Rosalyn, think about it. He only ever stayed with either of us two or three nights a week. He never lived with us. What if he has another woman he stays with a couple of nights? He could easily have two of us on the go. I don't drive, otherwise I would follow him and see just exactly what he does."

"No but I drive, an old car granted but good enough to follow him," Rosalyn was quite excited about the prospect of catching Eric out.

"Do you really think we should follow him?" Mary said with trepidation.

"Of course," Rosalyn answered, "We need to catch him out once and for all."

Mary thought for a moment, but only a moment, "The next time I see Eric, I'll telephone you just before he leaves and we can follow him, if you're up for it. I'll make arrangements to see him and let you know when he is coming to see me."

Rosalyn was definitely in favour of the plan.

By the time they left the restaurant the two women were quite excited about their plan. Mary joked that she felt like Miss Marple. Rosalyn gave Mary a hug outside the restaurant and thanked her for dinner and said she would see her soon. Mary told Rosalyn it was she who should be saying thank you, without Rosalyn's help, she could have lost everything.

Mary telephoned Eric the following day and they arranged to go for a meal in the village. Eric suggested trying the new bistro but Mary said she preferred another restaurant, too soon to go to the bistro again and so the surveillance began.

The next day seemed endless to Mary, and Ada and Annie were worried about her. Annie wanted to know all about Spain but neither Ada nor Mary said anything about their real reason for the trip. Annie left shortly after 1pm for the day and as soon as Ada and Mary were on their own, Mary told Ada all about their plan to a concerned Ada,

"I don't know Mary, Eric might prove to be very dangerous, after all he has no conscience by the sound of it. Who knows what he may do if he finds you are following him?"

Ada sounded very worried but Mary reassured her that this had to be done, "Look Ada, this man is a monster, look at poor Rosalyn, he's taken her money while making the pretence of being in love with her. He's planning to do the same to me and goodness knows how many other sad women."

Ada nodded and put her arm around Mary, "Just be careful Mary and if you need my help just say the word."

Later, while Mary was getting ready to meet Eric she was thinking that throughout all this deceit, she had found two friends, two good friends in Ada and Rosalyn and she knew how lucky she was. She didn't feel nervous about what she was about to do, on the contrary she felt confident that Eric had to be stopped.

Mary purposely arrived late at the restaurant, full of apologies to Eric about how busy she had been. They settled down with a bottle of good wine and Mary told stories, and stories they were, of her trip to London and the purchases she had made,

"Oh and by the way, I have instructed my solicitor to complete on the bungalow, isn't that wonderful?"

Mary thought she detected a slight look of horror from Eric but he agreed that it was wonderful and said he would enjoy helping her with any jobs that needed to be done. While they waited for desert, Mary excused herself and said she had to go to the ladies. Instead she went to the public 'phone box and quickly put in a call to Rosalyn. "Give me half an hour," was all she said.

When she returned to the table, Eric was again going on about Spain, and Mary nodded appropriately and smiled and looked enthusiastic. They left the restaurant just over half an hour later, Mary was about to say she was tired and needed an early night but fortunately Eric said he had to go home as he had a very early start the next day.

Eric walked her to her door and while Mary pretended to go inside, Eric got into his van and started to drive off. Rosalyn was as good as her word and stopped her car just long enough for Mary to climb into the front seat. Rosalyn was a proficient driver and skilfully followed the van, not too closely but enough to see where he was going. Not far as it turned out. Eric drove about three miles to the next village and pulled into the drive of a large detached house.

"This house must have cost a fortune," Rosalyn almost screamed, and Mary had to agree.

"What now?" asked Rosalyn.

"Well, we wait," Mary answered and Rosalyn grinned and produced blankets and coffee from the back of the car.

The two women waited all night. Fortunately, it was a warm night and far from being uncomfortable or bored, they chatted and laughed and drank coffee until the early hours. Mary sadly knew now that her first impression of Rosalyn was way off mark. Rosalyn was intelligent and witty, and she learned that Rosalyn and her husband had owned a successful newsagent until her husband had become ill. When Rosalyn's husband sadly died, she sold the business for a substantial amount of money. That plus the house they owned where they lived should have given her a good income for life.

At roughly 6am, the van left the house and Mary sarcastically remarked that at least he hadn't lied about an early start. They discussed their next move and decide they would investigate if there were anyone in the house, however as they were discussing what they would say, the milkman was about to make a delivery to the house. Mary and Rosalyn got out of the car and asked the milkman if Mr Bradley lived at this address. Mary wasn't sure how she would explain why they were lurking near the house at this early hour; she hoped Rosalyn would come up with a good story. As it turned out, the milkman didn't bat an eyelid, and certainly never questioned them,

"No luv, this house belongs to a Mr Greenhalgh, he's a builder you know, must be making a hell of a lot of money to afford a house like this."

Rosalyn was quick to ask, "Actually it's his wife we need to see, shame it's not the right address?"

The milkman smiled and nodded, "Definitely not right luv, Mr Greenhalgh isn't married, in fact he's not even here much, only a couple of pints of milk a week." With that information, the two women went home.

Mary met Ada when she arrived for work and told her of the night's events. Ada was horrified and insisted Mary get some rest, and as Mary bathed and got into her bed she smiled knowing they would get him eventually.

Chapter 21

Patsy and Ed finished their lunch and continued their journey through the country lanes. Patsy was in awe of the beautiful countryside and it seemed a short time later that Ed pointed out the coastline, followed by a small village with a harbour. Ed turned into a narrow lane and then onto a driveway. The house was a two-storey large house with a thatched roof.

"We are home at last," said Ed but before Patsy could answer, a tall distinguished looking man who looked like an older version of Ed walked out of the house and came over to the car and hugged Ed. "Welcome home you two," he said and he walked over to Patsy and hugged her saying, "Welcome Patsy, I'm Richard, Ed's dad. Come inside, I expect you're tired after that long journey." Patsy was ushered into a large, comfortable living room.

Patsy was now feeling even more nervous; the house was beautiful and so big. Richard invited Patsy to sit down and soon after they were all enjoying tea and scones with clotted cream and jam,

"These are a Devon specialty Patsy, try them," and Ed's dad offered the scones to her. Ed explained that the cream goes onto the scone first and then the jam and Patsy had to admit that they were delicious.

"I have a very good friend who insists on making these for me," said Ed's dad and Ed winked at Patsy. "Told you he had all these lady friends Patsy, you see now what I mean?" Ed was laughing and his dad fortunately saw the funny side too. "Dad I'm just glad you are getting on with your life, it's great. How are Ruby and Pete and the baby? I'll have to introduce Patsy to them."

"Well," said Ed's dad, "I'm taking you all out to dinner tonight so Patsy can get to know the family, and by the way Patsy, call me Richard. Dinner at the Kings head if that's OK. I shall see you both later." Richard grabbed his car keys and left the house.

Patsy was grateful for the warm welcome, she was not quite so nervous now, and Ed insisted on showing her around the house. There were lots of family photographs and Ed picked one up and told Patsy it was a picture of his mum.

"She is so pretty and stylish," said Patsy. "It's so sad she was taken from you all."

"Yes, we had a hard time, she was such a wonderful mum, and you're so right, she certainly was very stylish. She always looked immaculate even though she had a career and kids, and she was a great cook too so you have a lot to live up to," and Ed winked at Patsy and smiled.

They unpacked their things in a spacious bedroom with an en-suite. "My dad's broadminded so he put us in together, when I told him that you are the one I shall marry." Ed took Patsy in his arms. Patsy had never felt so at home and so loved at that moment.

They had a walk around the village. They walked down to the beach and walked around the harbour. Ed pointed out the small village primary school where he and Ruby had attended, and after a perfect afternoon they went home and sat in the garden with a glass of good wine. Later they went upstairs to get ready for the evening, but instead they sank onto the comfortable king-size bed and made love. As they lay with their arms around each other, they suddenly realised the time and then it was a mad dash for them both to get ready for the evening out.

Patsy had bought a new dress, which had cost her a fortune from one of the more expensive high street stores. She had learned a lot from Mary about colours and shapes and fashion, so she had taken care to choose just the right dress for the occasion. Although she didn't earn much money, she wanted to make a good impression on Ed's family.

At 7.15pm they walked hand in hand into the living room where Richard was waiting for them. He greeted them with a smile and another hug and after a drink they left to meet Ruby and Pete at the pub. The walk was just a short distance to the King's Head and Ruby and her partner were already seated in the bar area and as they entered. Ruby rushed over and threw her arms around Ed and then did the same to Patsy,

"I'm so glad to finally meet you Patsy, Ed talks about you all the time. You look lovely, I just know we are going to get on."

Pete was behind Ruby and after shaking Ed's hand; he gave Patsy a hug and introduced himself. "Ruby has been ready for ages, she couldn't wait to meet you," he said and rolled his eyes, which made Patsy laugh.

Patsy immediately saw the likeness to her and Ed's mother. Ruby also had the same sense of good style as her mother, Patsy could see that, plus she had amazing warmth and Patsy could sense that it came from a loving upbringing. They had a drink and then moved into a more formal dining area for dinner. Patsy was nervous, she wasn't used to fine dining but Ed's family were so welcoming and she thought about all the 'posh' places she had been with Mary, so she relaxed and she knew she would enjoy the evening.

Patsy learned that Ruby had an art degree and designed fashion clothing for a well-known middle range online company. Pete was an electrician with his own business. They also lived in the village and they had a baby girl of eight months called Belle.

"The life here is perfect for children Patsy," Ruby said. "The fresh air, the sea, the village life. When my girl is old enough she will go to the same school, Ed and I went to, and it's ideal for my job as I work from home mostly. Pete's mum is wonderful with the baby, she helps us out all the time if I have to meet clients."

Patsy noted that Ruby was the outgoing talkative one of the two, Pete didn't have a lot to say but it was obvious he adored Ruby. Whatever, Patsy liked them all and she felt as though she belonged, not inferior, not awkward as she had worried about, they seemed to just accept her for who she was. They left the pub late, Ruby made them promise to have dinner at their house before they went back to Manchester and gave Patsy a heartfelt kiss on the cheek along with a big hug.

The next few days went so quickly. The sun shone and they spent their days on the beach, going long walks and eating cream teas. Patsy had never experienced anything like it, she had never had a holiday so this was a new experience, and Richard was a perfect host, unobtrusive but charming, warm and hospitable. Ed wasn't wrong when he said his dad had female admirers. There were two ladies, Salina and Angela, both widows who lived locally who were constant visitors. Salina was a very good cook and brought food to the house daily.

Angela acted as an unpaid housekeeper, fussing around, always with a cleaning cloth or feather duster to hand. Strangely, some may say; both Salina and Angela were good friends and didn't appear to be in competition with one another, and Patsy wondered whether Richard would ever commit to any woman again.

Ed, Richard and Patsy went to Ruby and Pete's for dinner and Patsy met the baby, a beautiful little girl called Belle. She hoped that one day she would have children and she promised herself that she would never be like her mum, no, her children would know they were loved. Ruby and Pete had a large Victorian house on the outskirts of the village, which they were in the process of renovating, and it was a chaotic house. Patsy wondered why they didn't break their necks with bits of wood lying about and broken stairs, but funnily enough it was still a warm atmosphere, and the chaos certainly didn't appear to worry Pete or Ruby.

"Well, hopefully, one day we shall have a proper house, that's the plan," said Ruby, "When we ever get round to it."

They all ate in the kitchen, very relaxed and Ruby certainly was a good cook, she said her mum had taught her to cook. They sat around a big kitchen table and the wine flowed.

It was a great night and when they got back to Richard's, Ed and Patsy lay in bed laughing about the things said and the good time they had. The next morning Ed brought them both breakfast in bed. They were due to leave that day, and so the plan was to drop in at Ruby's first to say their goodbyes.

By the time they were both ready, Richard was just leaving for work. Patsy thanked him for the wonderful, hospitality and Richard hugged her and said he hoped he would see a lot more of her soon. Richard and Ed hugged goodbye and Richard told Ed to, "Look after this young lady, she's good for you." Ed remembered Mary saying something similar.

Car loaded, they called in at Ruby's as planned and again there were hugs and kisses all round, especially for Belle who loved all the attention. As they finally set off for home, Patsy was sad to be leaving, but Ed said he wanted to show her one more thing before they finally made the journey.

Ed pulled off the main road onto the coastal road and shortly afterwards into a small car park and invited Patsy out of the car. He was carrying a bag, and Patsy was a little puzzled. They walked along the coastal path until they stopped at a point where the view was breath-taking.

"This is amazing, Ed," said Patsy catching her breath as she looked out onto the coastline. Ed smiled, got down on one knee and produced a ring from his pocket. "Marry me, Patsy, I love you with all my heart."

Patsy just said 'yes' without hesitating.

"This is my mother's ring," Ed said. "I told Dad I was going to propose and he said you should have it." He put the diamond ring on Patsy's finger.

Patsy was so overwhelmed; she looked at the ring and said to Ed that she was honoured to wear it. They kissed for a long time and then they both sat down on the grass looking down on the view and thinking how lucky they both were to have found one another. Ed took a bottle of champagne and two glasses from the carrier bag; it was a perfect moment for both of them.

On the journey home, they talked about their future plans, where they wanted to live, their careers, how many children they wanted. As much as Patsy thought how fantastic it would be to live in Devon, they both knew their career opportunities, for the time being were in Manchester.

Chapter 22

Rosie was delighted at Patsy's news, loved her ring, and even offered to move out of the flat so that Ed could move in. Patsy said they were in no rush, they were taking their time, and that when Patsy decided to move in with Ed, they would be sure to give Rosie plenty of notice of their plans.

Patsy was excited to be back at work, she had wonderful news about her engagement, although she had put her ring away in a safe place, as her job did not permit her to wear an engagement ring for health and safety purposes. She understood the rules but it was a boring rule in her opinion. She wanted to show her ring to the world, she felt so happy and so in love.

The staff and residents were delighted for her, and Rita had more good news for her. She had passed her NVQ 2 and could progress to NVQ 3.

"The only problem I have," said Rita, "I'll probably lose you when you go on to other things."

Patsy smiled, "I'm going nowhere just yet, Rita. I've got some money to save now, getting married doesn't come cheap, although we won't have a big wedding."

Mary was delighted along with everyone else. She remembered Ed much to Patsy's delight, "The nice young man with the car and the lovely eyes," she said.

"We'll go out in the car again, Mary, with Ed and you can get to know him better if you would like that," Patsy told her. Mary smiled and said that she would like that very much.

After her shift, Patsy went to the library to tell Sonia her news and to collect some new books Sonia had ordered for her. As she walked into the library, Patsy noticed Sonia behind her desk looking very sombre.

"Hi, Sonia, are you OK?" Patsy knew there was something wrong. Sonia was tearful,

"Oh, Patsy it looks like I won't have a job here for very much longer, they are almost certainly closing the library. I'll be OK, I've been offered a job at the university library but I shall miss working here so much."

Patsy was devastated, "You've taught me so much Sonia, I don't know what I would have done if you hadn't helped me at every step, and you're a good friend." The two women hugged each other; both of them had tears in their eyes.

"We still have the demonstration Sonia and I am expecting a record turn out so there is still hope. I had so much to tell you," said Patsy, "but it doesn't seem appropriate." Sonia was eager to hear what Patsy had to say,

"Tell me anyway, Patsy, I could do with some good news. Come on, I'll make us a cup of tea, oh and I've found some good articles for you, and your books have come."

Sonia was delighted with the news of Patsy's engagement and said that the good news had cheered her up. She gave Patsy the articles she had found and said she hoped they were useful, Patsy knew they would be and couldn't wait to read them.

Patsy met Ed later and she told him all about the library almost certainly closing. Ed thought for a moment,

"I could have a word with my editor and see if we could cover the story and maybe start a petition at the paper. After all, so many people use that library, it's an important facility in the community so I should think we would get the support."

Patsy thought it was a great idea and hoped Ed's editor would be sympathetic. They talked about their day; Ed said he had been in court all day reporting on various different cases,

"I could do with a good murder," he said and Patsy thought that was a bit too drastic.

"You'll get your big story Ed, I am convinced you will be a successful TV reporter one day."

"How did the news of our engagement go with your colleagues?" asked Ed.

"Everyone, including Mary were delighted," Patsy said, "She remembered you, it shows how much of an impression you made."

"How could she not remember me?" Ed sounded surprised but Patsy told him he was being silly. Ed said that he would be pleased to take Mary out.

"She is a lovely lady, I really like her and she appears very sensible to me, after all she obviously likes me!" Patsy gently punched him on his arm.

"My news of the engagement went down well too," Ed told her.

"We had a pint or two at lunchtime, although some of the married guys told me not to do it, but I think they were joking, hope so anyway." Patsy laughed and told him he was outrageous.

"Any news about Mary's daughter?" he asked.

"Nothing yet," Patsy answered, "but hopefully they should be able to find her. She's probably married and has her own family. I wonder if she knows she was adopted?"

Ed, true to his word did arrange to take Mary and Patsy out to lunch. Mary seemed delighted when Ed arrived at the home for the outing; she shook his hand as best she could. The strength and the energy she once had wasn't there anymore, Mary knew that although she could never understand why.

They got into the car, Mary in the front, and they set out into the Cheshire countryside. Ed asked Mary if she had ever driven and she laughed and said that she never did learn to drive, but she had had some exciting times sat in a car with her friends. Both Ed and Patsy wondered what she meant but Mary did not elaborate. She just sat in the front seat with a cheeky smile on her face, and then she said,

"That's how I finally found out." Mary did not say any more, leaving Patsy and Ed bemused.

Ed chatted to Mary about their engagement and about taking Patsy to Devon to meet his family, and Mary said that was delighted for them both. "I expect both your parents are pleased too."

Patsy told Mary that she didn't have much to do with her mum,

"She wasn't a very good mother Mary and I didn't think she would be interested, only if there was money to be had."

Mary shook her head sadly. "I had a strained relationship with my mother too after Susan, but I wish I had the chance to be a good mum to my little girl. My advice dear would be, don't be too hard on your mother. I never forgave my mother for making me give up my baby but things were different then, she was a proud religious woman."

Both Ed and Patsy answered in unison that they thought Mary would have been a good mum. Ed said that he worshipped his mum, but that she had died in a car crash, and Mary touched his hand and said she was sorry.

Although the conversation had been on a serious note, by the time they stopped at a country pub for lunch, the mood had changed and they were all laughing, mainly at Ed's stories about University and his job as a reporter. Mary said that Ed should be on the television, he was so entertaining and Ed said that he hoped one day he would be on the television as a news reporter.

"If you want something badly enough, you will succeed young man," Mary replied. She knew that he would succeed too; she could see that he wanted it as much as she had wanted to buy her shop. She enjoyed the company of these two young people so much, they brought fun into her life and she needed that.

Mary insisted that she wanted to pay for lunch, "I'm not sure if I have any money though?"

Patsy answered her quickly, "Mary you have plenty of money, your solicitor looks after it for you, but we are buying lunch, it's our treat."

When they arrived back at the Home, Mary smiled at them both and said, "Thank you both, I have had a lovely time." Ed asked Mary if he could give her a hug and she replied with a grin that it had been a long time since a young man had asked that, and that she would like that. As Patsy took Mary to her room, Mary was talking about their outing, what lovely scenery, how much she enjoyed lunch and what a wonderful couple they were. Patsy said that they had enjoyed it too,

"I think Ed loves you almost as much as he loves me, Mary."

Mary laughed and said, "I wouldn't worry too much dear, I've never had much luck with men."

Ed had been waiting for Patsy, he had been chatting to the residents and the staff and as they got into the car. He told Patsy that he had actually enjoyed the whole day and he understood more about why Patsy loved her job so much.

"Mary is wonderful, Patsy, I do hope she finds Susan, I mean Jennifer, and she can finally find some peace."

Chapter 23

Mary told Ada about following Eric and about how he had yet another name he was also called Greenhalgh,

"I have been such a fool Ada, all this thought that he really did love me. How could I be so stupid?"

Ada put her arm around Mary. "He has fooled a lot of people, Mary, that's what men like him do. He's probably had years of practice, and you are so honest you would never think anyone is capable of such devious behaviour."

"The funny thing is Ada, I really enjoyed going out and spying on him. As bizarre as it may sound, it is the most exciting thing I have ever done, I can't wait to go out on surveillance again with Rosalyn, see what else we can find out. I feel like I have a new goal and it's exciting."

Ada wasn't as confident, she felt Mary hadn't yet grasped the full picture of what this horrible man was capable of, and she was worried that when the full story was out, Mary would be devastated. Ada didn't mention her feelings to Mary; she didn't want to worry her friend. Instead she said that she thought it was exciting too, and in a funny way it was.

Rosalyn and Mary made several more trips to Eric's house, but there were no new leads. To all intents and purposes, Mr Greenhalgh led a respectable, busy life. Rosalyn proved to be very good at casually speaking to neighbours without drawing any suspicion that she was anything but a very pleasant lady, but no one had anything bad to say about this respectable man.

There was no mention of any women staying at the house. He was a confirmed bachelor, he paid his bills, he hadn't tried to persuade any of his neighbours to invest in any properties plus, apparently he kept his house in immaculate condition.

"He's clever Mary," Rosalyn said. "Someone somewhere knows all about our Eric/Ronnie/ Greenhalgh, and we shall find them."

"Did you ever report him to the police Rosalyn?" Mary enquired.

"I felt such an idiot Mary," Rosalyn answered, "and anyway, I gave him money. He took it in front of my eyes and I, well, I thought he loved me and I wanted to share everything I had with him. He always had plenty of money and it never occurred to me that he was taking me for a ride, so no, I never went to the police. By the time I realised what he had done, I felt broken and ashamed, and I still do."

Mary thought that from Rosalyn's answer, this man had indeed done a good job of making Rosalyn feel humiliated and worthless.

The reconnaissance wasn't all bad. In the long hours that the two women spent watching the house, they talked about many things, they laughed a lot, trying to duck down in the car when anyone passed near the car. It was exciting and best of all they enjoyed each other's company.

Ada and Annie were brilliant looking after the shop and Mary, after serious consideration and discussions with Ada had told Annie the full story. Annie had said she thought something was amiss, "The b----d, sorry for the language. I can't wait for you to get him. Anything I can do Mary, you just let me know."

Mary was surprised at how easy she found it to pretend to Eric that nothing in their relationship had changed. Their routine carried on as it always had. Eric still never mentioned the bungalow, however he did talk frequently about the properties in Spain,

"Look at this weather, Mary, just think we could be sat by the pool in Spain, and living in a beautiful new apartment," Eric would say, looking doleful. Mary thought how convincing he sounded, if only he knew his lies had been found out.

They were sitting in a restaurant in Manchester having dinner; the conversation had flowed, like it always had. Mary used to look at other couples and wonder why they never spoke to each other. She and Eric always had time to talk to each other, and Eric was amusing and witty, they had always laughed a lot. With these thoughts in her mind, Mary suddenly turned to Eric,

"Oh, Eric, guess what? My passport finally arrived, so when would you like me to see these famous apartments of yours? I've never been abroad so it's all very exciting."

Mary was watching Eric closely, she was looking for any signs of lying, anything that would confirm her suspicions, but Eric didn't flinch when he replied,

"Mary, that's wonderful, let me check what work I've got on and then we shall arrange the dates. I know you will love the apartments and I'll be in touch with my friend Peter and let him know we shall see him in Spain shortly."

Mary was to say the least surprised. Had she and Ada looked at the wrong piece of land when they had gone on their trip? Was Eric genuine after all? Mary came to her senses and asked him to look in his diary,

"I'm excited now Eric, the sooner we go out there the better, and I'll have to arrange cover in the shop."

Eric said he would let her know by the next day, and, with that they finished the meal with Eric telling Mary all about what they would do in Spain.

The following day, Mary telephoned Rosalyn and asked her to come to the shop, and during their lunch hour, Mary told Rosalyn, Ada and Annie about the conversation she had with Eric on the previous evening.

"Maybe we've misjudged him," said Mary. "I know he behaved inexcusably to you Rosalyn, but he may have changed?"

Annie jumped up, "Oh come off it, Mary, you are blinded with love for this man, but he's out to rip you off! Think about it, it's what he does; take money from women, blinding them with his charm. I may be young but I can tell you he is no good."

Annie sat down and Mary noticed Rosalyn had been nodding in agreement with everything Annie had said. Ada had been sat quietly, listening carefully. She patted Mary's arm,

"We are only thinking of you Mary, he ruined Rosalyn's life, and took everything. None of us want you to go through that, and Rosalyn certainly isn't making this up, you know in your heart that he is a con man."

"I'm so sorry Rosalyn, what was I thinking?" Mary was looking at Rosalyn. "I know you are all thinking of me and yes, you are all quite correct when you say he is no good. I do know that, it's just that last night he was so convincing."

Rosalyn understood and put her arm around Mary's shoulder, "He is convincing, Mary, that's how he has to be. I believed him for years, but let's just wait and see if he will take you to Spain?"

The telephone rang and Mary answered, "Eric, when are we going then?"

There was a pause while Eric spoke and then Mary said,

"Oh, that's a shame, never mind dear we can always go later in the year." Pause again, "Yes I see, he needs a deposit to hold the apartment, yes I understand, but will I get that back if I don't like it?" Pause, "Oh, well if it's guaranteed, and he is a friend of yours so you know his word is good, yes leave it with me." Mary put the phone down and turned to her friends,

"Let battle continue, thank you each and every one of you for talking to me honestly. Eric informs me that he is too busy at work to go on a trip, in fact he's not sure when he can go. However, his friend wants a deposit as the apartments are selling fast. So now my friends where's the sherry? I think we all need a drink."

Mary saw Eric briefly two days later, although just long enough for him to apologise for having too much work on to go anywhere. He asked Mary about the £5000 deposit, which Mary thought was quite expensive, but she did tell Eric that she was seriously considering paying the money as long as she could have it refunded if she changed her mind.

"I've told you love," said Eric, "This guy, Peter is a friend of mine, he is a genuine businessman and he will refund the money if it comes to that, but you shall love the property Mary."

Eric rushed off, as did Mary, she was anxious to meet her friend.

Rosalyn was waiting in her car, ready to follow Eric. They drove at a safe distance behind him into the Cheshire countryside to another small village where Eric pulled into the driveway of a large picturesque cottage. Rosalyn reached into the back of the car and produced a flask of hot coffee and some sandwiches, "Thought I would come prepared, we may be here for a while." They both smiled and sat back to enjoy the feast.

Three and half hours later, both women were cold and tired and they were discussing leaving and coming back later. As Rosalyn prepared to drive off, Mary suddenly saw Eric standing at the door kissing an attractive woman, about the same age as Mary.

"Well, well, Eric, so she's the other woman," Mary said.

Rosalyn grunted, "I wonder how many others there are?"

"We need to find out who she is," said Rosalyn. "Let's go to the pub Mary, chances are someone will know her."

There was only one pub in the small village, and Mary and Rosalyn walked into the welcoming bar where a large log fire was burning.

"You sit by the fire, Mary, and I'll get us a drink. They do hot food here, we might as well enjoy a decent meal now we're here." With that decision made, Rosalyn went up to the bar and Mary studied the menu.

When Rosalyn returned with a sherry for Mary and an orange juice for herself, she was excited and couldn't wait to tell Mary.

"That was easy, the landlord knew her straight away. I told him I had fallen in love with the cottage and asked if he knew the owner, and whether he thought they would sell for a good price."

Mary was impressed, "You are good at this, Rosalyn, what did he say?"

"Well," said Rosalyn, "The owner is Vera Rowen, she is divorced, pots of money and she is probably moving to Spain with her new man, he's called Peter Greenhalgh and, he's a builder."

Mary was in awe at Rosalyn's ingenuity and shocked at the fact that he was planning on taking money from Vera, poor Vera she thought. With that thought, Rosalyn thinking the same thoughts as Mary, the two women were silent for a while. Mary broke the silence,

"What next? If we go to see Vera, she probably won't believe us, I didn't believe you at first, I thought you were mad, sorry Rosalyn." Rosalyn smiled and said she wasn't surprised. Mary continued her thoughts, "She may even alert Eric or whatever he is called, but if we don't warn her, she may lose everything."

Neither Mary nor Rosalyn had answers at that moment, so they settled for ordering some hot food and then going home to think.

Chapter 24

Patsy arrived at work to be greeted by a serious Rita, who told her she needed to speak to her. Rita sat behind her desk and took a deep breath,

"Bill has had news from the detective agency. Basically, they have discovered that Jennifer was married and then she divorced her husband, but since then, she seems to have disappeared and for the moment the trail has gone cold. Very sad, I really thought they might find her. Poor Bill is devastated, he really wanted this, and well I think we all did."

Patsy was upset but there was still hope, there had to be and she said so to Rita,

"She can't just disappear, I'm sure that they will find her." However in her heart, Patsy wasn't totally convinced.

Later in the day she was telling Rosie all about the news. Rosie's view was that it may take more time, but that there would be a positive outcome, but Rosie was always optimistic, and Patsy told her so.

"My glass is always half full, yes and so should yours be Patsy. You have done so much for Mary, she's a different woman, she has a quality of life these days and that's largely thanks to you and your books. If she hadn't met you, then she probably would never have found Jennifer, now at least there is a chance and Bill is spending a lot of money on this. The woman can't just disappear can she?"

"No, you are right, Rosie," Patsy said. "She has to be somewhere and Mary is happier, but it's not just me that made that happen, it's down to us all as a team. Everyone has really embraced my suggestions which has made it a lot easier."

Jess came into the staff room to get her coat. "Me and Iris are taking Edna and Alice out for a pub lunch. Hope Alice doesn't jump up on the table and start kicking her legs like she did as one of the Tiller girls."

Rosie and Patsy looked at one another and Patsy said, "Yeah, very funny Jess. Enjoy yourselves and make sure Alice and Edna have a good time and if Alice wants to dance, that's fine. Glad you've got Iris with you though."

Patsy went in to Mary with a cup of tea and some cake. She looked sadly at Mary and hoped Rosie was right about Jennifer being found eventually, she just hoped it wouldn't be too late. Mary had dementia and at some stage, Patsy feared that Mary might forget about her daughter before she found her, and some peace at last. At the moment, Mary was better than she had been for a long time. Everyone, especially Bill had seen such an improvement. Hopefully, Mary would remain well enough to be reunited with Jennifer, her Susan.

Patsy sat down with Mary to have a chat and Mary began talking about Devon. Perhaps talking to Ed had rekindled a memory.

"My aunt lived somewhere down there you know, well near there," she said. "Distant aunt, I didn't really know her, but she was so kind to me. She wasn't ashamed of me, she took me on long walks and I met all her friends and neighbours. She couldn't give a fig that I was, well you know, fat. It isn't fat though is it, when you are carrying a baby?"

Patsy realised that it was indeed in Somerset where Mary had been sent to have the baby. Slowly the story was emerging. Her parents had sent her away to avoid a scandal in the family,

"It must have been a very painful time for you Mary, I can't imagine what it must be like to have to give up your child." Patsy spoke gently and thought that although she had not had the best early life, she had never had to go through something as traumatic as that. It was a nice place.

Mary continued, "The beach was beautiful, and the countryside very pretty." She said nothing for a long time, lost in her thoughts and then, "I'm tired now dear, will you help me onto the bed so I can have a rest?" Patsy helped Mary to get comfortable in bed and before she left the room, Mary was asleep.

Ed and Patsy were invited to Rosie's parents' house that evening for dinner. As usual the house was full of family, and Rosie's mum was busy in the kitchen preparing the meal. Rosie's dad shook Ed by the hand and kissed Patsy and told them how delighted they all were by the news of the engagement they all were.

Rosie's mum appeared with a bottle of sparkling wine, and after kissing both Ed and Patsy she said that they must all toast the happy couple. Gemma and Andy voiced their congratulations and their two children joined in the celebrations with a glass of lemonade, Patsy felt so blessed to have met them all. "Have you too got a date yet?" Rosie's mum asked.

"We're still organising everything, but we have now decided that we don't want to wait too long," said Ed. "Andy, will you be my best man?" Andy beamed and replied that he would be honoured.

Patsy turned to Rosie, "Rosie, you will be a bridesmaid won't you?"

Rosie flung her arms around Patsy and said that she couldn't wait.

"The whole of your family is invited, if you can make it to Devon, we should love you all to come," Ed said, meaning every word and Rosie's mum said she would have to buy a hat for the occasion.

It was a happy time and throughout the meal, Patsy and Ed found themselves answering questions about the wedding and where they would live and was it going to be a church wedding, and where would they have the reception? So many questions that Patsy and Ed were laughing because they couldn't answer, "We've still not got that far," said Ed, "but hopefully we shall have answers soon."

Ed and Patsy said their goodbyes, and on the way home together with Rosie, Ed said that they had better sort out this wedding, everyone wanted to know their plans. Rosie agreed,

"You better had, you two, mum will be out tomorrow buying that hat, and we shall have to get you a dress Patsy."

When they got home they were still making plans. Patsy said that she was going to ask Iris to be a bridesmaid, and they talked about finding somewhere to live. Rosie said that she had thought about asking Jess to share the flat with her, much to Patsy's amazement.

"Well, she's a different girl now," Rosie said, "I like her and she's good fun. I'm certainly not ready to get hitched for a long time, so we can party. I'll miss you, Patsy, like crazy though, all the good times, the chats, you with your head stuck in a book, but no seriously, it has been great."

"OK, but you won't get rid of me so easily. Ed and I have to find somewhere near here if we can, so we can still get together and don't forget that we still work together."

Patsy felt a little sad, Rosie had been great but the two girls were both happy with that suggestion.

Both Patsy and Rosie were working toward their NVQ 3, Rosie was doing very well with Patsy's help, and Val was very supportive to all her students.

"Do you think I could apply for nurse training Patsy?" Rosie asked. Patsy was delighted, "Oh, Rosie, wouldn't it be great to train together? Of course you can do it and we can always help one another."

Rosie said that after careful thought, she should be striving for a career,

"I'd like to achieve something to build on. See what effect you've had on me Patsy, who would have thought that I could ever be a nurse someday?"

Patsy just laughed, she had the same feelings, and after all it had been just over a year since she hadn't got a clue where her life was going. She wished she could bump into the supermarket customer who had put the idea of becoming a carer in her head. What a debt of gratitude she owed that woman.

Besides the studying, there was the urgent task of saving the library. Ed had spoken to his editor and he had agreed for Ed to write a story about the threat to the library, and to publicise the forthcoming demonstration. The response from local residents proved to be overwhelming, the library was part of the community and it seemed that no one wanted it to close.

Then of course there was the wedding to organise. Neither Ed nor Patsy had the money for a huge wedding, and they both agreed that they wanted a simple no fuss affair. They agreed to make arrangements to go back to Devon and talk to Ed's family and see the vicar at the village church. It was a perfect setting, a small country church with the reception in the pub, which was just a short walk away from the church.

Ed kept asking Patsy when he could meet her mum and Patsy was trying her hardest to delay that meeting as long as she could. Her mum was embarrassing when she'd had a few drinks, and worse still she would bring her current lover to the wedding. Patsy cringed at the thought. This was to be their day, her and Ed's and the last thing she wanted was for her mum to ruin it.

Patsy spoke to Rosie about her concerns but Rosie just couldn't understand, well how could she when she had such a loving, supportive family?

"I'm sure your mum will be on her best behaviour, I mean she can't be that bad?" Rosie said. "Shall I come with you to see your mum and we'll both talk to her?"

Patsy was grateful to her friend and agreed to arrange a visit with Rosie before her mum was introduced to Ed.

Chapter 25

Mary and Rosalyn spoke to Ada about their findings and how they should move forward, but none of the women were sure what to do next. They all agreed that it was imperative that Eric had no suspicions that his devious plans were near to being exposed.

Mary thought long and hard, "I think I'll take a step back for the moment, I need to move into my bungalow and I still have furniture and fittings to buy. I keep up the pretence with Eric a while longer and I'm sure the answers as to what to do next will come to me."

The other two women agreed that it was probably a wise decision.

"We shall get him Mary, eventually and hopefully, because of our actions we shall stop other women from losing any money," Rosalyn said convincingly. "The situation with Vera worries me though. She may part with money sooner rather than later if she thinks she is moving to Spain with him, but there again I do agree we should take a breather and all have a think about our next move."

Ada pointed out that Vera hadn't yet put her house on the market so she thought that they had time to plan their next move.

"Let's go shopping Mary," said Ada, "Rosalyn you come too. We've got a bungalow to furnish and we need a break from all this and have a good day."

Mary telephoned Arthur and Isabel Stanhope and asked if she could measure the windows for curtains, they were pleased the sale was progressing well and a time for Mary to visit was arranged. On the day in question, Mary was welcomed warmly by the Stanhope's and taken into the cosy lounge, which overlooked the garden. One thing that Mary was sure of, and that was that she was doing the right thing buying the bungalow. She was so happy she felt like jumping for joy, but as usual Mary kept her cool business-like demeanour, although she was pleasant and friendly towards the Stanhope's.

Arthur Stanhope was very helpful when it came to measuring for curtains, and Isabel recommended a retailer who sold lovely fabrics and would make the curtains and fit them. Every room in the bungalow was a delight to Mary. She made notes of what she needed to buy as she pictured where her new furniture would go.

"Come and have tea Mary," Isabel said when Mary had all her measurements, and they had settled with tea and homemade cake.

Mary asked, "How about you? When do you think you will be ready to move?" Arthur told Mary that their new bungalow was ready for them to move into so they could be off very soon,

"Our daughter has overseen the build with her dad and it is wonderful. We can't wait to move. Strange really, it's a very quiet road but as our build was going on, the lady next door has had quite a bit of building work done too, but more interesting is that she seems to have fallen for the builder. She didn't strike me as the type of woman, very quiet you know. She even told our daughter that this new man, the builder, has persuaded her to buy a holiday home in Spain. Apparently he knows the developer."

Alarm bells were ringing for Mary, surely this wasn't Eric, but how many local builders were selling properties in Spain? Mary almost dropped her tea but she composed herself, laughed and asked Isabel if she knew anything about the builder,

"After all," she said as calmly as she could, "she should be careful before parting with money, and she can't have known this builder for long, can she?"

"I don't think she has. Mary," Isabel replied, "it seems he has been working at her house and, well, they got together very quickly. Quite exciting really, but you are right, she should be careful. Tell you what, why don't you come and see our bungalow? My daughter will make you very welcome and I should love you to see our new home."

Mary was delighted, but nervous. She might even meet the neighbour. She only hoped that she didn't bump into Eric, if indeed it was Eric. She readily accepted the invitation, even if Eric was there, she was only visiting friends, and it would be pure coincidence!

Mary couldn't wait to get home and tell her friends this possible new development. Surely Eric would not be stupid enough to start an affair with someone who lived in the same village as her. Just how many women could he be trying to extort money from at any one time? She kept asking herself how she could have been so gullible, so stupid. Had she really been so lonely?

Ada was the first of her friends she spoke to when she returned to the shop, but Mary had to wait for a while as the shop was full of customers and poor Ada was rushed off her feet.

"Sorry Ada," Mary said quickly, and she immediately took off her coat and went to assist a customer. When the shop became less busy, Mary told Ada her news and Ada's reaction was as shocked as Mary's.

"No it can't be him, Mary, so close to home, but if by chance it is Eric he is one bad man." The two women sat in silence, neither one quite believing what they had heard.

Later that evening, Mary telephoned Rosalyn who wasn't so surprised. "Well, well," she said, "I wonder just how many women he has had money from over the years. No wonder he can afford that house he lives in, he must have made a fortune. Let's stick to our plan and have a break and a think and we shall see if the Stanhope's neighbour can shed any more light."

The solicitor telephoned Mary with a completion date for the bungalow and Annie offered to cover the shop to allow the three women to plan a shopping trip. Annie was as horrified as the others to hear about the mystery builder. She actually said that she wanted to punch him hard if it turned out to be Eric. "I can't believe I have been so pleasant to him," she said, which made Mary smile.

Mary, Rosalyn, and Ada caught the bus into town and made for the shops. Fortunately, Eric had told Mary he was working all week on a job, so she did not had to see him. It was a relief not to have to pretend for a few days. The three had an enjoyable and productive day, Mary had all her purchases sorted out, and the others marvelled at her taste and expertise when it came to quality and colours. There was no doubt in anyone's mind that the bungalow was going to be a dream home.

They stopped for lunch, which Mary insisted on buying, it was so wonderful to have the company of real friends; she was actually having a super day, despite her problems. As they were sat enjoying the lunch, Rosalyn said that she had been thinking that if the Stanhope's' neighbour was involved with Eric, she and Ada should pay a visit to Vera and tell her just who this man was planning,

"I know we did agree to put this on hold, but this man needs stopping and fast. You keep pushing Eric, Mary to take you to see this apartment and we'll see what he does next," and they all nodded in agreement.

She was right. He needed to be stopped. They all thought it best that they should stop talking about him for the rest of the day and get on with enjoying themselves.

On the bus going home, Mary was excited. She had her moving date and offers of help from her friends, the mood all day had generally been happy and jovial. Eric was forgotten for the moment, and although it remained in Mary's mind, they all agreed it had been a good day.

Chapter 26

So reluctantly, Patsy and Rosie were on their way to visit Patsy's mum. Patsy hadn't seen her mum since; well she couldn't remember the last time she had even spoken to her mum. There were just too many bad memories, too many men, too much drinking, all Patsy's life. No Sunday lunches, no Christmas presents, birthday presents, good times of a normal family life, just poverty and plenty of embarrassment. Life was different now, good job with prospects, a lovely guy who wanted to marry her, good friends and a bright future, but Rosie was right, she had to go and see her mum.

They arrived at the block of high-rise flats, which were situated in a less than desirable area of Manchester. The lift was out of order, and there was an unpleasant aroma of cigarettes and urine on the stairwell as the two girls started the long climb to her mother's flat. Patsy hesitated before knocking on the door.

At first there was no reply and Patsy, sighed with relief and suggested to Rosie that they should leave. Rosie shook her head and knocked on the door again. This time, a middle-aged woman opened the door, attractive Rosie thought. She could see where Patsy got her looks, but too much make up and perhaps the mini skirt was a little too young for the woman stood before them.

"Patsy 'luv' come in, what a lovely surprise and whose this you've brought with you?" the woman spoke with a broad Manchester accent.

"Hi mum, this is my friend and flat mate, Rosie. Rosie this is my mum, Brenda."

"How are things, are you still with that same man?" Patsy motioned to Rosie to sit down on the thread worn sofa and the woman offered them a beer, which they both accepted. Brenda couldn't wait to tell them that she was now living on her own; the boyfriend had been no good and sometimes violent,

"I don't need a man, and I'm OK now on my own. But enough about me, what brings you here, Pats?"

Patsy wasn't so sure that her mum could ever live without a man, but she decided to just tell her news, "I'm getting married mum, in Devon to a lovely guy called Ed."

Brenda laughed and said she knew it wouldn't be long before Patsy got pregnant, "You're not that different from me luv, even if you think you are."

Rosie came to Patsy's defence, obviously annoyed with Brenda's attitude.

"Listen, Brenda, Patsy has a responsible job where she is well respected and making a difference to peoples' lives. She is marrying Ed because they love each other and together they will go places. If you want to be part of your daughter's life, I would suggest you change your attitude and look again at what a wonderful girl you've got."

Rosie mouthed the word 'sorry' to Patsy and sat with her arms folded. Rosie's outburst did seem to have an effect on Brenda. She was quiet for a moment and then apologised,

"I'm sorry, I never did know when to keep my mouth shut. I'm so glad you're making something out of your life Patsy. I always wanted that for you and I would love to meet Ed, if you're not too ashamed of me. Honest, I'll be on my best behaviour."

Patsy felt ashamed. Her mum had lived a hard life and really she should give her a chance, so she said she would arrange for Brenda to meet Ed, "Maybe we can meet somewhere neutral mum, somewhere nice where we can all chat like normal people?"

Brenda looked sheepish, "Let's do that and I promise to dress proper and not drink, I want you to be proud of me too, like I am of you."

Brenda came over to Patsy and hugged her, and patted Rosie affectionately on her arm, "Speak ye mind luv don't you? That's OK though, I'm a bit like that too."

They stayed a while longer and Patsy and Rosie talked about their job and Patsy's studies. Brenda listened and appeared to be genuinely impressed and happy for her daughter. They left with Patsy promising to be in touch.

"Give her a chance Patsy, I don't think she is a bad woman," said Rosie and Patsy smiled and said that she hoped Rosie's faith in her mum wasn't misplaced.

Patsy was telling Ed all about the meeting later that evening. Ed listened and said he thought Patsy would regret it if her mum wasn't there for the wedding, "She doesn't sound that bad Patsy."

But Patsy did have reservations.

"I only wish that my mum could be there, she would have loved it," Ed said sadly.

"You haven't really told me that much about your mum, I know she was a teacher but how did she and your dad meet?"

Patsy wanted to know so much more about Ed's family.

"Well, my mum already had Ruby when she met my dad, she had been married before when she was very young, but the marriage didn't last very long. It was my dad who handled the divorce. She had lived with her parents in Cornwall, I don't think she got on well with them, and she married a local boy, had Ruby and when the relationship broke down, she got a job in Devon. Anyway, she and my father fell in love and the rest as they say is history. My dad was offered a job in the United States, and mum and Ruby went with him where they got married.

"They came home after a year when mum was pregnant and dad started his own practice. Mum became a teacher much later after I was born. She had always wanted a career and from there they never looked back. Dad adopted Ruby, her dad didn't want to know her and dad has always been dad to her, it's never been an issue. Ruby never mentions her real father and dad adores her as she does him."

Patsy and Ed sat in silence for a while reflecting on what Ed had said. Eventually, Ed said that he had spoken to his dad about a visit, so the two checked their workload and came up with a weekend where they could travel down to Devon. They checked their guest list; a small intimate wedding was what they both wanted. The pub had letting rooms for the guests, and they could hire the restaurant for the reception.

"My mother did leave Ruby and I some money, we may even be able to buy a house or flat with a mortgage. We can make some enquiries and see if we can afford somewhere, what do you think?"

Patsy was speechless, a. place of their own, she had never imagined that would be possible, well not for a long time, "That would be fantastic Ed, but let's see. We've got the wedding to pay for and I'm happy to rent for a time. We've got all our lives to buy a house."

Ed nodded in agreement but still insisted that if they could afford to buy somewhere it would be better. He said he would make some enquiries and see just what they could afford. He kissed Patsy and said, "Now, when can I meet your mum?"

Chapter 27

Patsy was on her way to work, thinking how much her life had changed. Had it only been eighteen months since she had been working in the supermarket.

She thought about the wedding and decided she would ask Rosie to help her to find a dress, not expensive, not too fussy. Perhaps they could ask Mary to go with them, she had dressed so many women. Patsy wondered if she had ever helped any customer to choose a wedding dress. And she asked later as she was helping Mary to get dressed.

"I don't remember dear, I didn't stock wedding garments, specialist shops you know. Why do you ask?"

"Well, Rosie is coming with me to find my wedding dress and Mary, you have such an eye for knowing what would be the right dress, and I wondered if you would come with us?"

Patsy took a deep breath; this could be too much for Mary, especially when she noticed Mary had tears in her eyes. "I'm so sorry Mary, I didn't mean to upset you," Patsy said putting her arm around Mary.

Mary got hold of Patsy's hand, "On the contrary my dear, it would be an honour to help you choose your dress. You must look especially beautiful on your wedding day." Mary looked up at Patsy and smiled, "Would you ask the lady in charge of this establishment to come and see me?"

Patsy went to Rita and asked if she would go and see Mary. Rita grinned, and immediately went to Mary's room. When Rita left Mary's room, she was grinning even more broadly.

Rosie and Patsy arrived at the home to pick Mary up. They had spent hours poring over magazines to get some idea of what was on the market and most importantly, the prices. They planned to go to a large department store, Patsy knew her budget, it was small but she was sure she could find something special. She was glad Mary was coming with her; she certainly had an eye for what would suit. She just hoped Mary would appreciate that she couldn't afford a lot of money.

They had ordered a taxi to take them all into town. It was a bright, sunny day and Mary was fascinated by how busy the city centre was.

"I used to come into town quite a lot, with a man I knew, but I hardly recognise it anymore. So busy these days and everyone rushing about," and she looked out of the window again. Patsy and Rosie wondered who the man was, but they both said nothing, it was not the appropriate time and Mary would tell them when she was ready.

Mary was totally unfazed when she was wheeled into the busy department store and into the wedding department, 'Nicely laid out' and nodded her approval. Comments, which made Patsy, feel more relaxed. Patsy and Rosie, with the help of the friendly young assistant chose several dresses, all within budget and showed them to Mary.

"Try them on dear, then we shall know," Mary said assertively.

Mary came into her own when she was in the midst of fashion, this is without doubt the woman she really is thought Patsy.

Patsy modelled each of the dresses, they were all lovely and Rosie and the assistant said how beautiful she looked in everyone. Mary looked carefully but said nothing. Patsy liked one dress more than all the others. It was very simple but she felt comfortable, not overdressed and it was flattering, well that's what she thought, but she was worried because Mary had not said a word. Did she think none of them were right for her, or perhaps they looked cheap? Patsy certainly didn't want to look cheap on her wedding day. She wanted to look beautiful for her Ed.

Tentatively, Patsy asked Mary for her opinion.

"Well, they are all surprisingly stylish and reasonable quality but there is only one, I think which suits so well and shows off your beauty," and Mary chose Patsy's favourite dress.

Patsy flung her arms around Mary, "Do you really like it Mary, it's the one I want?"

Mary smiled and said, "I've taught you something then, of course it's the right one."

Rosie came over to them very excited and the three had a group hug.

With the dress packaged, Rosie ordered a taxi and Mary told them that she was paying for lunch. Patsy and Rosie said that wasn't necessary, but Mary said that she had spoken to the woman in charge, meaning of course Rita and she had the lunch money in her purse. Patsy could see that it was no use arguing, so the two girls graciously said a thank you and together with the precious purchase they set off for lunch.

They all got into a taxi again and Mary pulled out a piece of paper from her handbag,

"We have a reservation here," she said to the driver, handing him the paper.

They stopped outside one of the best restaurants in town, Patsy suggested to Mary that it would be expensive but Mary assured her that it had been highly recommended and it was her treat. With the help of Patsy, Mary who was totally at ease in the opulent surroundings ordered wine while they all perused the menu. During lunch, which was excellent, there was a lot of talk about the wedding, and Patsy told Mary about her planned trip to Devon to finalise the arrangements and to finally have a date for the big day.

"He is the one for you, that nice young man, I approve," Mary said.

When they got back to the home, they all had a tiny peek at the dress again. Mary said she had enjoyed every minute of their trip. "I can't wait to see the photos of your wedding," she said, but Patsy thought that she did look a little sad.

Patsy spoke to Rita and said that she hoped it was OK for Mary to have bought the lunch. "Mary was so adamant, I didn't want to argue with her," Rita answered.

"Mary spoke to me about it that day when she asked to see me," Rita explained, "she actually wanted to buy you the dress and she asked me to find a wedding shop, but I took the liberty of telling her that you wanted to buy the dress yourself. I suggested that she buy lunch instead. I telephoned her solicitor and he was agreeable to the idea. Mary insisted that you all go to a good restaurant, so I suggested Lesley's that is one of the best. I did check again with the solicitor though."

"Oh, thank you, Rita," Patsy replied, "I would not have wanted her to spend a lot of money on me, it wouldn't be right, lunch was expensive enough."

Rita nodded, "No it wouldn't Patsy. Mary is in our care and to some eyes it might look as though we were taking money inappropriately from her, although when I spoke to Bill he said that if Mary wanted to buy the dress with her money, then she should. I still think lunch was acceptable though, and a nice lunch at that."

Mary had a visitor a few days later, someone Patsy had heard about from Jess, but they had never met. The woman was in her 40s, very stylish and confident. Mary was delighted to see her, she recognised her straight away. The woman shook Patsy's hand, "I'm Annie, and I used to work with Mary in her shop. I loved every minute and Mary taught me so much about fashion. I live in London these days, but I still have to come and see Mary when I get the time. So sad that Mary became ill and had to leave her home."

Annie turned back to Mary and started talking to her about what she had been doing, and every so often Patsy could hear the two of them laughing.

When Annie came out of Mary's room she walked over to Patsy.

"She actually knew me," Annie said excitedly. "Usually she really has no clue who I am, but generally she is so much better. Mary was chatting away to me about old times, about the shop and Eric. She even remembered Ada and Rosalyn and their sleuthing."

Patsy was intrigued, "We know very little about Mary's former life other than she had the shop, and she lived in Oak hill in a bungalow. Bill, her brother lost touch with Mary for a long time so he didn't know a lot. We try to build a picture of all our resident's lives so that we can talk to them about their happy memories. It seems to help them and we can care for them better when we know who they were. If you can help in any way, ideally writing it down it would really benefit Mary."

Annie was only too happy to help, "Oh there's plenty to tell, Mary had a full life, she was a very successful businesswoman, and her shop was famous in the area. She fell in love with Eric, well that's a long story too. I can put it all in an email and send it to you, anything to help Mary."

"Oh thank you," Patsy said. "Annie, did Mary ever mention anyone called Susan?"

Annie thought for a moment,

"I do seem to remember that sometimes Mary would appear distant as though she were somewhere else, only occasionally of course. Mary was always sensible, but on those occasions I did hear her speak the name, 'Susan.' I remember wondering whom she was talking about, to my knowledge Mary knew no one of that name. I never asked her about it though because it seemed somehow inappropriate."

Annie said unfortunately that she had to leave, she had a train to catch, and she had to go home to London. She told Patsy that she had become a successful designer and that she had a family. Patsy mentioned that her future sister-in-law was also a designer, and as Annie said her goodbyes on her way out, she turned and said to Patsy,

"I owe Mary such a lot, so sad to see her like this."

Chapter 28

The date was fast approaching for Mary's move to the bungalow. Everything was set for delivery, all the curtains were made and arrangements set in place for the fitting. Mary was excited, but Eric still had very little to say about it, he constantly talked about the apartment in Spain and his friend needing the deposit.

One day while they were out having dinner and he was going on about how she really didn't want to miss out on such a golden opportunity, Mary turned to him and pleasantly said,

"Let's set a date now to go to Spain and you can show me this wonderful deal. I can meet and talk to your friend and if I am happy with the deal, then I shall be happy to pay the deposit. We had better make it quick though Eric, otherwise I will miss out."

Mary got her diary out of her handbag. "Let's see now, I move on the 9th, so I can go about the 16th. I'm sure you can spare the time Eric, after all it was your idea."

Eric looked shocked, Mary thought, Eric did not often lose his composure. He stammered a little as though he was thinking fast, "Yes, Yes, I see what you mean Mary but I have seen the development and this man, Peter, he's a good friend, there is no way he would sell me anything that wasn't perfect in every way. You've got enough to do luv, let me take the burden off you, I can deal with this for you."

Mary almost laughed. She felt like telling him then that she had seen the development, or lack of it too, but with every ounce of composure, it she answered him like a stupid lovesick teenager,

"Oh I know you can deal with this, darling, and believe me when I say that I am grateful." Mary hardened her tone, "But Eric, Peter isn't selling an apartment to you, he's selling to me and I want to see it before I part with money." Mary deliberately softened the tone again, "You understand I'm sure?"

Eric was not pleased; Mary detected a slight look of rage in his eyes. He looked away and when he looked back at her he was smiling, and he promised he would make the arrangements for them to go to Spain. He dropped her off at home; it was obvious from his demeanour that he wasn't staying, and he was beyond annoyed with her and trying too hard not to show his true feelings. Mary was so glad She almost hoped that she wouldn't have to see that man ever again; although when she thought about it she wondered just what Eric would do. As she watched him drive away, Mary went into her precious home, glad to be back. She made a cup of tea and discarding the tea she decided she needed a brandy. This detective work was taking a toll on her.

Life was busy as usual for Mary and moving day was fast approaching. Eric appeared to be incommunicado. Mary did wonder whether he had cold feet and disappeared from her life, but that didn't feel right. He still needed to be brought to account for the misery he had brought to, how many women? Mary couldn't imagine. After much consideration, Mary decided she would telephone him. He answered straight away and seemed genuinely pleased to hear from her.

"Oh, Mary," he said, "I thought about what you were saying, you want to see the Spanish development, of course you do, so I have been working hard so that I have the time to go to Spain with you. Funnily enough, only yesterday I was telling Peter, you know the developer, great guy. Anyway, I told him we'd be over very soon. Have to go, forgive me if I'm not in touch for a while but don't worry, we shall go to Spain."

Mary was confused, but she told Eric she completely understood and she had every confidence in him. Mary felt, well strange really, very mixed feelings. On the one hand she had listened to Eric and wanted to laugh, but she also felt nauseous. He must have had so many similar conversations with so many women.

Mary told Rosalyn, Ada and Annie about the telephone call. Annie was the first to comment, "The b——d Mary, sorry but I am so mad that he is putting you through this." Fair to say Annie was fuming.

Mary was not one for swearing but she was touched by this young woman's concern.

Mary put her arm around Annie, "Calm down dear, with my team we shall get him don't worry."

They all laughed, but Mary was right, they were all now so committed to stopping Eric, once and for all.

"Let's see what he does next, and then there's the visit to Iris to organise, and of course we have to get Mary settled in her new home." Ada remarked in her very organised tone of voice, and there was a consensus of agreement amongst all the women.

Mary did still have time to visit the Stanhope's' new bungalow and maybe she would get some more information. "Good idea, Mary," Rosalyn said, "Give them a ring and arrange the visit, but you need to get your skates on, moving day is not long away." So Mary arranged to go with the Stanhope's the next day before they all got too busy. They said that they would pick Mary up and drive her to their new home, and they did just that in the early afternoon.

The house was on a residential leafy road not far from the village, and Arthur Stanhope pulled into the driveway of a large detached house. A young woman greeted them and was introduced to Mary as their daughter Shirley. The garden was huge, and the new bungalow took pride of place but with plenty of privacy for the Stanhope's and their daughter's family.

The design was wonderful, a very large lounge, kitchen and two good-sized bedrooms. The bungalow had been finished to a very high standard and French windows led out onto a private area of the garden. Mary was very impressed but she still preferred 'her' bungalow, she thought it was more established; her new garden was mature and secluded.

The Stanhope's were obviously very delighted with their new home, they too had bought new furniture and furnishings, and there was no doubt that it all looked beautiful. After the viewing, they walked back to Shirley's house where they had tea and cakes. Shirley told Mary she was glad she could keep an eye on her parents,

"They are the only parents l have, and my family love the thought of them being so close to us. I know they weren't far away but they are getting older and I can keep an eye on them now. It was actually my husband's idea to build here," she paused, "We have too much land anyway, so it was the obvious answer."

Over tea, Isabel asked Shirley how her neighbour's building work was coming on.

"Yes, Eric is doing a good job, I'm a wee bit worried about the romance side though. She's fallen for him in a big way," Shirley explained as she offered everyone a cake.

Mary felt she was going to choke; surely he couldn't have called himself Eric. She tried hard to sound normal when she asked Shirley what Eric was like. Shirley thought for a moment,

"Ordinary really, probably late forties, fifties? But very pleasant and he works hard. He'd not been working there long when he asked her out. He took her out to a country restaurant, not sure why when we have good eating-places in the village but there we go. He has a friend who builds apartments in Spain and he wants her to invest in one. Still, it's her life and since the divorce, she has been lonely."

Mary was a speechless, lonely woman, yes that was the Eric she knew, the Eric who preyed upon lonely women. "I'll have to get his details," she managed to say, "I need a few odd jobs doing, nothing major, if of course he's interested in small jobs and it's always good to have someone who is recommended."

Shirley said that she would be happy to get his details, "Bradley," she suddenly said, "yes, that's his name, Eric Bradley."

The rest of the visit was a blur to Mary, she tried hard to remain interested and focused in the conversation. Shirley was telling her all about her family, and Mary nodded and smiled and gave appropriate answers. She wanted desperately to get home, to think. Isabel asked her if she was feeling all right, and Mary said that she was so sorry but she didn't feel very well.

"Better get you home Mary," Arthur said and he and Isabel helped Mary to the car. Mary managed to thank Shirley and apologised for their abrupt departure.

"Hope you feel better Mary," Shirley said sympathetically as the car pulled away.

The Stanhope's asked Mary if she could manage to go into her shop by herself and she assured them that she would be fine,

"I'll have a lie down and I should be much better. I've been busy planning the move, probably overdone it."

Mary repeated how lovely she thought their bungalow was and thanked them both for inviting her to see it. She walked into the shop to be greeted by Ada who noticed Mary wasn't well straight away. Mary breathlessly told her about Eric.

Ada was horrified and she insisted that Mary go upstairs and rest, "You've had a terrible shock Mary, I mean, that man is brazen."

Mary went to her flat but she couldn't rest. When the shop closed, Rosalyn and Ada came upstairs to check on her. Rosalyn asked Mary for the address and said that she would go to the house and have a look for Eric,

"It has to be him, but we need to know for sure. He won't see me, I'll keep a low profile, and mind you he probably wouldn't even recognise me. Must be hard remembering them all."

Mary gave Rosalyn the address and went to bed, she had to sleep and forget this mess, at least for a few hours.

At lunchtime the next day, Rosalyn confirmed that she had been parked near Shirley's house and the builder was indeed Eric. She didn't tell Mary that she had also seen Eric kissing Shirley's neighbour passionately at the front door.

"Just get into your new bungalow Mary and then we'll move in on him."

The move went smoothly, furniture, soft furnishings were all delivered on the day along with all Mary's belongings she had decided to bring with her. Mary still had her flat above the shop furnished; it was a haven to escape to in between busy times in the shop. The Stanhope's had moved out the day before and left the home in an immaculate condition. Rosalyn was a huge help and Ada called round after work.

By 7pm, the bungalow was looking like a home. Curtains hanging at the windows, the bed was made with the new bedding, pots and pans were put away, even pictures were in place, and a vase of fresh flowers brought by Ada. Annie came round with fish and chips and wine for everyone, and an exhausted Mary and Rosalyn sat with their friends around the new dining table and ate and relaxed for the first time that day.

Chapter 29

Annie was as good as her word and sent a detailed lengthy email. Rachael and Patsy read the email which told them all about Mary's shop, and. her close friends Ada and Rosalyn. There was so much information, the good times, and the friendship between the three women and how Annie came into their lives. Annie painted a picture of a lively, intelligent woman who was passionate about her business. How Mary was a respected, well liked and an important part of a community.

Then there was the story of Eric, how he met Mary and of course all about the infamous apartment in Spain, and what they all discovered about Eric. Annie had put lots of detail about Mary's sleuthing escapades, her friends and her love affair with her bungalow. Patsy was delighted; the information gave them so much more insight into Mary Reynolds, the person.

They showed the email to Bill, who laughed and said he never would have thought his shy, refined sister had had such a colourful life. Patsy emailed Annie to thank her for the history and asked what had happened to Ada and Rosalyn. Annie sent a prompt reply, saying that she would try and contact them, but she wasn't sure she still had their details.

Patsy wondered if Mary had photographs still in the bungalow. The solicitor was preparing to put the property on the market, but someone would have to go and sort through Mary's belongings. Rita said that she would telephone Mary's solicitor, which she did. He was agreeable to them going to the bungalow with Bill. Patsy asked Mary if she would like to go with them, she thought Mary might find the visit upsetting, but Mary said that she would like to see her home one last time, and there were a few things she would like to keep. Mary did seem to be finally resigned to giving up her home.

Rita, Patsy, Bill with Mary pulled up in the drive of the bungalow. It had been well maintained thanks to the solicitor organising the appropriate workmen Patsy asked Mary if she was OK, Mary's expression gave little away, but Mary assured everyone she was fine. Patsy thought the bungalow was lovely, a little old fashioned, but still charming with so much attention to detail which showed off Mary's talent for interior decorating.

"This is a proper home Mary," Patsy said, a statement which obviously pleased Mary.

Mary asked to be taken over to dresser, where she looked in a drawer and pulled out photographs, "These are my friends," she said showing a photo of four women. Patsy recognised Mary and Annie, much younger of course. The others, she presumed were Rosalyn and Ada and she mentioned their names to Mary.

"Oh yes," Mary said sadly, "Rosalyn and Ada, my dear friends, what good times we had." Mary giggled at the recollection.

Patsy had been recently reading about memory boxes, just as the name suggested, the boxes could be filled with photos, letters, anything which would remind people with dementia of their lives before their illness. With this in mind Patsy suggested to Mary that she keep these photos, and as they went around the bungalow, Patsy picked various items and asked Mary if she wanted to take them with her. They spent some time looking around and left with photos of the shop, the bungalow with the garden in full bloom, pieces of jewellery, a hat, three handbags, a lovely bedcover and some ornaments. As they closed the front door and helped Mary into the car, Mary waved goodbye to her home, no tears, and more an acceptance of what must be.

They stopped off at the little cafe Patsy and Mary frequently visited and over tea and cakes, they talked about the items Mary was taking back with her.

"How about I get those photographs framed Mary?" Bill suggested, "You could put some on your bedroom wall or your door to make it more your room, more homely."

Mary was delighted, "Oh yes, that would be lovely dear." and she quietly sipped her tea, Patsy noticed, much to her relief that Mary looked content.

When they got back to the home and Bill had said his goodbyes, Patsy, with directions from Mary, put her belongings in appropriate places in Mary's room. Patsy offered to get the bedcover laundered and Mary was in agreement. Patsy asked Mary if she wanted to rest, and to Patsy's surprise Mary asked for some of her jewellery to wear and said she would like to join some of the others in the lounge. Patsy left Mary chatting to Doreen, Doreen doing most of the chatting and Mary looking and nodding back at Doreen.

The day of the library protest arrived and Patsy, Ed and Rosie arrived, not sure of how many people would turn up. Sonia was waiting for them, also apprehensive. Thanks to Ed's piece in the paper, so many people, families, older and young people all arrived complete with banners and ready for peaceful battle. The photographer from the newspaper took his photos, as the crowd chanted that they needed their library.

"Save our library!" everyone chanted over and over.

Sonia was delighted and amazed at the turn out, Patsy, arm linked to Ed said,

"Wait till Ed writes about this Sonia, they can't close the library now."

The response was even more amazing after the story was published. Letters of support for the library poured into the newspaper offices and soon after that they heard that the council had agreed that the library would remain open.

Sonia was so grateful to Patsy for helping to save the library, she remarked that she knew it was a good day when a young girl, eager to study walked into the library and asked for help,

"How could I possibly have known that day that you would be the one to help me?"

Patsy laughed and said she was glad to help, "I need this library Sonia and I need you."

Ed and Patsy had arranged to go to Devon the next weekend, they were both looking forward to the trip but Ed said he was worried, "Dad and Ruby have gone a bit over the top with their suggestions, and we can't afford what they are proposing. With our budget, we'll be lucky to afford a cake. Maybe we should go with fish and chips for the wedding breakfast."

Patsy laughed and said that was a great idea, "It doesn't have to be a grand affair, and we'll make that clear, after all we have said we want a simple wedding. I've got a beautiful dress and Rosie and Iris are buying their own dresses, bless them. The pub, and fish and chips sounds just great."

Ed kissed her. "I picked the right one, I knew you weren't a spendthrift," and he winked at her.

They travelled to Devon on a Saturday in February, a cold crisp day with plenty of winter sunshine. Richard Clifton, Ed's dad gave them both a hug and ushered them inside to a roaring log fire. Over tea, and after establishing everything was good for his son and Patsy, Richard proceeded, with excitement to offer suggestions for the wedding.

"Ruby and I have spoken to the vicar, he still has limited dates for May or June, and we can hire the restaurant for the wedding breakfast. Then we thought we can come back here, possibly we can make use of the garden, and later in the evening, the pub can sort us out with a buffet, which they will deliver. I'll get plenty of drink in and the hotel; The Regent is an ideal place for some guests to stay.

"Uncle David and Aunt Beatrice are coming from the States, but it will still be a small wedding as you requested. What do you think?"

Richard was speaking so fast, he was breathless. Ed looked at Patsy and decided his answer must be tactful, "Dad, it all sounds wonderful, but we have such a limited budget, we were thinking more on the lines of wedding, then fish and chips in the pub. We do appreciate the work that you and Ruby have put in though, and the Regent is fine for those who can afford it, but some may want a room at the pub and then we thought some guests could stay here or at Ruby's if that would be OK?" Patsy nodded in agreement and thanked Richard.

Richard sat back in his chair and clasped his hands, "I want you two to do exactly what you want, but I am paying for this wedding and that is non-negotiable. I want to do this and I've got all the costs. It still won't be anything fancy, a small family and friend's wedding in hopefully sunny Devon. Your mother would want that and we can't let her down."

They all thought about Ginny for a moment, and how she would have organised the wedding. Ed said he hoped it would be sunny and then he went very quiet so Patsy took the lead,

"Thank you, Richard, we are very happy with your arrangements, it sounds perfect."

Richard smiled and then Ed thanked his dad and agreed it would be a very special day.

Ed and Patsy went for a walk, past the church, the pub, and then walked the mile or so to the hotel Regent.

"It's so good of your dad, Ed, when he was telling us about the restaurant and the garden, I was secretly wishing it could be just like that."

"I know. I felt the same." Ed agreed. "Right, well let's arrange an appointment with the vicar and then plan this wedding, although dad and Ruby have done all the hard work."

Later that evening, Richard, Ed and Patsy walked over to the pub. Richard had booked a table in the restaurant and shortly after they arrived, Ruby and Pete came in. Ruby ran over to Patsy and hugged her,

"Can't wait to see the dress, what do you think of the arrangements, sound good don't they?" Ruby was clearly excited. While they ate, Ruby said they should talk about numbers for the wedding. Rosie and her boyfriend, Jamie, Rosie's mum and dad, and their family, Patsy's mum and friend, Iris and husband, David and Beatrice.

Richard looked pleased, "Well, all we need is the date and we've got ourselves a wedding." He suddenly looked down sadly, "I only wish your mother could be there, but I know she'll be keeping an eye on us, of that I'm sure." Everyone had a moment of thought, Patsy wished she could have met this woman who had been so loved, she was sure she would have liked her very much.

They discussed floral arrangements and spoke to the restaurant manager about menus and the buffet. The manager said that the restaurant would be decorated for the wedding, and he asked about a colour scheme. Patsy had never had to think about so many things at the same time, but Ruby had plenty of suggestions, as did the restaurant manager.

Richard was getting a marquee in the garden and Ruby said she knew a good band. Patsy was worried about the costs and said so, but Richard told her he wanted it to be a perfect wedding. By the time they left and walked home, Patsy was exhausted, but very happy.

The following day, Ed and Patsy met the vicar, an older man who Ed had known since he was a child. After a lengthy but heart-warming meeting, the date of the wedding was arranged. The 26th May at 2pm. The vicar graciously accepted that Patsy was not a regular churchgoer, but he said that he had heard of her work and she had a good heart, which was good enough for his 'boss.

Chapter 30

Eric picked Mary up from her new home. Mary insisted on showing Eric around the bungalow and he said that he liked it all very much, although he wasn't very enthusiastic. He said that he was anxious to get to the restaurant where his friend would be waiting. Mary sounded enthusiastic, but secretly she couldn't wait for the evening to be over.

When they entered the restaurant. Eric's friend, the developer was already seated and was introduced to Mary as Peter Summers. Peter was a well-dressed portly man about the same age as Eric, very charming, a bit too much actually, Mary thought, but of course she knew why. They ordered drinks and Peter wasted no time in giving Mary the hard sell. She must move quickly otherwise she would lose this wonderful deal, the bargain of the century; Mary listened intently to Peter's patter. She asked if anyone had moved in yet, Peter said buyers were moving any day now. He had been amazed at the demand, so if Mary was serious about buying, she must act quickly. Eric said very little, letting Peter do all the talking but he nodded and smiled at Peter's every lie.

Eventually they ordered their meals, and Peter told her about all the wonderful restaurants in the area, so much cheaper than in the UK. Mary looked suitably impressed, and then she asked Peter when she could actually view the apartments,

"I've recently moved house Peter but now that I'm settled I can fly out anytime." Mary took a mouthful of her dinner and waited for the response.

"Of course, Mary," Peter did not appear surprised. "Eric could bring you next week, the apartment he chose for you is one of the best in the whole development, but it will sell very soon, so come and see it."

Peter looked pleased with himself and Mary noticed that he looked at Eric and they both nodded. "That's settled then," Mary said and raised her glass to both men. Eric paid the bill and they all walked out of the restaurant. Mary sensed that both Eric and Peter were surprised that the discussions had gone so well.

Peter gave Mary his card and said he looked forward to seeing her in Spain. Mary shook his hand and said that she too was looking forward to it, and that she was excited to see the apartment.

On the way home, Eric was congratulating Mary on her wise decision, "You won't regret it, I'll book the airline tickets and off we go."

Mary turned to Eric, "I know you'll think me silly, but I want to go with Ada, I'd like my friend to see the apartment, see what she thinks. You don't mind Eric do you darling?"

Eric was shocked, Mary could see that, but he quickly composed himself and said he understood and anyway he said he was busy, he had plenty of work on,

"Peter will look after you, and there will be lots of trips for the two of us," and with that, Mary opened the door to her bungalow. She didn't invite him in, just said she would see him when she got back.

Mary made tea and telephoned Ada, who asked, "What are they up to, Mary?" Mary said she was puzzled too. "I need you with me Ada and we shall find out."

Ada was only too happy to accompany Mary and said she would make all the arrangements.

"We might even enjoy the trip Mary like last time." Mary smiled and said she would see Ada in the morning.

Rosalyn and Annie were also perplexed by this news.

"Just what is this Peter chap going to show you. We know there are no apartments?" Rosalyn asked, and added, "Be careful you two, we are dealing with devious people here and we still don't know exactly what they are capable of. Eric took all my money, but this, this is all very strange, he's going to a lot of trouble, I don't like any of it."

Mary was very calm about it all, "Devious. Yes, but they won't get a penny from me, of that I am very sure. Rosalyn, will you come too, after all three heads are better than two, you've never met Peter have you? Of course I shall cover all our expenses."

Ada thought it was a good idea and Rosalyn was delighted and said she would love to go.

"I'll speak to my aunt but I'm sure she'll be OK for a couple of days on her own, she is so much better."

Rosalyn left and telephoned later and said that her aunt was keen for her to go; in fact she was delighted that this evil man was going to finally be caught out.

Mary, Ada and Rosalyn were sat on the aircraft on their way to Spain. Mary felt guilty because she was actually enjoying all this. She explained her feelings to her friends as they settled in their seats with a drink,

"I've found out the man that I loved is a crook and here I am on my way to Spain with two good friends to find out what he is up to and I'm enjoying every minute of it. I feel alive," she paused to see their reaction. "Is that bad?"

Rosalyn and Ada started laughing, and Mary joined in.

"No, Mary," Ada said, still laughing, "I think we're all enjoying this too," which for some reason set them all off giggling like three dizzy schoolgirls.

They checked into the same hotel that Mary and Ada had stayed in previously. Ada had insisted on paying for herself again, despite Mary's pleas to let her pay, but Mary had paid for Rosalyn, ignoring her protests. She was more than happy to pay for her friend. They unpacked and went for a walk to see the sights, and by early evening they had found a little restaurant, which came highly recommended. They were all tired, but at the same time they felt elated. The sun, the sea, the company, they all felt good.

They were meeting Peter the following morning, he said he would pick them up at their hotel and all three were wondering just where Peter would take them and how he would pull this one off. The next morning they didn't have long to wait, Peter was prompt, and very charming. Mary introduced Ada and Rosalyn to Peter and they were soon on their way in Peter's luxury car to see the what? They weren't sure.

Peter pulled into a very smart new development of apartments, not too far from the barren land they had viewed, however these were much closer to the sea, and there were other similar developments in the area. Peter was quick to point out to the ladies that he had played a large part in developing all of them, and the three friends appeared suitably impressed.

Peter showed them the swimming pool, the tennis courts and a restaurant, which was part of the apartments complex. It all looked beautiful and Mary felt a little sad that it wasn't the real thing. All the apartments looked to be unoccupied, there was no doubt they were brand new, and no one else was on site.

Peter led them to an apartment on the first floor, beautifully appointed and with a sea view. The rooms were spacious as was the balcony.

"Well, Mary, what about this? I told you Eric had chosen well," Peter said smugly.

They had a good look around, Mary's two friends made a point of telling Mary she should proceed with the purchase. The three women kept looking for anyone else on site but they didn't see anyone, Mary was beginning to think that Peter, if not Eric could be genuine.

Peter dropped them back at their hotel, and Mary said she would discuss everything with her friends and let him know the following day. Peter was quick to remind her how he had noticed that her friends were very enthusiastic about the apartment, and Mary smiled and said she would make a decision before she left Spain. The friends were all a little confused so Rosalyn suggested that they return to the complex later in the day, "They must have someone there at some time, maybe security, someone may be able to tell us more?"

After dinner and a walk to clear their heads, they haled a taxi and headed back to the apartments.

It was about nine pm and dark by this time. As the taxi approached the complex, they were in luck; two security guards were patrolling the well-lit grounds. The guards approached the women, and Ada asked if they spoke any English.

Both men spoke very good English and were reasonably friendly, if not a little suspicious. Ada explained about 'Peter Summers' the developer showing them an apartment earlier in the day. She asked them if they knew him or anyone connected with the building. The two guards looked puzzled and asked them how Peter had obtained a key, they knew the developers, they were a reputable Spanish company but they had never heard of Peter Summers. They also said that the building had security twenty-four hours a day, so strangers wouldn't have access.

Mary felt honesty was the best policy so she openly explained to the guards that they thought this Peter was not genuine. She told them about the plans she had been given, different from this location and about how she thought Peter and another man were trying to take money from her for a non-existent apartment. The men both nodded sympathetically and said they had heard of similar scams, and that they would inform their managers, who would probably want to speak to Mary. Mary readily agreed and gave them her name and details of their hotel.

The mood was sombre as they drove back to the hotel. Mary wondered how Peter had gained what appeared to be complete access to the apartment complex, despite the twenty-four-hour security she had been told about, it was all very confusing. When they reached the hotel, Ada suggested that they all needed a drink, a suggestion that appeared to everyone to be a good idea.

Over drinks on the hotel terrace, the three women discussed the day's events, but not one of them had any answers.

"Well, Mary," Ada said, "Those apartments are beautiful, I almost feel like buying one myself, though not from Eric or Peter."

Mary and Rosalyn both laughed, something they had all needed after such a stressful day. They decided to see what tomorrow would bring, and as they retired to their rooms, they were in a much lighter mood.

The following day, Mary was in her room getting ready to meet the others when her room telephone rang. It was Peter asking her if she had made a decision. Mary explained that she had yet to make a final decision, but that she did love the apartment,

"I am nearly ready to sign Peter but let me make my mind up in my own time." Peter sounded slightly irritated but he assured her that he fully understood. He reminded her yet again that the properties were selling fast so she needed to bare that in mind. Mary was relieved when the call ended and with a deep breath she went to meet her friends.

Chapter 31

Mary, Rosalyn and Ada were just finishing breakfast and discussing what to do next when a waiter approached their table and said that there was a telephone call for Mary at reception. Mary hurried off to see who was telephoning her; she hoped that it wasn't Peter again. It was in fact a gentleman introduced himself as Pablo Mendez, a director of the development company who had built the apartment complex. He was very concerned about information he had received from security about someone selling apartments illegally, and he asked if Mary would visit his offices. Mary readily agreed and Seigneur Mendez said he would send a car to pick her up. He also said that if she was more comfortable bringing her friends then to do so.

Mary hurried back to her friends, anxious to tell them about the meeting. The car didn't take long to arrive, and the driver introduced himself and opened the car doors for them. The journey was short and they pulled up in front of a large modern office complex. A lady who introduced herself as Maria, personal assistant to Seigneur Mendez, met them at the door and she led them into a lift to the top floor. There, they proceeded to a door, and Maria ushered the three ladies in. The office was very grand, but comfortable with not only a huge desk but also a comfortable seating area.

Seigneur Mendez was an older man, probably late sixties, Mary noted that he was of slight build and very tanned. He greeted them warmly. After introductions were made they were invited to sit on the comfortable chairs and offered coffee. Seigneur Mendez and Maria explained about the company, which had been responsible for several apartment complexes in Spain. The company was well established and reputable. They were obviously shocked and both expressed their concerns that someone was showing people apartments on the development and attempting to sell properties.

Mary took a deep breath and told them the whole story.

She explained how she knew Eric and Peter, and how she felt they were up to no good. She told them that there were other ladies they thought were being conned. Mary explained all about the previous visit to Spain to the actual site she was shown on the plans and the fact it turned out to be just barren land. She felt as though she was relating such a far-fetched story, but she hoped she would be believed.

Seigneur Mendez nodded, and he looked even more concerned. He said that he had made enquiries and had found some serious discrepancies in his security. He had yet to investigate fully, but it appeared that one or more of his security staff had been paid to turn a blind eye to certain people visiting the site. In particular to two men, one of whom, from the description resembled Peter and the other man, from Mary's description could be Eric. Maria added that so far, they had no idea how many of the apartments had been fraudulently sold. Mary smiled, a strange reaction some would say, but she felt relieved. Relieved that all her suspicions, all the months of wondering, all the months of doubting herself were over. Eric was a thief, a confidence trickster, and oh such relief. She looked at Rosalyn and Ada and yes, they were smiling too.

Seigneur Mendez thanked them all and asked if Mary would repeat her story to the police, and Mary was only too happy to agree. He came over to her and took her hand,

"This is all very distressing for you, Miss Reynolds, but without your information we might never have discovered this criminal act and it may well have brought our company very bad publicity. I am very grateful that you have agreed to help us bring this to our attention."

Mary answered that although it was distressing, she was glad that she had found the truth.

"Of course," Maria said, "If you still want to purchase an apartment, I am sure we can offer you a very good deal."

"The apartments are beautiful," Rosalyn said, "Just how much are they?"

Maria explained that they were different prices depending on the location, view etc., "…but the apartment you were shown is," and she told them the price. Mary was shocked; Eric and Peter were asking far more money.

They left after Seigneur Mendez had established when they were flying home and he assured them that the police would surely be in touch. Maria showed them out of the building and reiterated how grateful they were. The driver was waiting and offered to take them on a tour of the sites before dropping them off at their hotel. An offer, all three were happy to accept, and as he drove them, all the while showing them the area in this large comfortable car, they all finally relaxed, at least for a while.

Later Rosalyn, Ada and Mary were sitting by the pool discussing all the events, which had brought them to this point. They laughed as they talked about the 'stakeouts' and Mary said that she had enjoyed the flasks of coffee and the sandwiches if not the long cold hours of waiting in a car.

A hotel receptionist walked into the pool area with two men and came towards the three ladies. The men introduced themselves as police officers; they had spoken to Seigneur Mendez and they wanted to hear Mary's account.

The officer in charge introduced himself as Inspector Rodriguez, and asked many questions while the other officer took notes and Mary asked if they had received other complaints,

"We did have a complaint from an English lady about twelve months ago about a similar operation, but although we investigated, nothing came of it. It was a different apartment complex but we had very little information at that time. We are questioning the security guards and we have alerted all developers to tighten their security. I am hoping we might get these men this time with your help."

"I do hope so," said Mary, "Who knows how many women they have fooled with their devious plans?"

The officers promised to keep in touch with Mary and let her know if there were any new developments. They took all her details and after thanking her they stood to go but Inspector Rodriguez stopped briefly and said,

"I'll make some enquiries with the British police, they might have further information, and my guess is that these two have been doing this for a while." He was about to leave when he suddenly stopped again,

"Miss Reynolds, would you be prepared to help us to collect evidence against this man? If we could witness him taking money from you, we can arrest him? I wonder, can you phone Peter and ask him to meet you? I realise it's a lot to ask but we would be there watching all the time, there would be no danger."

Mary thought about it for a moment and then readily agreed. She said she would let the Inspector know where and when she was meeting him.

Mary did not have to wait long. Before she had a chance to telephone Peter, he telephoned her. Peter was quick to ask her if she had made a decision, and Mary told him that she would like to meet him again to finalise a deal. She confirmed that she was ready to purchase the apartment but it would have to be soon because she was flying home the next day.

Peter was delighted, and he suggested that if it were convenient, he would come over to the hotel at 5pm that same day. Mary made a big effort to sound excited too and she said that she would look forward to seeing him again. "Can't wait can he?" Ada said, and Mary immediately made another call and left a message for Inspector Rodriguez.

The Inspector was back at the hotel at 4 pm with another officer,

"We do need to see you pay him money Miss Reynolds," he stressed and Mary told him she would be sure to hand him a deposit for an apartment,

"I have been to the bank and the money shall be paid in cash, but Inspector, please make sure I get my money back?"

Inspector Rodriguez reassured her they would arrest Peter as soon as they witnessed the money had changed hands. Mary spoke to Ada and Rosalyn and said that she would meet Peter on her own. Her friends thought it would be better if they were with her but Mary was adamant,

"He's got to think I am serious about the purchase, better if I meet him alone."

Her friends reluctantly agreed. The Inspector stressed to Mary to keep Peter in the bar area of the hotel,

"Do not, under any circumstances let him lead you anywhere else, inside or outside the hotel."

At promptly 5pm, Mary greeted Peter at the hotel reception and suggested they have a drink in the hotel bar and discuss the details. Peter was happy to follow Mary into the bar, and having found a discreet table, he ordered them both a drink, "So, you decided my dear to buy, very wise Mary?" He said, smiling at Mary. Mary was not happy with his endearment, but she smiled back sweetly and said she had decided the offer was too good to miss and she was more than pleased to pay the deposit. She added,

"Eric will be pleased too, and Peter, I can't thank you enough for your help, Eric was so right telling me that I could trust you."

Peter grinned like a Cheshire cat and made a toast with his Martini in hand,

"To many sunny days in Spain my dear." Mary raised her glass of sherry to his glass. Mary counted out the money very carefully, making sure she could be seen clearly handing over money. Peter gave her a receipt stating the money was a deposit for the apartment and told her as soon as the paperwork was complete, she and Eric could move into the apartment.

He added, "You can pay the balance to Eric, easier for you I think, I trust him to pay me." Peter laughed, a little too loudly Mary thought.

They finished their drinks, Mary felt like choking but she kept up the pretence and talked about purchases she would be making for her holiday home. Eventually, and to Mary it seemed forever, they said their goodbyes and Peter and Mary got up to leave. Mary exited as quickly as she could, but not before witnessing Inspector Rodriguez and his colleague approach Peter and after a brief discussion lead a shocked Peter away to a police car.

Rosalyn and Ada rushed over to Mary and hugged her,

"You did so well," said Rosalyn, "We were watching the whole time, so brilliant Mary, and they got him. Let's hope Eric is caught too."

"I really do need a drink now," Mary said, "I feel a bit shaky now."

Rosalyn and Ada linked her arm and guided Mary to a table. Mary quickly recovered and the three spent their last evening enjoying a meal and afterwards a walk along the seashore. The following day, the three boarded their flight home.

They arrived back home in the late afternoon to be greeted in the shop by Annie who looked very busy helping various customers. Mary immediately took off her coat to help while Ada and Rosalyn went straight home. When the shop finally closed, Mary thanked Annie for taking care of the shop and then she told her about their escapades in Spain. Annie was impressed and also slightly amused at the thought of these amateur sleuths she knew so well tracking down criminals so efficiently,

"I always thought of you all as refined ladies," she laughed, "not hardened private investigators. No word from Eric by the way."

Mary laughed too and said she agreed she didn't know just what she was capable of until she had to, "I must say though Annie, I have enjoyed it all. Now you get yourself home and thank you once again."

Later, back in her bungalow, Mary was unpacking her suitcase when she received a telephone call from Inspector Rodriguez,

"Well, Miss Reynolds, Mr Peter Summers sang like a bird. Your Mr Bradley has several aliases just as you said and has been in many fraudulent deals over the years. Bradley extorts money from women in many different ways, and he always has accomplices, names of some of these Summers has given us. Of course Summers says he was dragged into all this unwillingly, although I do not think so for a minute. I have been in touch with the British police force and they will look into Bradley and establish if they know him. Thank you Miss Reynolds for your assistance."

Mary felt so relieved, she had her money, the Spanish police had Peter and hopefully Eric would be caught before long. She telephoned Ada and Rosalyn straight away.

She was just about to finish her unpacking when the telephone rang again and it was Eric, wanting to know how she had got on in Spain. He said that he had not heard from Peter.

Mary took a deep breath, "Oh Eric," she said, hoping that she sounded normal, "You were right. The apartment is stunning, and I couldn't resist. I paid the deposit to Peter before I left Spain, I'm so excited."

Mary knew at this point that Eric must be jumping for joy, but he of course kept control in his voice as he answered.

"I knew it was right for you Mary, now you can relax in the sun whenever you like. Peter is a good chap; I've done loads of deals with him in the past. Now, when can we get together, I've missed you darling?"

Mary said that she was tired, it had been an exhausting journey, but she would 'phone him the next day. As Mary got into bed, she hoped she would never have to see Eric ever again.

Chapter 32

"She looks beautiful in her dress," Mary was telling Bill. "That nice young man, I should have loved to see them get married, that's a marriage made in heaven." Mary looked sad, she was thinking what might have been, but the two men in her life had let her down badly.

"I'm sure there will be lots of photographs and Patsy will tell you every detail," Bill answered sympathetically. Mary nodded and brother and sister then spent a long time deciding on a wedding present, it was Mary's wish and Bill was only too happy to agree.

Patsy went into Rita's office to make the call to Annie, who was pleased to hear from her. Patsy thanked her for the email and told her how helpful it was. She explained that they had taken Mary to her bungalow and Mary had chosen some photographs and jewellery to take back to the home. Patsy asked Annie if she had any contact with Mary's friends and Annie said she had not seen them for some time,

"I haven't seen them since I moved away, and I'm struggling to find their contact details. Such a shame, they were such good friends and they went through a lot together. I miss them all too, even though I was a lot younger we had many a laugh, sad times too."

Later in the pub with Ed, they went over some finer details for the wedding. They arranged a date when they could buy Ed's suit, after all the wedding day was getting closer. There was also the task of finding somewhere to live and Ed showed Patsy some photographs for sale that the estate agent had given him. They had applied for a mortgage, but although Ed was using the money his mum had left him as a deposit, all the houses were expensive. They agreed to view the most suitable and affordable properties, but they both knew they might have to move to an area, which was more affordable.

On a whim, they decided to go and see Mary's bungalow. Patsy wanted to show Ed where Mary had lived and the trip meant they could both relax a little, away from their busy schedules. "We can dream that one day we shall move to a lovely area. We may be old by then unless you become a famous reporter." Patsy said laughing.

Patsy and Ed pulled up in the car outside Mary's bungalow. A FOR SALE sign was placed prominently in the garden.

"Great area Patsy, the bungalow must be pretty expensive, out of our price range sadly," Ed put his arm round Patsy.

"I know Ed, but Mary worked hard to afford this, just like we will. Wouldn't it be wonderful to someday be able to afford somewhere like this one day, in a prime location?" Patsy sighed, but she was thankful for all she had at that moment.

They sat outside the bungalow for a while just taking in the area.

"How does Mary feel about selling her home, has she talked to you about it?" Ed sounded concerned.

"Not really," Patsy said sadly, "She seems resigned to the sale though, it's such a shame because she loved her home." She was silent for a moment, deep in thought. "I wonder what we'll be like when we get old?"

"Oh, we'll be partying when we're old, celebrating the kids have all left home," Ed quipped, and Patsy said that she hoped he was right, but she knew from her work that life was a lot different for many old people, but for now youth was on their side, and they had things to do.

On the way home, Ed asked how the search for Mary's daughter was going. Patsy sighed. "Nothing yet. I know we've not been searching long but it's not looking too hopeful, although Jennifer can't just disappear." Ed said he had a good feeling about finding Jennifer and that it would end happily.

Chapter 33

The day Patsy had been dreading arrived, the day when Ed would meet her mother. Patsy had arranged to meet her mum at a restaurant, she and Ed were treating Patsy's mum to lunch. Patsy was nervous, she so hoped her mum would have toned down her attire and not be drunk. Patsy chastised herself, this woman was her mother after all, and she shouldn't be so judgemental.

Ed and Patsy were sitting in the restaurant when Brenda arrived looking smartly dressed in a knee length dress and a jacket. Ed stood and shook Brenda's hand,

"Lovely to finally meet you Mrs Bennett," he said. Brenda smiled at him,

"Likewise Ed, but please, call me Brenda."

Patsy hugged her mum and after they were settled and ordered drinks she told her all about the wedding,

"Ed's dad said you can stay at his house, and you can travel down to Devon with us." Patsy tentatively waited for the response.

Brenda paused before answering, "Actually luv, I would like to come to the wedding with my friend, a new friend, Ernie if that's OK, you'll like him I know. Ernie has a nice posh car and we'll drive down together."

It was no surprise to Patsy that Brenda had a new man, she always had to have a man no matter how rubbish they all were. However, despite her feelings she told her mum that would be fine, and Ed said that he was looking forward to meeting Ernie and that he was very welcome.

Their drinks arrived, noticeably Brenda was totally sober which Patsy was so glad about, and they ordered their meal.

"Such a lovely treat for me Ed to be taken out for lunch, it doesn't happen very often, still it's not often your daughter is getting married I suppose," Brenda said as she nervously took a sip of her drink.

Ed recognised that Brenda wasn't very comfortable so he resorted to tales about his job at the newspaper and proceeded to relate some funny incidents that had happened to him while he was in pursuit of a story, in the hope it would relax the mood.

"Ed hopes to become a reporter or presenter on the TV mum," Patsy said proudly, and Brenda, now more relaxed, but with an empty glass said she couldn't wait to see that, "Oh get you Ed, my son-in-law on the tele." Ed ordered another round of drinks.

They chose some food from the menu and Patsy suggested to Brenda that they could go together to choose a wedding outfit,

"I'll help you pay for it, Mum, but let's get you something nice to wear for the big day."

Brenda smiled and said that she would like that,

"Ernie will give me some money luv so don't you worry, but it would be smashing if you could help me choose. You know what I'm like with fashion and I would like to look nice for you and Ed."

Patsy felt that they were finally getting somewhere and settled down to enjoy the lunch. Brenda was by this time somewhat inebriated, but she was managing to hold it together.

Ed did most of the talking, he told her all about his family, Brenda was genuinely sorry to hear about Ed's mum, and Ed said Patsy was so lucky to have her mum at their wedding. He told her about them trying to find somewhere to live, to buy somewhere if possible and Brenda was impressed, "I've always had to rent somewhere," she said, "I always dreamed of owning my own place."

Finally, and it did seem to Patsy a very long time, they got up to leave. Ed offered to take Brenda home, but she insisted that she was meeting Ernie. She kissed Patsy and gave Ed a hug, "I really hope you'll both be very happy," she said and with that off she went.

Patsy looked at Ed, "I am sorry, Ed, but I did tell you what she's like."

Ed was quick to answer, "Don't apologise, I actually think that was very hard for her and under the circumstances she did very well."

He shook his head, "Sorry Patsy, that sounded very patronising and I didn't mean anything."

Patsy put her arms around him, "I know Ed, and she would have found that an ordeal but I didn't want to meet in the local boozer. She will struggle at the wedding, she'll be totally out of her comfort zone and goodness knows what Ernie is like."

They saw the funny side but Patsy was genuinely worried for her mum and how she would cope with the wedding.

After they left the restaurant, they went to look at a couple of houses in their price range. Both properties were in an area some distance from where they lived now, but one terraced house they saw was a possible contender.

"The Street looks quite nice," Ed observed.

"Quite a large house, in good condition, not bad, and not too far for work," Patsy agreed, "We could make this really nice Ed, a real home, let's have a good look at the area."

They walked around the area, looking at the other properties, the shops; they spoke to some of the people on the way. They were close to all the amenities, a short bus ride for Patsy to get to work; all in all it did look promising.

"Let's think about it, Patsy," Ed said, "If we decide we still like it, we can put in an offer. Otherwise, we keep looking, we'll find something."

Patsy was happy with that, after all she thought, they had to start somewhere and the house would be theirs one day. She thought about what her mum had said about always renting and she felt bad about being embarrassed about Brenda and Ed meeting. Her mum had not had a good life and she should remember that and be kinder.

Patsy was working a late shift the next day, and on her way to work, she stopped by the library to invite Sonia to the wedding, so much for a small wedding, the numbers were growing. Sonia was clearly very touched with the invitation and said she would love to go and would book a room at the pub if there was one available. Patsy thought that would not be a problem, "Bring someone of course, Sonia." Sonia said she would come alone and she was happy to drive to Devon.

"I'm really looking forward to it Patsy, and it'll be a nice break for me."

They talked about the wedding and the search for a house, and Sonia had some new research articles for Patsy. "Have to dash Sonia, I'm working," Patsy said putting her coat on and she rushed off to work.

The home was busy, quite a few of the residents had colds and chest infections and some were too poorly to get out of bed or leave their rooms. Chest infections were particularly dangerous to older people and there had been several doctors' visits during the morning shift.

Patsy listened to an extensive report about each resident, given to her and other staff by the nurse in charge. Antibiotics had been prescribed for those most ill, and fluids were to be encouraged. As many of the residents were too ill to get out of bed, they discussed the importance of care of pressure areas; the areas of the body most vulnerable to pressure sores from being in one position in bed.

With such a heavy workload, she didn't have much chance to chat with residents in any length. She helped Mary to get ready for bed and told her she couldn't stay long. Thankfully Mary was fine and seemed to understand how busy all the staff were. Mary settled in bed and sleepily said to Patsy, "When is the wedding dear?" and closed her eyes. Patsy smiled and wrote down the date and left the message next to a sleeping Mary.

The next few days were busy for all the staff, more of the residents were going down with a 'flu like illness. Alice, the London lady who had been a dancer in her younger years was taken into hospital, which upset everyone. Also, many of the staff had to go off sick not only because they were ill, but also their absence lessened the spread of the infection. All the staff were reminded about the importance of hand washing, and all trips and social events were cancelled.

Mary had so far escaped the illness, but she was getting very agitated because she couldn't go out. Patsy explained the situation to Mary on numerous occasions, but it did little to pacify her. Patsy decided to stay after her shift one day, and armed with fashion magazines, she sat with Mary showing her some fashions. Mary was interested to a point but insisted,

"Yes, dear, very nice, but I need to feel the quality and it is imperative that I try the garments before I buy."

Patsy said that she had brought in the magazines to get some ideas, and as soon as the illness was under control and she had more time, she promised they would go out. This did seem to settle Mary a little and she commented on several outfits in the magazines that she liked.

Bill arrived for a visit and Mary said to him, "I shall be going out soon to buy a new outfit."

Patsy winked at Bill and he smiled and sat down with Mary to look at the magazines.

When Bill came out of Mary's room to make a cup of tea for himself and Mary. Patsy asked if he had any news about Susan/Jennifer. Bill shook his head,

"The investigators are working hard to find her, they are confident, and it's just a question of time which is worrying. We don't know how much time we have."

Patsy nodded and said, "Mary is doing really well, Bill. I'm sure she will get to meet her daughter." Bill nodded and said he hoped that she was right.

Sad news the next day, Alice had passed away in hospital, always sad for staff and residents to hear when one of their friends had died. Close relationships were made, not only between residents, but also between staff and residents. To care for someone daily, helping them with personal care and talking about all sorts of things every day for a long time, then to lose that person was always very sad. It was also unfortunately part and parcel of the job, but new residents would arrive and be assured to receive the same amount of care and love.

Chapter 34

Mary's wish that she would never have to see Eric again was not to be. The very next day after Mary's return from Spain the local police had made arrangements to come to her home. Mary was worried again.

Ada, as always was very understanding, "Don't worry Mary, take all the time you need and be sure to tell them everything. Just come in when you can, I'll be fine and Annie is in this afternoon."

Mary was expecting a police constable to visit her, but it was in fact a detective Inspector Granger, a smartly dressed, attractive middle-aged woman who said she was part of the fraud squad. She said that the Spanish police had alerted them.

Mary told her story, how she met Eric, how Rosalyn told her what he had done to her, the aliases that she and Rosalyn had discovered. Also the Spanish apartment saga, and how their investigations had discovered two other women who Eric could be trying to defraud.

Inspector Granger listened with interest and took notes. She said they would look into Mary's allegations, and she took down addresses of the other women, and included Rosalyn. Inspector Granger explained that Summers had set his loyalties aside, and he had a lot to say about Eric and his dodgy dealings.

The Inspector got up to leave. "Thank you, Miss Reynolds, hopefully with your information, we shall be able to put Mr Bradley away for a long time," and with that, the Inspector shook Mary's hand.

"What happens next?" Mary tentatively asked, "I really don't want to see him again, what do I tell him?"

Inspector Granger looked sympathetic, "You have done a great job Miss Reynolds, but with your permission, we may need you to meet him again depending on the evidence we can find on him. If you could carry on and act as though everything was as normal it would be helpful. I do know that's a big ask.

In the meantime, we'll speak to all the women you found and of course continue to liaise with the Spanish police."

Mary showed the Inspector to the door. She went into her lounge and uncharacteristically, she burst into tears. Admonishing herself for being so stupid, Mary telephoned Rosalyn, told her about the visit from the police and asked her if she could come over,

"I know I'm being silly Rosalyn, but I don't want to be on my own tonight, my head is in a whirl." Mary sounded tearful. Rosalyn listened to Mary, knowing that this strong woman she had come to know and love needed her help, "Of course I'll come Mary and I'll bring some wine and a casserole."

Mary was so grateful, she needed support, "Sounds wonderful Rosalyn, just what I need, I'll see you soon."

As promised Rosalyn arrived with a beef casserole and a good bottle of red. They sat at the kitchen table eating their meal and enjoying the wine, and they talked and talked about anything and everything. Mary felt so much better, and by the time Rosalyn left, Mary knew she could face Eric again if she needed to. He had to be stopped, and she was determined that she would stop him once and for all.

Mary and Ada were in the shop as usual, Annie was dressing the windows and they looked fabulous with an autumn display of the latest pieces. The shop was very busy, mostly with regular customers. Mary noticed a woman who didn't look familiar so she approached her and asked if she needed any assistance. The woman looked nervous, "Are you by any chance, Mary?" she said quietly. Mary didn't think her question unusual, a lot of new customers wanted to meet the shop owner, she was well known in the village for her expertise.

She held out her hand, "Mary Reynolds, yes that's me, how can I help you?"

"Lovely to meet you, I am Shirley's next-door neighbour, Alison Miller. I believe you met Shirley and you bought Arthur and Isabel's bungalow. Isabel has told me how wonderful your shop is, and today I need some cheering up so I'm here to buy clothes please."

Mary was shocked, so this was another of Eric's conquests. Mary decided to remain professional, not a difficult decision, it came naturally to Mary in her business capacity. "Yes, of course, Alison, what can I show you?"

Alison proceeded to lose herself in fashion and spend a considerable amount of money.

Mary was busy parcelling the purchases and chatting to Alison, Alison suddenly burst into tears. Mary took her to the back of the shop where there was a small office and offered Alison a cup of tea.

"I'm so sorry," Alison said, still upset. "I have had such a bad day. I just have to tell someone," and she paused. "You have been so kind, would you mind if I talk to you about something?"

Mary felt so sorry for this woman and sympathetically said that she didn't mind at all, after all she had a good idea what had upset Alison.

Allison took a deep breath, "You see, Mary, I have a friend who I am deeply in love with and, this morning, well I had a visit from a police officer asking questions about him. They knew I was thinking of buying an apartment in Spain. Eric, my friend knows the developer and can get a good price. We are planning to move there soon. Well, then the police asked me lots of questions about Eric and then told me not to tell Eric about their visit. They seem to think Eric may be trying to extort money from me. I feel so stupid, I don't know what to do, I'm such a fool, and I think he's not been very truthful from what the police said. I bet you've never fallen for his type." Alison laughed half-heartedly and then looked at Mary.

Mary touched Alison's hand and thought about what to say next. "I'm sorry, my dear, I know Eric too and I also loved him. He tried to sell me an apartment in Spain, but I was suspicious and I went to Spain and found out he was a confidence trickster. It was me, who went to the police, and I'm sorry, I knew he was tricking you too. Shirley told me about you and Eric, but the police told me not to say anything."

Alison looked shocked but Mary went on to say that they were lucky, he had not robbed them of any money, "You haven't handed any money over have you Alison?" Alison said that she hadn't but she was about to very soon, money for the deposit.

"It is difficult," Mary said, "Believe me I know, but we're not the only ones and it is important that Eric does not find out that we are on to him."

Alison nodded and said she would keep quiet. "Take your clothes Alison," Mary said gently, "and enjoy them and you will enjoy seeing Eric getting his just rewards soon, I promise."

Alison finished her tea, took her purchases and squeezed Mary's hand,

"Thank you, I feel a little better now I've spoken to you. At least I'm not the only foolish one, oh sorry Mary." Mary smiled and nodded. Alison continued,

"Thank goodness you found out about him." She smiled, "Don't worry, my lips are sealed, and thank you for helping me. If you hadn't, goodness knows how much of my money he would have taken?"

Mary put her arm around Alison, "He shall pay for his crimes."

As Alison left the shop, Mary relayed the conversation to Ada who said she hoped they wouldn't have to wait too long until Eric was arrested,

"The misery that man has caused," she reflected. Mary nodded, she so hoped this would soon be over.

When Mary arrived back home to her bungalow, she felt exhausted. The stress over the past weeks was telling on her, and she wondered just how long she could cope. She dreaded the phone ringing in case it was Eric, although noticeably he was definitely not around as much as he used to be. She hoped he hadn't detected anything unusual in her behaviour.

Just as she was mulling all these things over, the phone rang. Taking a deep breath, Mary answered. It was Eric asking her if he could take her to dinner the following evening.

"Lovely Eric," Mary answered, "Just what I need. Yes, see you at 7pm."

Eric sounded his usual cheery self, "Yes luv, not heard from Peter but I'm sure you can complete on the apartment very soon. Not like Peter, not to be in touch, not like him at all. Was he OK when you met him?"

Mary answered confidently, "Charming as ever and very helpful, he looked fine when I saw him. He's probably just snowed under with work like the rest of us."

Eric seemed to relax and said she was probably right, and he would look forward to tomorrow.

Chapter 35

Spring was in the air and there were much fewer residents going down with chest infections. A new resident had arrived called George. He had been diagnosed with Alzheimer's and was very confused. He apparently had no relatives, and he was very wealthy, but there was no knowledge of how he had amassed his fortune.

He had been living in a very large house, which was in a poor state of repair. He hadn't been eating or washing and was unable to care for himself. At night in particular, he was often found by the police wandering the streets, unkempt and in his pyjamas.

George moved into Alice's old room and settled almost immediately. George liked all the attention and care, and very soon his physical health improved. After months living with no one to care for him, he appreciated the food, the warmth and the company. He quickly became a firm favourite with the staff due to his amazing sense of humour. George had something funny to say about everybody and everything. Some of George's jokes were totally inappropriate, but no one took offense: he had a way of saying things.

With the work not as pressured and the improved weather, all activities were resumed and Patsy and Mary were off to buy yet another outfit for Mary. Mary was very excited and she asked Patsy if they could go to her favourite shop in the village. They arrived at the shop in a taxi, and as Patsy pushed Mary's wheelchair through the door, Fiona, the shop assistant greeted Mary like a long-lost friend,

"Oh, it's so lovely to see you again, how can I help you today?" she said.

Patsy smiled, a good commission day for Fiona, she thought. Mary smiled back at Fiona, Patsy wondered if Mary recognised Fiona, but it didn't really matter because she was being spoken to like a real person and not a lady with dementia, sitting in a wheelchair.

"Beautiful lines as always," Mary said knowingly, "and the fabrics are perfect."

Two hours later Mary had yet another outfit complete with hat, gloves, and comfortable but stylish flat shoes plus a handbag. The cost of all the items made Patsy gasp, but she was happy for Mary. It was inbuilt in Mary to be stylish and she had the money to spend on herself.

As Patsy and Mary were getting ready to leave, a woman in her thirties came into the shop. Patsy thought how beautiful she was, tall and willowy, long perfectly styled hair and her clothes were stunning. Fiona introduced the woman to them,

"This is Louise, the shop owner. Louise these are the ladies from the home, you know, I told you about them. Miss Reynolds is one of your best customers, she has just bought a lovely outfit."

Mary looked pleased and Louise bent down to shake her hand, then did the same to Patsy,

"Yes, Fiona told me all about you. How exciting about your wedding, and I believe you want us to do a fashion show at the home, I'd be delighted."

Louise spoke in a very well-bred voice, unlike Fiona's peculiar accent, which by now had turned into normal Mancunian, which Patsy decided, was much better.

They spoke about the fashion show, Louise said she might have difficulty getting these models, but Patsy suggested the staff at the home could model the clothes. "Excellent," Louise enthused, "I shall check my diary and be in touch and I can give discounts for purchases or make a donation to the home."

Patsy suggested to Louise that she telephoned Rita to sort out the details, which Louise was more than happy to do.

After leaving the shop, Patsy and Mary were having lunch at the pub. Mary was excited but said suddenly, "I should have loved to be there when Susan got married, what a wedding that would have been! I do hope she found a good man." Mary looked sad, but only for a few seconds. She looked at Patsy, "Well, I can't be at Susan's wedding but I shall be waiting to hear all about yours my dear. I'm so excited I feel like I shall be there. In fact I shall wear my new outfit on the day," and Mary beamed.

Patsy was touched, but she felt guilty that she had not invited Mary to her wedding. She would have loved Mary to be there but she also felt that it would be a step too far for Mary to travel all that way, "We'll video the wedding for you and all the other residents and have tea and wedding cake when I get back." Mary was more than content with that.

When they returned to the home, George was pacing up and down in the hallway. He stopped when he saw them come in and immediately said to them, "Two roses in between all those thorns, what a picture."

Mary and Patsy both laughed and Mary graciously thanked him. George followed them and as they went into Mary's room, Mary sensed his uneasiness and said to him that she would be in the lounge shortly and they could have tea together. Patsy directed George to the lounge where he sat contentedly waiting for Mary.

The friendship between Mary and George grew. Mary seemed to know how to settle him and appeared to be completely oblivious to some of George's rude remarks. He paced less often and he also had a calming effect on Mary. She laughed a lot more and she loved his frequent compliments. Everyone remarked on what an unlikely friendship it was. Mary was such a lady and George, well George could be quite blunt with his remarks, however not so with Mary. She found his remarks as funny as everyone else, and there was also no doubt that George had a warm personality despite his sarcasm. Mary and George had an understanding and were indeed friends, even Bill remarked that Mary had finally found her beau.

Fiona and Louise arrived at the home on the arranged evening for their fashion show. They were early so that they could dress their models and there had been no shortage of volunteers from staff to wear the high-quality clothes. Louise, it transpired had worked in top fashion houses, and she proudly demonstrated how to walk a catwalk with maximum impact. Residents, staff and visitors gathered in the main lounge. The catering staff had prepared a special buffet and this was offered to spectators along with a selection of alcoholic and soft drinks.

Fiona was in charge of the sound system, which she managed expertly. Mary sat at the front with George sitting next to her, although every now and again he would go for a wander around the room, always to return to Mary. Mary patted his hand and spoke softly to him and George smiled contentedly. Louise introduced the proceedings and mentioned that it was due to 'her good customer Miss Mary Reynolds' that they were honoured to be at the home Louise stood to one side of the floor, which had been dressed especially with a red carpet and the show commenced.

Fiona started the music, tasteful and appropriate for her audience and one by one the staff, now models for the evening, paraded the fashions with Louise explaining all about each of the magnificent gowns. The audience applauded politely, although some of the residents fell asleep. George did his usual outlandish remark, "Have you got knickers on love?" while Mary was telling him to 'shush'.

Mary, well Mary loved it, every second of the show, she was as always oblivious to George's inappropriate remarks. The fashion was her world, a world she understood completely and she was sorry when they broke for an interval. The models enjoyed it too and afterwards some of the visitors made purchases for themselves and their relatives who lived at the home. Of course Mary bought too, only one purchase, a very lovely cocktail dress in a small size, which puzzled Patsy.

"Mary, it is gorgeous, but it won't fit you, you know that?"

Mary just smiled and said she was buying it anyway, and Patsy knew it was pointless arguing with her. Ed called in as the show was ending. He went over to Mary and she whispered something in his ear. Ed nodded and winked at Mary.

On their way home in the car Ed had some bad news, "The estate agent telephoned me. Someone has offered the full asking price on 'our' house Patsy, so that's that. There isn't much for our price unless we move much further out of the area."

Patsy was sad to lose the house, she had imagined them living there and being happy, but it wasn't the end of the world. The house could wait,

"It is sad Ed, but let's just rent somewhere for a while, a property will turn up and as long as we're together, that's what is important."

Ed thought again, not for the first time that he really did love this girl and said he would start the search for somewhere nice to rent, "Not sure we shall have time for another visit to Devon, but dad and Ruby seem to have done everything anyway."

Life certainly was hectic, but they resolved not to panic. With their combined earnings, they could afford a nice place to rent. "More bad news I'm afraid Ed," Patsy moaned. "Mum wants us to meet Ernie at his local on Friday, not looking forward to that."

Ed laughed. "He can't be that bad. Can he?"

Chapter 36

No sooner had Mary put down the phone after speaking to Eric, the doorbell rang. Mary wanted to make something to eat and relax; she was mentally and physically tired. However she made her way to the front door. It was Inspector Granger.

"Sorry to bother you again, Miss Reynolds. May I come in for a moment?"

Mary invited the Inspector into her lounge and offered tea. Over tea and biscuits, Inspector Granger told her what she had learned from the Spanish police,

"Seems Peter and Eric have been taking money in various scams for several years. Peter of course insists it is Eric who finds the targets and plans how they take the money, Peter, according to him plays a small part and receives a fraction of the money they steal. Even Peter, and that is his real name, has no idea who Eric really is. He has several aliases and judging by his account. Eric is very secretive and tells Peter very little. Peter only found out about the other people he uses for his scams by chance."

Inspector Granger took a sip of tea before continuing. "Unfortunately," she said, "We only have Peter's word that Eric is involved, and we don't know who Eric really is. We have tracked down some of his so-called colleagues, but they won't tell us anything useful and none of them have criminal records. What we need is some hard evidence against him, and that's why I'm asking you Miss Reynolds to help?"

Mary took a deep breath and thought for a minute, "What do you want from me? I've told you what I know."

The Inspector nodded sympathetically, "Your information is very valuable Mary, may I call you Mary?"

Mary quickly answered, "You may," she said. The inspector nodded and continued, "From what you told me Mary, you still have a good relationship with Eric, and there is still the matter of the rest of the money for the apartment to pay for. He wants that money and we really need you to give him the money, just as you did to Peter in Spain. We need hard evidence Mary."

The inspector looked at a horrified Mary, "We shall be there with you all the time, and once we see the exchange take place, we can arrest him for extortion. Hopefully, we can also find out his true identity. Once we know who he really is my guess is we shall find other women." Inspector Granger paused and asked,

"Will you help us?"

Mary explained that she had done all this before with Peter, and how stressful that had been. She said she had told the Inspector about Alison, Vera and of course Rosalyn. "You can get evidence from them, surely." Mary was angry and confused. Why should she have to do all this again, and with Eric? This was much harder.

Granger was sympathetic, "Unfortunately not, Vera and Alison haven't handed over money, and although they would have I'm sure. Rosalyn was a victim a long time ago and we have no proof. Of course I believe that he stole from her but we can't prove it. To be honest Mary we really need your help. You are a strong woman; certainly Inspector Rodriguez was very impressed. We need you to get Eric to take your money."

Mary thought about it, long and hard, this man had to be stopped, she was sure of that; she eventually looked directly at the inspector,

"He's taking me to dinner tomorrow, but he's worried he has not heard from Peter and he has not asked for any more money yet so I'm not sure what I can do. You can't know Inspector just how hard it is for me to meet him and keep this pretence up, but yes, I will help, you."

Inspector Granger nodded, "I admire you, Mary, it can't be easy but I think Peter may be persuaded to contact Eric and tell him he needs the balance for the completion of the apartment. Can you get hold of the money quickly?"

Mary was now determined. "I can," Mary said, "that is not a problem and, yes I know I have to do this so I am willing to help you."

The inspector thanked Mary and asked her to telephone Eric and postpone the dinner,

"Can you come up with a good excuse until we can get Peter to phone him?"

Mary smiled. "I'm sure I can come up with an excuse, after all I'm getting practiced in this lying business."

Inspector Granger smiled back and thanked Mary, "Let me know what you come up with and we'll be ready to move. Here's my direct number, call me anytime, and Mary; we shall arrest him and put him away for a long time."

The Inspector left and Mary went into her kitchen, she was suddenly hungry and she needed to eat first and then think. After eating an omelette and pouring a glass of sherry, Mary picked up the phone to speak first to Rosalyn and then to Ada. Both were worried about Mary being involved yet again with a police operation, and both knew it needed to be finished, once and for all.

The police had visited Rosalyn and she had told of her involvement with Eric. She also told them of the two other women they had discovered and of their escapades in Spain,

"I know it sounds terrible Mary, but all this, this getting our revenge has given my aunt a new lease of life. She's actually so much better, not that it's much consolation to you."

Mary laughed and said that she was glad Rosalyn's aunt was feeling better, at least something good had come of this mess. "I want to do this," Mary told both her friends and they both knew that when Mary was determined to do something, there would be no stopping her.

Next, Mary took a deep breath and telephoned Eric, "Eric, I really don't feel well, I think I'm going down with some sort of virus, so I shan't be at the shop tomorrow and I wondered if we could put off our dinner date tomorrow. I'm going to rest and take some paracetamol."

Eric said that he completely understood and that he would telephone her the next day to see how she felt,

"Would you like me to do anything for you luv?" he said in a pathetic voice. Once, Mary would think he was sympathetic, now Mary could think of a few things she wished he would do, get lost? Get locked up? But she remained calm,

"Thank you dear, I am better on my own when I feel ill, I'll have an early night and probably a day or two in bed and I should be fine."

They said their goodbyes and Mary breathed a sigh of relief. She took another glass of sherry with her to bed, but sleep eluded her.

Mary had a bad night but managed to go to sleep thankfully at about 6am. She was wakened at just after 11am by the phone ringing. It was Inspector Granger, "Good news Mary, Peter has agreed to telephone Eric and tell him all is well and Eric should now get the rest of the money. I expect he was getting worried not hearing from him. What did you come up with to tell Eric?"

Mary explained that she had told Eric she wasn't feeling well and that she was not meeting him tomorrow, she mentioned that Eric sounded worried that he had not heard from Peter.

"Well done Mary," the inspector replied, "I suspect Eric will be in contact very soon after talking to Peter. Let me know as soon as you hear from him."

"How soon do you want me to meet him?" asked Mary.

The Inspector was quick to answer, "Is Thursday too soon? I can have a surveillance team ready to go, and of course I'll be there."

Mary's heart missed a beat, Thursday was the day after tomorrow. Mary took a deep breath and said, "Yes Thursday will do nicely I'll withdraw the money and let you know where and when I am meeting him, oh and Inspector, after this, I don't want to see him again, ever."

"You won't, Mary," Grainger reassured her, "We'll do our job and get him."

Mary telephoned the bank and asked that they have the money ready for her on Thursday morning, although they were surprised that she wanted such a large sum of money in cash. She made tea and toast and kept her friends updated with the latest developments.

Eric telephoned her that afternoon, "How are you, luv?" Mary reassured him that she was feeling much better. "Good, glad you're over it. I have good news, the apartment is all yours, and just the completion to sort out and then you can move your things in. Peter telephoned this morning, everything is fine." Eric was jubilant.

Mary faked her excitement, "Oh Eric, that is good news, I can't wait to plan the move, think of the good times we'll have in Spain. Now, you'll need me to pay the balance? I'll write you a cheque."

Eric laughed again, like Peter, much too loudly Mary thought, "Oh, darling, I've already sent the money to Peter, sorted it as soon as he phoned. No, if you give me the money in cash, I prefer cash, can't have the tax man snooping can we? Now, when shall we meet for dinner?"

They arranged to meet on Thursday, 7pm at their favourite restaurant in the village for a celebration meal. Mary assured him she would bring the cash, and Eric said jokingly, "Don't forget now."

Mary immediately telephoned Inspector Granger who reassured her that the police would be there, and that Mary had done well. Still, despite the kind words, Mary was nervous that something would go wrong. Ada, Rosalyn and Annie visited Mary at her home that evening to offer support. It was agreed that Rosalyn would drive Mary to the bank and bring her back home, "It's a lot of money, Mary, to be walking about with."

Mary couldn't sleep again on Wednesday night. She paced up and down, tossed and turned in bed, got up and made tea, but nothing helped her relax and sleep. Mary wondered what Susan would think about her mother now. An old sleuth who had got herself in yet another mess? She would have supported me though, Mary was sure about that.

On Thursday morning, Rosalyn arrived as promised and together they went to the bank where the manager handed her the money, "Is everything all right, Miss Reynolds, it is a lot of cash and so unlike you?"

Mary smiled and assured him everything was fine, "I am thinking of going to, Spain," she offered as an explanation, "luxury holiday you know?"

The manager smiled and told her she worked too hard and he was pleased she was treating herself. Money safely in her bag, Rosalyn left with Rosalyn. Rosalyn suggested they go back to her house for lunch and Mary gratefully accepted the chance to wait with friends.

Mrs Johnson, Rosalyn's aunt looked so much better and she had prepared a delicious lunch, "This is all so exciting. Rosalyn keeps me up to date with the plan; you've all done an amazing job. Just get tonight over with Mary and let the police do their job, I for one can't wait to hear he is off the streets. Oh, and Mary, so well done."

After lunch, the three women chatted, well there was only one topic of conversation, and it played on all their minds. At 5pm, Mary asked Rosalyn to drive her home so she could get ready,

"I want to look especially nice tonight."

Eric was prompt as usual to pick her up and was quick to ask Mary if she had the money. Mary nodded, grabbed her coat and her handbag and within five minutes, they were sitting at a not too discreet table in the restaurant, despite Eric's plea for somewhere quieter. He argued that he didn't want people seeing all that money on view. Mary told him he was being silly, that they would be quite safe in the restaurant. Eric noticed Mary was nervous, but Mary said she had been worried about carrying all this cash around with her before they had met. Eric laughed and said that if it made her feel better she could hand over the cash now.

Mary looked around the restaurant. Everything looked as it always did, and she hoped the police were there. "Yes, good idea Eric, I'll just go to the ladies.

Sorry Eric, back in a minute. Order some drinks will you?" And Mary took her handbag and got up from the table.

In the ladies' room, Inspector Granger who just smiled and nodded met her. Mary was relieved. Returning to the table, Mary took a sip of her drink and took the money from her handbag and very deliberately, and hopefully in full view of the police, she handed the money to Eric. Eric thanked her and counted the money carefully. He was smiling as he put the money in a bag he had with him,

"All sorted luv, here is the contract for you to sign," and he produced a biro with a contract and gave it to Mary.

The transaction completed and suddenly out of nowhere two police officers came over to the table and cautioned him. "What?" he said, looking confused, "What's going on? Mary what…?"

The officer read out the reasons for the arrest and Eric, protesting his innocence was handcuffed and led away, turning to stare unbelievingly at Mary as he was led away. Inspector Granger appeared and sat with Mary.

"Well done, Mary" she said, "that can't have been easy for you."

The manager of the restaurant also came over to ask Mary if she was all right. Mary was shaking, and the inspector offered to take Mary home, but as they were leaving, Rosalyn, Ada and Annie appeared and led Mary back into the restaurant. "Let's have dinner," Ada said, "we can all relax now."

Mary was reluctant, the last thing she wanted to do was eat, and other customers were staring at her. Mary took a deep breath and ignored the stares, they had succeeded, and the man who had caused so much grief had been arrested. Mary needed this, her friends and a celebratory relaxing meal. It turned out to be a good decision because finally she did relax with her friends and together they celebrated. Their investigation was complete; they must wait and hope that Eric would be convicted.

Chapter 37

Patsy walked to work with Rosie, both of them were excited about the impending wedding and the fact that they had both completed NVQ level 3 in record time.

"We can start applying for nurse training Patsy, I never thought I could do it. You have inspired me Miss Bennett." Rosie had changed her voice to what could only be described as 'posh.'

"Well get you," Patsy said laughing, "I didn't do anything Rosie, except perhaps show you what you can do if you want to. Let's face it, if I can do it anyone can."

Rosie suddenly became serious, "No, Patsy. You have studied hard, studied when I only went out to enjoy myself. What you have achieved through your books has taught me that there are better things in life if you apply yourself instead of messing about. My social life has tamed, I need to grow up."

Patsy felt so lucky. Rosie had always encouraged her and been there for her. Furthermore, both Rosie and Iris had secretly bought their bridesmaid dresses, and still insisted they were paying for them. Patsy was touched by their kindness and loved the dresses.

"Really looking forward to this wedding," said Rosie, "it's going to be fantastically wonderful."

Patsy hoped she was right. Everything was organised, she was marrying a great guy, she had a beautiful dress, why was she so nervous about the whole event?

She had read articles about disastrous weddings, guests getting food poisoning, the bride falling over, all sorts of stories, the worst being the groom backing out at the altar. No, Ed wouldn't do that to her, but still she was so nervous and sometimes she almost wished it was all over. She spoke to Rosie about her worries, but Rosie said it was normal for brides to worry.

"Do me a favour though Patsy, don't turn into Bridezila."

Patsy answered seriously, "I'll try not to."

Patsy met Ed after work, they grabbed a pizza and then went off to view some flats. They were all local which was good, but rents were quite high because of the area, however they had worked out their finances and decided they could afford somewhere nice to start married life.

They looked at three prospective flats, all quite large, well decorated and all were on tree-lined roads and had communal gardens. The firm favourite for both of them was the second one they viewed. It was hard to describe, but they both felt at home. It was a first floor flat, and had an open plan kitchen/ living area, a large bedroom with fitted wardrobes and lovely views from all the windows.

"That's the one then," said Ed and Patsy nodded as they headed off to the local pub for a drink.

"I'll ring the letting agency first thing tomorrow and then we'll have to think about buying some furniture," and Ed gave her a hug.

Excited, they spoke about what they needed to buy. The flat had window blinds and flooring, plus a fitted cooker, so they decided all they needed a bed, a chest of drawers, a sofa, coffee table, and for the time being, that would be fine for them.

Patsy was on a late shift the following day so as soon as Ed had spoken to the letting agency and they had given references and a deposit, they drove into town and bought the furnishings they needed. They arranged for the goods to be delivered when they had a moving date. The shopping trip was a rush and Patsy was late for work, however she explained to Rita why she had not been on time. Rita looked up, with a stern face, and then smiled,

"I suppose I have to give the bride to be some leeway, but that will cease young lady after the wedding though."

Patsy went about her work, she told everyone about the flat, including Mary.

"If you can find anything in my house you would like dear, you are very welcome to have it," Mary said sadly. "I shall not be going home again."

Patsy felt touched by the offer but also guilty at feeling so happy. Here she was, young and active with a life in front of her and here in the home were older people with their health failing, unable to go home. She resolved to be more empathic in the future and she apologised to Mary.

Mary shook her head, "Oh no dear, I for one love hearing from you young ones about your busy lives. Don't forget, I was young once, starting on my journey, and I do like it here, sometimes. I just so wish I could see Susan."

Patsy quickly said, "Bill has it all under control and hopefully we shall have some news soon. Now, shall we have another look at your new outfit Mary?" Patsy said and opened Mary's wardrobe and Mary gave her a beaming smile and said, "Oh yes dear, let's."

It was the day Patsy was dreading, meeting her mum's boyfriend, worse still, taking Ed to meet her mum's boyfriend. Patsy knew she should be kinder to her mum, but all her life, all Patsy knew was meeting the latest new boyfriend and there had been too many to count.

The men, the drinking, the lack of care from her mother, especially when she was young, nothing had ever changed. Brenda would think nothing of giving Patsy a packet of crisps for her dinner and then going out for the night, her mother was a fool where men were concerned, but Patsy knew that was Brenda's life, always searching for the right guy.

The pub where they were meeting Brenda and Ernie was in a run-down area of the city. The pub, 'The Mucky Duck,' looked very shabby from the outside; a For Sale notice was displayed on an outside wall. As Ed and Patsy entered the pub, they noticed the worn furnishings and peeling wallpaper.

The man behind the bar was very friendly and asked what they would like to drink. Patsy asked for a glass of white wine and asked what wines they had, another trait she had picked up from Mary. The barman looked totally shocked, he obviously wasn't asked for wine very often. "Ooh," he said, "We don't do wine, luv" and he paused and looked awkward. The pause was a long one, but eventually he said optimistically, "Might have a box in the cellar, I'll have to look. No call for wine here you see, luv." And he beamed at Patsy.

Ed thanked the man and said they would be grateful if he could find some wine, and off went the man to the cellar.

Patsy noticed a group of people sat at the far end of the pub. There was a lot of laughter coming from the group and then Patsy spotted Brenda, who came over with a man. "Patsy, Ed, meet Ernie." Just then, the barman came back with a dusty box of white wine, obviously very pleased with his find. Ed thanked him and asked for two wine glasses. The bar man paused, he looked distraught. "Ooh we don't do wine glasses." but without a pause this time, he smiled and produced two tumblers. Ed paid for the drinks, which were very cheap, and Brenda ushered them to a table.

Ernie was a small, very plump, balding man, scruffily dressed and obviously very drunk. He nearly fell over as he sat down on a chair. Brenda and Ernie were drinking pints and Brenda was also very much the worse for wear. Brenda explained they had started drinking early in the day. Ernie had arranged a weekend away for them and they decided they needed to celebrate.

Patsy was so embarrassed; she wanted the floor to open up so she could disappear, whereas Ed seemed totally at ease with the situation. He said that he was pleased to meet Ernie and he was glad Brenda was bringing him to the wedding. Ernie grunted and looked daggers at Brenda who coughed nervously,

"The thing is Patsy and Ed, Ernie wants me to go away with him, on the day of the wedding as it happens so, we won't be able to come, I'm sorry Patsy, you do understand don't you? You know me luv; I'm not very good at those sorts of functions. I thought I could do it, but Ernie suggested we have a weekend away, he doesn't like weddings either. He's been married three times." Brenda laughed, "Not surprised he doesn't like weddings." Ernie, whose facial expression remained miserable, grunted and then nodded.

Patsy did understand, only too well. She was angry and understood that Ernie was far more important than Brenda's only daughter's wedding, but hey, what was new about that?

"It's OK, Mum, I'm sorry you can't make it though, it would have been nice if you'd been there, you know being the bride's mother."

Brenda looked suitably embarrassed and reached for Ernie's hand. He brushed her off and told her not to be daft.

Ed tried hard to diffuse all the emotions and asked Brenda where they were going? Brenda, obviously feeling a touch guilty but trying hard to hide it said lightly, "Blackpool love, aren't we, Ernie? We're staying in a hotel." Ernie grunted and finished his drink in one gulp and got up to go for a refill. Patsy motioned to Ed that they were leaving, what was the point? "We've so much to do, Mum, only popped in to say hello to Ernie. Have a good time in Blackpool."

"Glad you could come, don't worry about us, Ernie is a great laugh and we'll have a ball, nice to see you again Ed."

Brenda waved and went over to the bar to see Annie, while Patsy and Ed made their way to the door. The barman gave them a cheerful wave. Brenda never looked back.

Once outside, Patsy broke down crying, "My own mother does not want to come to her daughter's wedding, how bad is that? I bet you're wondering why you want to marry such a loser." Ed gave Patsy a big cuddle.

"Patsy, you're anything but a loser. You are a beautiful intelligent girl who I am crazy about. Come on let's find a pub that might just sell decent wine."

Over a drink, and feeling more relaxed, Patsy could see the funny side of the encounter with her mum and Ernie. "What does she see in him? And come to, think of it that pub! Typical of Brenda, she always knew how to pick them." And she started laughing.

"Come on, Patsy, the people in the pub were very friendly and the barman did try," Ed said wryly, which made them both laugh.

"Manchester hospitality at its best," Patsy explained to Ed. "We might not have much but we are friendly, and that poor barman did try," Ed replied that he loved Manchester and he meant every word.

They were both looking forward to their new flat, and the wedding was only two weeks away. Patsy and Ed went over the arrangements; Patsy said they were very lucky because Ed's dad and Ruby had arranged everything beautifully. Both grateful beyond words because a further planned quick trip to Devon had not materialised as they were concentrating on their new home.

Patsy told Ed about Mary offering to give them whatever they wanted from the bungalow. "It was such a nice gesture, and she meant it Ed, but it made me realise that she has had to give up her home which she loved and worked so hard to have. We couldn't possible take anything, it wouldn't be right. I wonder if that will ever happen to us?"

Ed agreed and they sat silently for a moment. "It teaches us that we need to live every minute Patsy, while we can," Ed said optimistically, and with that thought they discussed their future plans.

Chapter 38

Over the next weeks, Mary concentrated on her business once again and started to appreciate her new home. She planted bedding plants in her garden, and on sunny summer evenings; she loved to take her evening meal and a glass of sherry into her garden and sit listening to the quiet and peace of her garden.

The police had kept her up to date with developments. Eric's real name was Roger Griffin, although he had several aliases, many more than Mary had discovered. He had extorted money from many women, some of whom had come forward with new allegations. Inspector Granger said he had shown no remorse and he had boasted about how irresistible he was to women and how easy it was to take their money. The fraud squad was still not sure how much money he had taken, but it was well over a million pounds.

Vera had been about to hand over a large sum of money to Eric, she was ready to move to Spain with him, and never detected anything amiss. Apparently, her relationship with Eric had started about a year ago when Eric was doing some work for her. Alison was also luckier than others, she had held onto her money, but she admitted that she was very much in love with him and but for Mary's intervention, she would have given him money. Rosalyn too had been interviewed, much to her delight. She was relieved that finally, after telling her story she could put an end to her distress and move on with her life.

As Inspector Granger put it, "That man has taken a fortune by preying on vulnerable, lonely women."

The word lonely struck a chord with Mary Was I lonely? Mary asked herself, I suppose I was but I didn't know it at the time, I just went along with the situation, glad I had someone and fell in love with him.

He would serve a long prison sentence. "He did admit that out of all the women he took money from, he only loved one woman, and that woman was you Mary, if that's any comfort, although he still wanted to steal from you," Inspector Granger told her, but that made Mary sad.

It wasn't any comfort to her and she vowed never to fall in love again and decided that it wasn't meant to be. She always made bad judgments when it came to choosing a man.

Sad as it all was, another lost love, Mary resolved to get on with her life, and that's what she did. Mary's social life went from strength to strength. She and her friends went for meals, to the theatre, spent cosy evenings at each other's houses and holidaying together. They had a real friendship and Mary was more than happy with that.

One evening, Mary had a telephone call from a hysterical Rosalyn. Rosalyn's aunt had complained of feeling tired and had gone for a rest. Rosalyn had gone up to wake her aunt for their evening meal to find her aunt dead in her bed; apparently she had suffered a massive heart attack. Rosalyn was devastated,

"She was doing so well, Mary, and she was over the moon that we Eric had been arrested."

"Your aunt had a good and a long life," Mary said sympathetically. "You know Rosalyn, our investigation did spark excitement in her life Rosalyn, and she was so happy that you went to stay with her. Would you like me to come round and stay with you? There will be arrangements, I could help with that, whatever you think?"

Rosalyn was grateful and said she would like Mary to be with her, "This house is so big without my aunt, I keep expecting her to come in from the kitchen and I'm rattling around on my own, I could use some company."

Mary packed a few things, telephoned Ada who sent commiserations and also said she would call round later.

"Annie and I are fine at the shop, you go to Rosalyn's and I'll see you both later."

Mary walked into the village, stopped to buy flowers for Rosalyn and soon after, she and Rosalyn were sat drinking tea. It felt strange that Rosalyn's aunt wasn't there; she was always such a warm, friendly person. Rosalyn was clearly shocked; she said that her aunt would have to have a post-mortem.

"She hadn't seen her doctor for a while, and she was so well. I should have taken more care of her."

"Nonsense," Mary told her, "Your aunt was very independent, she wouldn't have wanted to be wrapped in cotton wool, and you did take very good care of her"

Rosalyn nodded, "I know you're right Mary, it's just, well such a shock."

Despite the tragic circumstances of Mary's visit, they did eventually switch the conversation to happier topics and by the time Ada arrived with Annie, the mood was not as sombre.

Mary spent a couple of days staying with Rosalyn. The post-mortem was quickly carried out confirming the cause of death was a heart attack. Mary helped Rosalyn arrange the funeral and Rosalyn assured Mary she was content to stay on her own,

"I'll be fine now Mary, better after the funeral but I've accepted my aunt's death, and you're right, she did have a good life."

Some weeks after the funeral, Rosalyn told her friends that her aunt had left her the house and a considerable amount of money and she insisted on paying for them all to return to Spain, "If it's not too painful for you Mary, I know for me it brings visions of Eric rotting in a prison cell."

"I totally agree about Eric and, yes, let's go to Spain," Mary said smiling.

"I'll organise it," Ada offered, the others were all for that, Ada knew how to organise a holiday.

They were staying at the hotel they were all too familiar with. Mary thought about the first trip she had made with Ada, looking for the apartment complex, and finding a sparse piece of land. Then of course there had been the next trip, looking at the lovely apartment shown to them by the charming Peter. Mary had to admit the plan was clever, both Peter and Eric were plausible, how could anyone not trust them?

As if reading Mary's thoughts, Rosalyn tentatively suggested that they go back and look at the apartments. "Well, they were lovely, I fell in love with them."

Ada laughed, "Now Rosalyn has some money, she'll buy an apartment, I bet."

Rosalyn was quick to answer, "You never know?" Mary could see that Rosalyn was very happy to see the property again.

They arrived at the apartment complex. Nothing had changed, it all looked just as impressive. Seigneur Mendez met them and greeted them warmly. He led them to the very apartment shown to them by Peter. Rosalyn was delighted,

"I don't understand, is it still for sale?" Seigneur Mendez explained that it had been sold, the buyer had furnished the apartment and then had to sell very quickly due to personal reasons.

"He is selling very cheap, just wants a quick sale, and the furnishings are included."

Rosalyn jumped in, "Then I shall buy it." And then turning to the astonished Mary and Ada she said excitedly, "Ladies, welcome to our holiday retreat, you two can stay any time you want, and I have decided that I shall move here permanently so, welcome to my lovely new home."

Both Mary and Ada advised Rosalyn to 'think about it' but Rosalyn was adamant.

"I have the money now, thanks to my aunt, and I can start a new life. It's about time."

Although she was surprised, it did make some sense to Mary. Rosalyn had suffered years of hardship, why shouldn't she move here and enjoy life? And she clearly wanted just that.

Rosalyn completed the paperwork with Seigneur Mendez, and arranged for a deposit to be paid, she certainly had a bargain. The present owner was selling exceptionally cheaply. The three women celebrated with drinks at the hotel, Rosalyn was so excited. Mary was happy for her friend but she would miss her and she told Rosalyn, but Rosalyn, unperturbed said that her friends could pop over for weekends,

"It's not far, and you have a place to relax, and get some sun."

They spent a few more days in Spain, this time it was a holiday, no sleuthing necessary on this trip. When the time came to leave, Ada and Mary were a little sad that their friend would be living so far away even if they could visit, and they agreed that they would visit often.

Chapter 39

It had arrived so quickly Patsy thought. She and Ed were on their way to Devon a few days before they were to be married. Patsy had her dress and had accompanied Ed to buy his new suit. They had moved to their new flat and life felt good for them both.

Patsy would be staying at Ed's father's house with Rosie and Iris and her husband. Ed would be spending the night before the wedding at Ruby's house, as would his best man. Rosie, with her family and Iris and her husband were travelling the following day to help with the final arrangements, the other guests would arrive the day before the wedding.

The journey passed quickly, Patsy was familiar with the route now, but she still marvelled at how pretty the countryside was. The last few weeks had been so hectic, moving into their new flat, buying last minute wedding items and checking that their guests had sorted their accommodation and travel arrangements. They had so much to do that they both appreciated the calmness of their journey, which was only interrupted for a lunch stop at 'their' country pub.

They pulled up at Ed's family home; Richard and Ruby came out to meet them. Ruby was talking very fast telling them everything was ready, and Richard took them into the large garden to show them a huge marquee, ready to be decorated for the guests. Patsy was lost for words, Richard and Ruby had really pulled out all the stops for them, and it was amazing.

They went into the house, and Ruby helped Patsy fully unpack her wedding dress and hang it up neatly.

"It's beautiful Patsy, gosh I'm so excited, can't wait to meet your friends."

Salina was busy in the kitchen cooking an evening meal for them all, "I thought you might appreciate a quiet family meal before all the excitement." She said, "Now, tea and scones I think."

"The dinner smells delicious," Patsy commented, and Salina beamed.

Pete and the baby arrived and the family discussed the final 'things to do' Patsy was amazed at how little there was left to arrange, Ed's family had done a fantastic job. Patsy also reflected at how comfortable she now felt with her new family. How lucky Ed had been growing up in such a loving environment, she just wished Ed's mum was here with them all.

Ed was staying with Patsy until the night prior to the wedding, so after a wonderful home cooked meal, they walked over to the pub to speak about the catering arrangements for the wedding. The restaurant manager showed them the cake that was stunning. Patsy decided that it was the best ever wedding cake and she said so, much to the delight of Ruby. There were no problems, the food and drinks were sorted and the restaurant would be decorated just as they had requested.

Chapter 40

Life continued to be good to Mary, she had her friends, her business and despite Rosalyn leaving for Spain, Mary was happy for her friend and planned to spend more time visiting her in her new home. She thought about her life. It had been eventful, perhaps not the life she would have chosen. She would have been happy with a good man and her daughter Susan, and perhaps a chance to have more children.

The money she had was unimportant, she would have given every penny she had just to be reunited with Susan. Realistically, now Mary knew that reunion was unlikely to happen. I'll never give up hope though, Mary said to herself, Susan might still find me. Mary thought long and hard about selling her shop and retiring. She had enough money, more than she needed. She loved her bungalow and she would have time to visit Rosalyn in Spain without always worrying about the business.

Mary spoke to Ada and asked her whether she thought it was a good idea to retire. Ada thought for a minute, "I never thought I would hear you say that Mary, that shop has been your life. On the other hand, why not enjoy your life now? You have worked hard, now you can relax and do other things. I shall miss the shop, I've loved it too, but my husband does moan about the hours I work. It's your decision, and you have my support whatever you decide."

So Mary made her decision and put her shop up for sale and was surprised that it was valued so high. Her customers were shocked at the thought of their shop no longer being there. Some said they would never find a shop as good, others said they might have to travel further, many of them asked Mary to reconsider. Mary told them that she would do her best to sell to the buyer, who could guarantee that they would continue to sell high quality clothes,

"I'm sorry, it's the best I can do, I need to retire now after all these years, but I am so lucky to have such loyal customers."

Mary reflected on all the comments, she had loved the shop, her shop. It was such a big part of her life. It was supposed to bring security for her and Susan, instead there was only her, and Mary was resigned to the fact that there would probably always be only her.

Mary confided in Annie. "I do hope I'm doing the right thing," she said, and Annie said that maybe Mary needed to put her feet up now and enjoy life, although she added that she had learned so much working with Mary and that her time spent there had been a joy. Mary was touched by Annie's kind words. Annie was young; she would move on and have a fantastic career, and Ada, bless her, well she needed to spend more time with her husband. They had both always been so loyal to her. She was lucky. She didn't think she could run the shop without them.

The interest in the shop was amazing, Oak hill village was a prime location for businesses for the more discerning customer. The village had grown so much since Mary first opened her small shop. There were good schools; low crime rates and properties in general, though always high were now selling for ridiculously high prices. The estate agent did his job well, arranging viewings at convenient times, and keeping Mary well informed. Mary met all of the prospective buyers. She was horrified that some wanted the shop for restaurants, wine bars, beauty treatments. No, she had promised her customers she would sell to someone who continued to sell quality clothes, and she was determined to honour that promise.

The estate agent tried to persuade her otherwise, "You have to think about the offers Miss Reynolds. This chap wants to open a wine bar, the property is ideal and believe me he is willing to pay, and he's offering cash."

Mary smiled, "No wine bars, Mr Davies, only fashion, I've promised my customers and after all these years, I am not going to let them down now."

Mr Davies sighed and said he would do his best to find the right buyer, "But I must warn you Miss Reynolds, it does limit the market considerably." Mary shrugged and that was that.

Mr Davies did however find a buyer only a few weeks later. Natalia was an ex-model who was now married to a very rich premier league football player. Natalia wanted to open a high fashion shop, she was bored with staying at home, and as she told Mary, she did know about fashion. Mary didn't quite know what to make of Natalia. This young woman was very stylish, and obviously not without money, but she was very pretentious and full of herself. Mary didn't like her very much, and when Natalia swept through the shop and told Mary she would have to rip everything out and virtually start again because she thought it was 'very dated' Mary liked her even less.

Mary asked Natalia what kind of fashion she was proposing to sell, and to Mary's surprise, Natalia appeared one day, bringing with her several pieces, which Mary had to admit she did like. Mr Davies said that Natalia had made a generous offer for the shop and he advised Mary to accept.

"The problem is Mr Davies, I don't really like Natalia, and she's not what my customers are used to."

Mr Davies looked exasperated, he was used to difficult clients, part and parcel of the job. He knew of Miss Reynolds, she was very well known in the area and respected for her good business sense, but this woman was driving him mad.

"You do not have to like her Miss Reynolds." He was very red in the face by now and in danger of becoming unprofessional. He composed himself and softly said, "She has the money, even you said that you like what she is proposing to sell, and her customers, and I do mean her customers, they will decide for themselves whether or not they like her."

Mary had to agree, she had to let go, and after all it was her decision to sell her business. Natalia would run the shop differently so Mary had to accept that. So the sale went ahead and Mary was amenable to Natalia's requests to allow her builders to visit the shop with her to plan the alterations for when she took over.

The day came when Mary had to say her goodbyes to her beloved shop. She, Ada and Annie bid farewell to their last customer and with hugs all round, Ada and Annie left, saying they would meet Mary later for dinner. Natalia had graciously paid for any stock left, saying that although the clothes were not to her taste, she was sure she would sell them. Mary reluctantly had to agree that in the end, Natalia was not such a bad person, but as Mary closed the shop for the last time, she took a last look and walked home tearfully. Later that evening, Mary met with Annie and Ada for a farewell dinner. They were all subdued, but they spoke of their future plans and agreed that they would always remain friends.

Over the next few weeks, Mary kept busy in her bungalow. She tended the garden, had some decorating done, bought various items for her home, and in between kept close contact with Ada and Annie. Isabelle Stanhope visited her regularly, she told Mary that she loved her new home, but she also loved what Mary had done to her former home. Rosalyn telephoned her every week; she was happy living in Spain and had become very friendly with the man next door. He was a widower, a retired policeman, and they shared similar interests. Mary hoped that Rosalyn had finally found a good man.

Mary could not resist walking to the village to watch the progress of the building work they were doing to her shop. The outside looked very different, but Mary reluctantly had to admit that it was very tasteful. The day the shop was due to open for business, she and Ada arrived together. Natalia's husband, the footballer officially opened the shop, so he had drawn quite a crowd. There were canapés and drinks on offer and a spectacular fashion show choreographed by Natalia. Natalia graciously greeted Mary and Ada and ensured they had a good seat for the show. She also introduced them to her husband, who was actually very charming, and afterwards Mary breathed a sigh of relief and decided the shop was after all in good hands. In fact, Mary became one of Natalia's best customers and the two women were never to be friends but both were always very cordial to one another.

Chapter 41

Ruby arrived early the next morning to find Salina and Richard in the kitchen making breakfast and shortly afterward Angela turned up to help with the preparations. The flowers arrived with a team to decorate the marquee in the garden. A delivery of drinks, more flowers for the house and of course for the wedding party. Thankfully, it was a beautiful day, sunny and warm.

Salina took breakfast upstairs to Patsy, and Rosie. Ruby and Iris burst into Patsy's room with champagne and an order to eat quickly and have her bath, so they could begin getting the bride ready. Rosie skilfully styled Patsy's hair, they had practiced many times before and Ruby proved to be a talented makeup artist. Meanwhile, Iris made sure the wedding outfits were ready and crease free, while her husband helped Richard with the preparations in the house before they went to get ready.

At the appointed time, the wedding party walked the short distance to the church. Villagers were out in force on route to give their best wishes. Patsy looked stunning, walking arm in arm with Richard, while Rosie and Iris, also looking wonderful followed behind. The church had been decorated with an abundance of flowers and as Patsy walked up the aisle with Richard, she had never looked happier as she smiled an undeniable smile of happiness at her guests.

Ed was waiting for her at the altar, looking very nervous, but proud, Andy next to him with the all-important rings. Rosie took the bouquet from Patsy and Richard stepped back to his seat. As they made their wedding vows, there was a hush in the church, even from Ruby's little baby. Andy dutifully produced the rings, which Ed and Patsy placed on each other's fingers and after the blessing, the vicar pronounced that they were now husband and wife.

The congregation applauded the newly married couple. The wedding party then made their way to sign the register, while Louis Armstrong sang about a 'Wonderful Life, 'a favourite song of Ginny's.

The wedding reception went to plan. Everything was perfect, food, the tables, the speeches, and afterwards they all went back to the marquee where the band played all night starting with Ed and his wife starting the dancing, "Mrs Clifton, did I tell you how beautiful you are?"

Patsy moved closer to her husband, "Not so bad yourself Mr Clifton."

After a perfect day and the guests had left, the family had one last drink and discussed the day. Ed and Patsy were spending their wedding night at the hotel, but before they left, Richard produced a parcel and an envelope. "This arrived a few days ago from Bill. He said that it was a wedding present from Mary and him. You apparently have to open the envelope first."

Patsy was embarrassed, and shocked, "Oh, that is so good of them but they shouldn't have bought us a present." Patsy tentatively opened the envelope and gasped. It contained a letter from Bill and two airline tickets and booked accommodation to Paris. "We can't accept this Ed," Patsy said tearfully, "It's too much."

Richard laughed, "Yes, Bill said that's what you would say. I telephoned him after he wrote and he told me this was Mary's idea. She said all newlyweds should honeymoon in Paris, but that they both wanted you to have this. Now you have to open the parcel."

Ed took the parcel from his dad. "I think I know what this is," he said grinning. "Mary wanted you to have this, now I know why."

It was the cocktail dress Mary had bought from the fashion show, the one not in Mary's size but perfect for Patsy. Patsy was overwhelmed.

"Look you two," Richard said. "Bill was most insistent you had the gift. He told me that you have done so much for him and his sister, oh and he said he would be in serious trouble with Mary if you didn't go and have a brilliant honeymoon."

"OK, OK, I get it, but it is too much." Patsy was laughing and then she paused and said, "Paris, here we come!"

The following morning, Patsy and Ed were back at the family home with Ruby and her family. All were enjoying a huge breakfast before the newlyweds left for their flight to Paris. The telephone rang and Richard left the table to answer, "It's Bill, Patsy, he wants to speak to you and he sounds worried."

Patsy jumped up from her seat and ran to the telephone. "Bill, is Mary OK?"

"Mary's fine, Patsy, and congratulations," Bill answered, "but I have some news about Susan, I thought you would want to know." Bill did sound serious and Patsy was worried and said so.

"It's just strange Patsy," Bill continued, "The investigators have discovered that Susan/Jennifer married again in the US to a man called Richard Clinton. This is silly but isn't Ed's father, Richard Clinton too? I mean it just could not be the same man, could it?"

Patsy was so stunned she had to take a moment to answer. Bill asked if she was still there. "Sorry Bill," Patsy eventually said. "It must be a coincidence, let me speak to Richard and I'll phone you back, it's too ridiculous but I almost wish it were true. By the way, thank you and Mary for the wonderful wedding gift, so kind of you both. Let me phone you back, we're here with Richard now."

Patsy took a moment before returning to the others. They were all still talking about the wedding and what a success it had been.

"It was everything and more Patsy and I could have wished for," Ed told everyone.

"Yes, it was," Ruby answered, "What wonderful wedding planners you had. Could have cost a fortune!"

Everyone laughed but stopped when they saw Patsy's face.

"Patsy, what on earth?" Ed went over to his wife and guided her back to her chair.

"Are you all right my dear?" Richard asked looking concerned.

Patsy took a deep breath. "That was Bill with an update about Mary's daughter. This is going to sound ridiculous, but apparently Susan, well Jennifer married again in the United States to a man called Richard Clinton." Patsy laughed, "Isn't that a coincidence?"

Ed and Ruby laughed too but Richard was very quiet, he looked shocked, the colour drained from his face. He sat down and after a silence; he spoke to Ruby and Ed,

"I don't think we ever told you two that your mother was adopted. Her adopted parents called her Jennifer but she always called herself Ginny. The fact that she was adopted was something Ginny never wanted to talk about. When I met her, she told me early in our relationship that she had not had a very happy life with her adopted parents, and that she always wanted to find her real mother." Everyone looked stunned.

"As you know, I worked in the States for a while, Ginny and Ruby came over with me and that's where we were married. When we found out that Ginny was expecting with Ed, we both decided to come home and I started my law firm here in Devon. Your mother never wanted to live in Somerset or Cornwall again, but she was always happy here in Devon."

Richard had tears in his eyes as he spoke and everyone else was stunned by the news.

Eventually Ruby said, "So Mary, the Mary who we've heard so much about could be our grandmother. That's amazing." She added tearfully, "So sad mum never met her."

Richard was very thoughtful. "I need to speak to Bill and arrange to meet him. If Mary is Ginny's natural mother, this needs to be sorted, for everyone's sake. If Mary is part of our family we must all love and take care of her."

There was a silence in the room as everyone gathered their thoughts. Patsy was so stunned. Mary had asked her to find her daughter and by the strangest chance, she, Patsy had met and fallen in love with Mary's grandson. Why had she not even seen any signs this was happening? She had thought Ginny reminded her of someone, now she could see that Ginny had Mary's eyes, and there was an instant connection between Ed and Mary? Why did she not see it for what it was? Patsy wasn't the only person in the room wondering the same thing. Patsy went to telephone Bill. He too was shocked, but happy for his sister.

Chapter 42

Mary decided that she was actually glad she had made the decision to sell her business. Much as she loved it, it had to a large extent taken over her life. Nowadays, she could take her time, sleep late if she wanted to and visit Rosalyn in Spain. She was packing her suitcase to visit Rosalyn, a trip with Ada, which they were both really looking forward to. Ada was only coming for a couple of days, while Mary was staying two weeks. Mary had never been away for so long and she pondered about what she should take with her, but eventually she finished her packing, ready for her trip. Ada was calling for her later that day and together they would travel by taxi to the airport.

The flight took off on time and the two women settled on the now familiar journey. When they landed and collected their luggage, they gave the taxi driver Rosalyn's address. Ada asked Mary if she felt strange going back to the apartment where so much had happened, and Mary agreed that it did indeed feel very strange retracing all the events. Mary said that in a way, she was sad because the last time, although traumatic, it had also been exciting.

Ada felt the same, "Yes Mary, it certainly was exciting, a bit too exciting at times."

Mary giggled, "Oh yes, but we did well didn't we?"

An excited Rosalyn was waiting outside to greet them, she ran up to the taxi and practically dragged them both out. "Come on you two, I'm dying to show you the apartment now."

As they walked inside, Mary was impressed, Rosalyn had made the apartment very homely, and it had lost the 'holiday home' interior and become a tasteful comfortable home.

"I too learned so much from you Mary, I'm glad you approve." And Mary did approve, very much.

Ada and Mary unpacked in the guest bedroom and they all decided to visit one of their favourite restaurants that meant so much to them.

"We visited many times when we were the detectives," Mary said, and she knew that she was so glad to be back.

After a lovely dinner, they returned to Rosalyn's and sat on the balcony reminiscing and talking about their lives now.

"So tell us all about your man next door?" Ada said. Mary was embarrassed, but Ada always was quite forthright. Rosalyn didn't seem to mind Ada's comments,

"He's called John. He was a detective inspector before he retired. He bought an apartment here in Spain with his wife when he retired, she had always wanted to live in the sun, but they weren't here long when she died suddenly and then he was on his own. He found that he couldn't stand to stay any longer in that apartment, too many memories. So, he sold up and moved here.

"John was really helpful when I first moved in, you know, hanging pictures, telling me the best places to shop, and we, well we became close."

No one spoke; they were all thinking the same thing. Rosalyn looked sheepish,

"I know what you're thinking, I thought the same, after what happened, but John is different, and I'm not as stupid anymore, he's not getting my money so don't worry."

Mary and Ada said that although they were worried about Rosalyn, they hoped that John was a decent man and they wished her every happiness.

The following day, Rosalyn introduced John to her two friends and they all went out to lunch together at a restaurant John had recommended. John was slightly older than Rosalyn, a large man with a full head of grey hair. He spoke a lot about his career in the police force and told them about his most interesting cases. Rosalyn had told him all about the infamous Eric, he thought they were taking many chances when they decided to catch Eric out, but he congratulated them on the outcome.

John then told them about his wife, their long happy marriage and their dream of retiring in Spain.

"I never imagined I could love another woman," John told them, "but then I met Rosalyn."

They strolled back to the apartments; Mary liked John, as did Ada. He was not a particularly charming man, nor did he make jokes all the time, but he did appear to be honest and kind and very sensible and he certainly seemed to think the world of Rosalyn. The two of them looked into each other's eyes like two teenagers. Ada left the next day, she was sorry she had to go home, but she wanted to get home to her husband.

Rosalyn and Mary spent long happy days enjoying the sunshine and the local sites. Mary got to know John much better; he was very much a part of Rosalyn's life. The more she saw of him, the more convinced she was that he was indeed a good man and right for Rosalyn. The two weeks past all too quickly, John drove her to the airport and there were tearful goodbyes between Rosalyn and Mary, but Mary promised to return soon.

When Mary had boarded her plane, Rosalyn said to John, "There's something wrong with Mary, she keeps forgetting things, it's not like her." Rosalyn said that Mary seemed to have moments when she forgot who Rosalyn was, forgot who Ada was, things that were so uncharacteristic.

John said that he liked Mary, and he hadn't noticed any strange behaviour, although he didn't really know her. "It's probably just an age thing Ros."

Rosalyn thought that was probably it. However, the more she thought about it, the more she worried. Mary had changed and she wasn't that old, in fact she had always been so meticulous and organised, and she was happy to be retired. No, her friend had changed. Mary was ill she knew it.

Rosalyn continued to worry about Mary's forgetful spells. She telephoned Ada and asked her if she had noticed. Ada thought about it,

"Well sort of, I mean Mary is certainly not as sharp as she used to be. A couple of times we've arranged to meet somewhere and she hasn't turned up, but I can't say I'm worried, I mean we're all getting older, I forget thing myself these days."

Rosalyn thought again that perhaps she was worrying unnecessarily and got on with her life.

Mary went back to a quiet life with no regrets. She enjoyed the Spanish trips but she had no wish to live in Spain. She was content with her lovely bungalow, which she had wanted for so long. She liked John too and she was happy for Rosalyn, her happiness was long overdue.

Susan was never far from her thoughts and she did think about hiring an investigator to try and find her daughter, but she dismissed that idea as she had many times before. "She'll find me if she wants to, I only hope she will one day." She said out loud and then she was annoyed for talking to herself.

Over the next two years, life did change again for Mary. Ada's husband was asked to move abroad to Dubai with his company, Mary was devastated. "How long will you be away?" she asked. Ada looked sheepish and replied that it would be a minimum of two years, possibly longer. They were renting their house for the time being but they may sell at a later date.

"I shall really miss you Mary," Ada said and Mary wished her friend well and said that she too would miss her. Mary was very sad about Ada moving away but after all Ada had given her friendship and loyalty and it was time to spend some time with her husband and support his decision to work abroad.

Then a few months later, Annie had a job offer from a magazine based in London. "It's the chance of a lifetime," she told Mary. "I'm sharing a flat with two other girls, the rent is extortionate, but it'll be worth it, the job sounds wonderful, just a dream job!"

Mary was of course happy for her young friend, but she was losing all three of her friends, her life would be lonely. I've lost everyone I ever cared for she thought, but I shall be all right, I always am.

So Mary was once again on her own, although Isabelle Stanhope invited her for a visit a few times, but Mary was reluctant to go. She would rather stay at home these days, and she hadn't felt too well lately. She had noticed that she couldn't remember everyday things, not like her at all. She thought that it must be something to do with her age and perhaps she should speak to her doctor, but then she decided against it. No, that was silly, how could she explain without looking stupid. She must make more of an effort, get a notebook and write things down more. Mary had never kept a diary; she had her diary in her head and prided herself on her excellent memory. Perhaps it was time to buy a diary; after all, no one needed to know.

Mary visited Rosalyn several times, and each time it became harder. She found the airport confusing and once or even twice missed her flight, telling Rosalyn that there had been a delay. Even packing for the trip was a chore and she forgot to pack basic necessities like her toothbrush or her best blouses.

John had asked Rosalyn to marry him, and Mary was invited to the wedding. It was a very small affair, no fuss with few guests, but Roslyn had never looked happier. Mary was careful and wrote everything in her diary, she did not want her friend to know how forgetful she was. However, each time Mary visited, Rosalyn became more worried. She asked Mary if she was unwell, but Mary would answer, "Never better dear, just a bit forgetful sometimes."

John offered to take her to see a doctor in Spain, but Mary insisted that her own doctor saw her regularly and she was in excellent health. Mary justified the lie. Deep down, Mary knew that she wasn't very well, but then she would always shrug and convince herself that she was just being silly. One thing Mary was sure of was that she would not give in, she didn't want people to pity her, and pity wasn't in her vocabulary.

Back in her bungalow, Mary sat in her comfortable chair and once again thought about her daughter, she had given her up without a fight. Why had she given in so easily to her parents? She should have kept her baby, she would have managed, and she knew that now. Feeling very sad as she always did when she thought about Susan, Mary decided she should make the effort and walk to the village.

She walked along the high street, had a coffee in one of the chic wine bars, and afterwards spent some time window-shopping. It was getting dark and Mary decided it was time to go home, but instead of going home to her bungalow, she walked to her shop. The shop window was in darkness and Mary suddenly realised that she had been out much longer than she had thought. She was getting hungry now and it had started to rain.

Mary looked in her handbag and took out her keys and put the key into the door of the shop, but it just wouldn't open no matter how many times she tried. Mary couldn't understand why her key didn't open the door. She looked around the high street, someone would help her, this was silly, but the high street was deserted.

"This is ridiculous, you silly woman," Mary spoke out loud, why would the door not open?

Mary was upset and thought the best thing to do, the only thing to do, would be to break the window. She took out her umbrella and crashed it repeatedly against the shop window but the window stayed intact. Now Mary was very upset. She banged on the door, very distressed, crying and shouting, "Help me, please help me!"

Mary was making quite a commotion, lights went on from flats above other shops, and a woman who Mary didn't know appeared and asked if she could help. Mary explained to the woman that she wanted to go home and she couldn't get in. The woman tried the key to the shop door, but the door remained shut.

By this time there was no consoling Mary, and more people had appeared. Someone recognised Mary and tried to explain to her that she no longer lived above the shop.

"You sold the shop Miss Reynolds, some years ago now. Tell me where you live and I'll take you home." Mary thought this woman, whom she didn't recognise, was mad. Of course she lived there, had done for years, and she had to open the shop the following morning.

Mary pushed the woman away and started walking down the street to find someone sensible to help her. She paced up and down the street, but everyone she met, could not understand what she was saying.

"This is beyond a joke," Mary shouted, "Why can you not understand that I live above my shop? Everyone knows me, I am Mary Reynolds."

A police car pulled up and the policeman, seeing the commotion, got out of his car to establish what was happening.

"This lady thinks that she lives in this shop, but she sold the shop, some time ago, she's very confused," a woman explained. The police officer tried to talk to Mary.

"Come on love, let's find out where you live and I'll take you home. Do you live alone?"

They're all mad, Mary thought, she turned to the policeman, "I LIVE HERE" she shouted, "Where is Susan?"

The police constable eventually persuaded Mary to get into his car, and he sat talking to her to calm her down. He remembered well his grandmother who used to forget things constantly and also became very distressed, Mary reminded him of her. He told her he was driving her to the police station while they sorted this out, and at the station, while Mary was given a cup of tea and a sandwich, the police found out Mary's address.

They drove her home and took her into her house. The police officer noticed straight away that the house was in total disarray, dirty dishes and rubbish everywhere, clothes strewn all over the floor. The bed was unmade, the bathroom filthy. The constable wondered how long this woman had lived like this and felt that he needed to make an urgent call to social services. He tried to explain to Mary but Mary had had enough. She asked the officer to leave, took herself into her bedroom and she lay on the unmade bed.

Chapter 43

The next morning, her doorbell ringing wakened Mary. She got up from the bed and wondered why she was still fully dressed. Not like me she thought, I never sleep in my clothes, I always put my nightdress on, clean my teeth, and take my makeup off. Mary shrugged and went to answer the door. Her GP greeted her and introduced a woman with him as a social worker. Mary told him she wasn't ill and asked why he was visiting. Her doctor asked if they could come in and she told him that of course he was welcome. They all sat down in the untidy lounge and both visitors declined an offer of tea.

Mary's doctor had known her for many years, and the state of Mary and her home was totally uncharacteristic. He explained to Mary that the police had brought her home last night because she had become very distressed; she was convinced that she still lived above the shop.

Mary laughed. "No," she said, "I didn't go out yesterday, there's been a mistake."

The doctor continued, "The police officer was so worried about you Mary, he telephoned social services, and they contacted me. Can I take a look at you, just to check that you're not ill?" Mary couldn't understand what all the fuss was about. She thought that they were all mad, as if she would think she still lived at the flat. The idea was ridiculous when she had her bungalow, but she allowed the doctor to examine her.

"You have a nasty chest infection Mary," her GP gently said after examining her. "I need to admit you into hospital. The house is normally so neat and tidy, have you been feeling ill for sometime?"

Mary was astounded, "Excuse me doctor, I am not ill, and as for my house, well I happen to be very house proud."

The woman with the doctor introduced herself as Jill, a social worker.

"We only want to help you Miss Reynolds. If the doctor thinks you need to go to hospital, then you should go, I can come with you, there's nothing to worry about."

Mary thought for a long time; she had to admit that she had felt lethargic recently and she had lost her appetite. She looked around the room, it looked OK, and then she looked again and knew they were right. It was a mess.

"What's happening to me?" she said, "I need Susan, and she'll help me."

Jill asked who Susan was and Mary was silent. The ambulance arrived, the doctor patted her arm and told her she would get the treatment she needed to get well and Mary, accompanied by Jill was taken to hospital.

It wasn't that Mary disliked this woman, (Jill); in fact she was quite kind. It was just that she asked a lot of questions. Mary answered the best she could, but her memory wasn't what it used to be and some of the questions she couldn't answer, which was very frustrating.

"Can I call you Mary?" Jill asked. Mary thought that a little impertinent considering she had only just met the woman, but she nodded to her that it was acceptable.

"Do you have any relatives Mary or friends?" Jill wanted to know. Mary asked herself, did she have relatives? There was of course Susan.

"Susan," Mary answered confidently.

There were more questions, too many, Mary felt overwhelmed, she couldn't think, actually she had changed her opinion; this woman was intrusive and annoying.

At the hospital, Mary was examined. The noise in the accident and emergency department was too much for Mary. She was used to a quiet life nowadays, plus the fact that she couldn't understand what was happening to her. They all asked her questions, questions she couldn't seem to answer. What was wrong with her? She knew she must pull herself together. She was put into a cubicle and different staff kept coming in and going. Mary felt even more confused and lonely.

Eventually, a doctor who confirmed that she did have a nasty chest infection just as her own doctor had said saw Mary. They told Mary they would admit her and treat her with antibiotics. Jill spoke to the doctor,

"A lot of social problems with this lady, we may need to find her a place of safety."

Mary overheard Jill saying her house was messy and that she, Mary, had forgotten where she lived and the police had been involved.

"Poppycock," Mary said angrily, "My house is beautiful, and of course I know where I live."

Jill put her arm around Mary, Mary was not impressed, and whom did this woman think she was, intruding in her life and asking personal questions? Jill said she would be back to see her, well that was no consolation. Mary was eventually transferred to a ward and given tea and something to eat along with some medication. She felt better after the refreshment and she was so tired, soon after she fell asleep.

There were lots of people asking Mary questions over the next days. Mary was feeling physically much better, but half the time she was asked about things, which she knew nothing about. One man, who said he was a doctor, asked her what year it was, and, if she knew who the prime minister was? Mary answered reluctantly. It was a silly question, of course she knew the year and who the prime minister was. It was all so ridiculous; she had always liked Maggie Thatcher.

Mary wanted to know where Susan was and asked. He responded, "Who is Susan, Mary?" Mary sighed, what a waste of time this conversation was, as if he doesn't know that my daughter is called Susan.

Mary was taken for a scan; they were looking at her brain. Well, Mary knew for sure that there was certainly nothing wrong with her brain. It was a strange experience and the machine was noisy and quite frightening. She was worried and confused. Mary certainly couldn't understand why she had to have all these tests; she felt so much better, well enough to go home. Mary remaindered herself to ask when she could go home.

One day, Mary had a visitor, a man who she recognised by appearance, but not by name. "Mary, it's Bill, Bill your brother." And he sat by her bed.

"I don't want to see Bill," Mary said, "He would not help me when I needed him." And she closed her eyes and refused to speak to him. Bill left looking upset.

Bill spoke to the medical staff; the social worker Jill was present. The doctor explained to Bill that Mary was physically fit enough to be discharged, but that after extensive investigations, Mary had been diagnosed with vascular dementia.

Jill spoke to him, "Your sister really needs to be in care Mr Reynolds, she wasn't coping well at home. The house was filthy and she had no food to speak of. I realise that this is hard to take in, but you can view different homes, I'll give you a list. Have a look at the staffing levels, see what the residents are eating, look at how the staff interact with the people in their care, you'll know when you find the right place. We have also discovered that Mary has a solicitor, it may be worth speaking to him or her about her finances. She may have to pay for her care, she may even have to sell her home eventually." Jill explained how the finances were determined, and then said,

"Mary is not safe to look after herself anymore, she needs help 24 hours a day."

A nurse added, "Mary had quite a lot of bruising when she came to us, and we have noticed that she is prone to falling. She may well have had falls in the past."

Bill was upset, Mary didn't deserve this, she wasn't even very old, but he agreed to see the solicitor and look at homes.

"If Mary needs care, I am willing to pay, I've not seen Mary for years and I've let her down in the past. I can assure you all that I will help her in any way I can."

Bill wasted no time in looking at the various homes, a nursing home was specified, and it had to be a home where there were trained nurses. Many of the homes, Bill thought were terrible. The smell of urine when you walked through the door, residents looking dishevelled and uncared for, food that was unappetising and lacking in nutrition. He was beginning to despair and then, following a recommendation from a doctor friend of his, he visited a home and met Rita the manager.

This was a comfortable, clean home, it wasn't too far from Oak hill, but Bill was not sure if Mary was familiar with this area. Nevertheless, the staff were friendly and were kind to the residents, and from what he saw of the food; it looked good. The room he was shown was adequate, if slightly clinical, but this home was certainly the best he had seen. It had a homely feel about it. He told Rita he would be glad for Mary to come there and Rita said she would go and assess Mary in hospital. Bill said that there would be no problem with the fees.

Bill then contacted Mary's solicitor, who told him that Mary had been a very good businesswoman. Mary had appointed her solicitor as her enduring power of attorney, which meant that he could access and handle Mary's finances if she was no longer able to do so herself.

"Your sister has plenty of money, Mr Reynolds, there is no problem with the finances," he added, "Please gives my kindest regards to Mary when you next see her; she is a lovely lady." Bill assured him that he would.

Rita wasted no time in going to visit Mary and after looking at her medical notes; Rita went to speak to Mary and found her to be a very withdrawn lady who said little. When Mary did finally speak, she asked repeatedly when she could go home.

"I have a beautiful bungalow you know, and a lovely dress shop," she said to Rita.

Rita smiled and gently tried to explain that Mary needed some rest at a nursing home, and for the time being she would be more comfortable with people to look after her. Mary did not reply, just nodded reluctantly that she would go. "So you are happy to come to the home Mary, to stay." Rita wanted Mary to understand. Mary mumbled that she would come.

Mary did move into the home soon after all the arrangements had been made. She protested strongly and constantly asked, "Why can I not go home? I am a grown woman, I don't want all this fuss, and I want to go home."

She blamed Bill, he'd let her down again, but after she had been in the home for a while, there didn't seem much point in complaining, no one listened. They were kind enough, well most of them, but they didn't listen to her, not really. Mary was convinced that the world had gone mad, why would they not listen? She tried many times to leave but they always brought her back.

At first, Bill visited regularly, but the visits were always difficult. Mary made it clear that she didn't want to see him; he had not supported her when she needed him, and now he had put her in this place. Bill would leave the home, always upset. He knew he had let his sister down badly and he wondered if it was too late to repair the damaged relationship.

Over time, Mary became even more withdrawn and hardly spoke and appeared to resign herself to her situation, and she remained that way, until she met Patsy.

Chapter 44

It wasn't until Ed and Patsy were on their way to Paris that they had the chance to discuss just how perfect their wedding was. Then there was the amazing discovery. Quite by chance, Patsy had met and married Mary's grandchild, and to top that, they were now on their way to Paris, thanks to Mary and Bill. They were sitting on the plane, both going over everything that had happened in the last few days. It was almost too much to absorb.

"I knew there was something about that lady," Ed said, "I don't know why but I did feel a connection with Mary straight away. Why I couldn't see the resemblance, I don't know? I couldn't see how much my mum looked just like her."

"I know," Patsy said, "I saw the picture of your mum, and I didn't see it either. When you think about it though Ed, who could have possibly imagined that your mum would be Mary's missing daughter? By the way, did you know about the dress that Mary bought for me?"

Ed just nodded and laughed, "Can't argue with Mary."

The plane was landing, and they were soon on their way to their hotel, which turned out to be a five-star hotel in a central location. Patsy, who had very limited experience of hotels, certainly not five star, was concerned that the clothes she had brought away with were definitely not suitable for such a high-quality establishment.

"I have got the beautiful cocktail dress though thanks to Mary, it is definitely the nicest dress I've ever owned."

Ed laughed, "Yes, and you are beautiful my love. Don't worry about clothes Patsy, we'll be out sightseeing and enjoying our honeymoon, we don't need to be dressed up all the time, just relax and enjoy it all."

Patsy knew Ed was right, after all, the hotel was paid for and she looked respectable enough and she did have at least one good dress for evenings out.

"I can't believe Bill and Mary paid for all this," she said, "We were all set to stay in b&bs in Devon, which would have been lovely, but Paris, it's so exciting. We've certainly started married life in style Ed." And she hugged him tightly.

"OK, Mrs Clinton," Ed said, "Let's see Paris."

They spent their time seeing all the sites, walking along the Seine, and the busy streets of Paris. They loved the architecture, the pretty apartments and watching the Parisians collecting their bread daily from the many patisseries. When they were tired of walking, they would sit in one of the pavement cafes just talking to one another and people watching.

Honeymoon over, Patsy was back at work and Rita was asking to speak to her.

"Congratulations first Patsy," Rita said smiling. "Rosie told me all about the wedding, and goodness me, the shock of it all. Who could have thought that Mary would find her family in such circumstances? Tell me all about it, and how does Ed feel, must be quite a revelation?"

Patsy told Rita how they discovered that Ed's mother, Ginny was probably the lost Susan, and how delighted they all were.

"Ed said that he always felt a connection, I don't know why I didn't see the resemblance because they do have the same eyes. I just wasn't looking I suppose. I just hope it is confirmed but both Ed and I are convinced that Mary is Ginny's mother. I can tell you Rita, we were all stunned, and all this just after the wedding."

"We all talked to Mary about the wedding, reminding her when it was and on the day, she insisted on dressing up, and she has talked about it all day and every day since. She was like a new woman and she certainly didn't forget," Rita told Patsy and laughed.

Patsy said a quick hello to Mary, who she found chatting to George. Patsy kissed her on the cheek and said she would be back to see her when she had some time. "Better get to work Mary, but I'll see you later." Mary smiled,

"I want to hear all about the wedding and Paris," she said, and she carried on chatting with George.

Patsy was busy all day, and although she saw Mary, it wasn't until much later that she had a chance to sit with her and tell her all about Paris, the sights, the food, and the fashionable shops. She thanked Mary for giving them such a wonderful gift and she handed Mary a thank you present from Ed and her.

"It's nothing much," she said, "But I thought you might like a reminder from Paris."

Mary was delighted and she opened the gift-wrapped package. It was a Hermes scarf, which she said she really liked and would treasure. "This is a gift, I never expected, it' so lovely thank you my dear."

Mary and Patsy hugged one another, and Patsy could not wait to give her the news, but not yet.

Later that evening, Rosie came over to the new flat to see Patsy and Ed. She too, wanted to hear all about the honeymoon. Patsy cooked a meal and they sat in the cosy flat eating the food and drinking wine. Rosie raved about the flat, and how lovely they had made it.

After hearing all about the Paris trip, Rosie said her parents had really enjoyed the wedding too. "It was magical," she said, "and of course how fabulous to have found Mary's family right under your nose, what a lovely shock."

"My dad and Ruby can't get over it," Ed said taking a sip of wine. "They are all planning a visit up hear very soon, mainly so they can see Mary, so many years of catching up to do. Dad gets a progress report on Mary nearly every day, he knows my mum would want that."

Patsy wanted to know how the flat share with Jess was going. "Fine," Rosie said hesitantly, "I mean, she's not you, she's good fun. Very untidy though, hey we're getting used to each other slowly."

Patsy laughed, "I bet you two get up to all sorts, bet you don't get to bed until the early hours?"

"Too right," Rosie said laughing, "One thing Jess can do and that's party! I know now I can party a little and study a lot."

Ed asked them both if they had thought any more about applying for nursing courses. Rosie said that she would like to apply soon,

"We'll apply together Patsy and then with a lot of luck and hard work we shall qualify together. Anyway I need you to keep me on the straight and narrow."

Ed insisted on driving Rosie home, it was by that time very late and they all had to work in the morning. "Our first visitor in our new home," Patsy said to Ed when he came home, it was a good feeling.

A couple of days later, Bill telephoned with the news that the investigators had confirmed that Mary was indeed Ginny's mother.

"There is no doubt that Ginny and Susan are the same person. The agency have all the documentation from the adoption through to the marriage to Richard Clinton."

Chapter 45

Rita quickly organised a meeting with Dry Morris. Bill, Patsy and Ed were present, as were Rita, Rebecca and Dr Morris. The big question on everyone's' mind was if and how to tell Mary. How would Mary react to the news that 'Susan' had died and would the news affect her health?

A lengthy discussion where everyone gave his or her opinion began. Patsy explained how much it mattered to Mary to find her daughter.

"I believe Mary needs some closure after all these years, and the loss of Susan has affected her cognitive impairment, I know this because she constantly asks about Susan and becomes distressed. The fact that she knows we are all doing our best to find Susan has given Mary hope and that has helped her health to improve. That is my opinion."

Patsy thought back to her days in the supermarket. She would never have had the confidence to voice her opinion. Her knowledge had given her an educated voice, and hopefully her view would help Mary.

Bill agreed with Patsy, "I do think that living here and everything the staff have done, taking Mary out, encouraging her to socialise and of course her very special relationship with Patsy who I can't thank enough. All this has certainly helped Mary. Underlining all this hard work, the fact that we are trying to find Susan has been a driving force for Mary's improved health, in every way. She didn't speak; she had no idea who I was or anyone else for that matter. She didn't know where she was and now, she has some control again over her life. Since Mary learned that we were actively looking for her daughter, she now has a goal, something in her life to look forward to."

Ed assured everyone that Mary would have a loving family in her life,

"After all Ruby and I now have a grandmother and I know my wife and, in particular my mother would not be happy if anybody in the family thought otherwise. I think Mary must be told about my mum, and what happened to her.

We can fill in so many of the gaps and we have hundreds of photographs and memories we can share."

Dr Morris listened intently to everyone and then eventually she spoke, "I commend the work this home has done for every resident. In Mary's case she has improved beyond all expectation, largely due to the dedicated staff and Bill's generous funds, but also, I believe the hope she has that her daughter will be found has given her something to enrich her life. Now, Susan has been found, and unfortunately Mary cannot meet her daughter. But, she can meet Susan's husband, her grandchildren and her great grandchild. You all seem to think that Mary should be told the truth about her daughter's life, and her death and I agree. I think Mary is a strong lady who has coped with many difficult life experiences. I have no reason to doubt that Mary has certainly inherited a new loving family, and Patsy and Ed already have a close relationship with Mary. I think that Mary will cope with the news and her life with her family around her will enrich her life. I also think that Patsy and Bill should be the ones to tell her."

Bill and Patsy took time to gather their thoughts and then, tentatively they made their way to Mary's room, where staff had taken her so they could talk privately. Mary was in good spirits, pleased to have their company. Rosie followed them into Mary's room with a tray of tea and biscuits. Mary insisted Bill see her new scarf, she hadn't forgotten the gift from Patsy and Ed. Mary also insisted that Patsy should tell her and Bill all about the wedding and the Paris honeymoon.

They all sat drinking tea, Patsy felt sick with nerves. She needed to tell Mary the news, but she knew this couldn't be rushed. So she cheerfully told Bill everything about the wedding, how thrilled and surprised she and Ed were at the lavish gift to Paris they were given by Mary and Bill. She told them all about the hotel, the sites, the people they met and the cocktail dress which she wore with pride on many occasions. Mary beamed throughout, and Bill nodded and smiled appropriately although he too wanted to get to the main event.

Patsy took a deep breath and looked at Bill. He took hold of Mary's hand,

"Mary, Patsy and I have some news, news about Susan."

Mary looked shocked, "Have you found her, found my Susan? Tell me please."

Bill was searching for the words, Patsy could see that so she stepped in. "Mary," she said gently, "The agency did finally track down Susan. Sadly, Susan was in a road traffic accident a couple of years ago. She was driving her car and there was a terrible accident and Susan was killed instantly. Susan died Mary, but we know that she couldn't have suffered, she died quickly."

There was a long pause while Mary processed this shocking information.

Then Mary started crying uncontrollably, "I'll never see her, I'll never get the chance to explain why I gave her away. I'll never know if she had a happy life. Oh Susan, my Susan."

Bill wiped the tears from Mary's eyes. "Mary, we know Susan did have a happy life. She married a wonderful man called Richard and they lived in Devon. Susan was an art teacher; she obviously inherited that talent from you. Susan had a daughter from a previous marriage she called Ruby, and she and Richard had a son they called Ed."

Bill paused for a second and Mary, who had been listening carefully suddenly said quietly, "Ed Yes, I know Ed, that lovely young man who comes to see me."

Patsy spoke, "Yes, Mary, Ed who I married in Devon. Ed who we now know is Susan's son, your grandson, and Ruby; Ed's sister is your granddaughter. Mary, you have a family and we are all so pleased you have all found each other."

Mary looked at them both. She was totally confused, so Patsy and Bill told Mary the whole story several times until at last Mary understood, and when she did, Mary stopped crying. She looked hopeful and said, "So I lost Susan, but you have found her family, how wonderful is that? This is a bad day and a good day. I have grandchildren, and my grandson is married to you, my dear kind friend? Is that correct?" Mary was smiling at Patsy as she spoke.

Patsy smiled back, "Yes, Mary, we are now officially related and I for one couldn't be happier." The three hugged one another, and much later after more discussion and Mary was finally in bed asleep. Patsy and Bill left the room.

The next day, Ed visited Mary. She was in the lounge with George when he arrived, but Mary's face lit up when she saw him. The staff at the home had been reminding Mary all day that she now had a family and when Ed approached, Mary told George,

"My Grandson is here, I shall be back in a short while."

Ed put his arms around Mary. "When I met you Mary, for some reason I felt an instant connection, and now I know why. I have brought photos, lots of photos of mum for you to see," and he helped Mary to her room.

Ed and Mary went through all the photos, and at long last, Mary saw her daughter. Ed carefully explained where and when each photo was taken, and Mary was overjoyed at the happiness she could see with each photograph.

When they had looked at all the photographs, Ed said, "You have now met all the family Mary, well you have an idea what they look like. Soon, very soon you'll meet them in person."

They spoke at length about Ginny's accident and Mary could see how it had affected all the family. Mary refused to acknowledge that Susan was known as Ginny even though Ed kept reminding her in a good-natured way, but to no avail. In the end, he gave up and realised that understandably Ginny would always be Susan to Mary.

Chapter 46

The next few months passed quickly. Patsy and Rosie set about filling out applications to study for a nursing diploma. Ed and Patsy settled down to a busy married life, Patsy continuing with her dementia studies and Ed was applying for better jobs in journalism. Ed became a frequent visitor to the home to see Mary, and he and Patsy took her out whenever they could. Mary's relationship with Patsy was well established, but she was also becoming close to Ed. Looking at him now, Mary could see the resemblance to his mother from the photographs. She also thought he looked like her.

Patsy and Ed invited Mary to their home; after all she was family. Mary was delighted and she had many ideas about decor and soft furnishings, which she shared with them.

"They don't have to cost a lot," she said reassuringly. Mary would have loved to give them everything they needed but despite her illness, she knew it was wise to be cautious and not embarrass them. "Susan would have loved this," she said to them tearfully.

"She would indeed," Ed said, "But she would be happy that you were here to see us in our new home. Mary." He hesitated. "Mary would you be offended if I called you granny?" Ed looked sheepish and hoped he hadn't overstepped his position.

Mary paused, smiled and with tears in her eyes she answered that she would love it if he called her granny, "It's a title that I never thought I would be honoured to have."

"Why not write a piece on Mary's story Ed, you don't have to use real names?" Patsy said to him one evening when they were sitting in the flat having a quiet evening. "You never know, it might help people understand dementia better and it is a human story with a happy ending." Ed thought about it, nodded and agreed, "I may just do that."

While Patsy was at work the next day, she received a telephone call from Annie saying that she was sorry but she had no contact details for Rosalyn or Ada. She sounded genuinely upset that she couldn't be more helpful.

"I've looked and looked, I'm sure I had them, but I have moved about a bit. Have you got access to Mary's bungalow? Mary was always so organised, so my bet is that she has all the contact details of her friends somewhere."

"Thanks, Annie, yes I think Bill has the key."

Patsy told Annie the news about finding out that Susan was Ed's mother. Annie was amazed, "I can't believe that, who would ever have thought? But I'm so happy for Mary. She hasn't had an easy life. Oh, very successful with her business but such a lot of heartache and now this terrible illness. Hopefully, now she can enjoy the rest of her life."

Patsy thanked Annie and immediately rang Bill, who said straight away that he would have a look. "Do you think Mary might remember? She is much more alert these days?" he asked and Patsy said that she would ask, which she did.

"Oh yes dear, they are my dear friends," Mary replied, "Of course I know where they are dear, I'm not stupid even though everyone seems to think I am. Their details are in my address book, top drawer of my bureau in the lounge. They all moved away you know. It was a sad time in my life. I should so love to see them again." Mary laughed, "The things we did, we shared many good and bad times, but we did laugh."

"Would you like Bill to get that address book, Mary?" Patsy asked. "We could try and contact your friends and let them know where you are, I'm sure they are worried, not knowing."

Mary thought for a minute, "That would be nice dear, I should so like to see them but I don't want them to worry about me."

Patsy patted Mary's hand. "My guess is that they'll worry a lot less if they know you are well and living here, being looked after," and Mary nodded and smiled.

A couple of days later, Rita told Patsy that Bill was in her office, he had found the address book, just where Mary had said it was. The three of them looked through Mary's neat entries and Patsy didn't recognise any of the names until she saw the name, Rosalyn.

"I know one of Mary's closest friends was Rosalyn. There's a phone number here, with a foreign code. Shall we give her a ring?"

Bill thought that Patsy should phone her and said so, "You ring her, Patsy you know Mary best and you can explain Mary's situation better than I can."

The code for Spain was included with the phone number and Patsy nervously picked up the phone and dialled Rosalyn's number. Almost immediately a woman answered and Patsy asked her if she was Rosalyn.

"Yes, I'm Rosalyn, who is this?" the woman replied sounding a little perplexed.

"Hello, Rosalyn, I am sorry to disturb you but my name is Patsy and I am a carer in a nursing home in Manchester. I look after Mary, Mary Reynolds. Mary hasn't been well for some time and she wanted me to contact you, also she wanted to tell you not to worry. Mary has been very ill but now she is much better." Patsy hoped that she had been sensitive, but she was reassured to see that Rita and Bill were nodding approvingly.

There was a pause and Rosalyn sighed and said that she had been very worried about Mary.

"Oh thank you for contacting me. I rang and rang her, then I wrote, but she never replied to my letters. I've been frantic with worry, is she really all right, I knew she wasn't well, but she kept saying she was fine?"

Patsy thought Rosalyn deserved an explanation, after all Rosalyn was a close friend of Mary's.

"Mary has dementia, she forgets things and she couldn't cope on her own living in her home. She has been here a while now, but she keeps us all on our toes these days with her trips out, and she loves to buy clothes, she still has an amazing eye for fashion. She would love to see you if that was possible?"

Patsy liked the sound of this woman, even though she hadn't met her, it was obvious that she was very fond of Mary.

"I'll have to speak to John, my husband first Patsy. He's not been well either, heart problems, but he's much better now too. I was so worried about John; I couldn't have come back to England to find Mary. But, you try and stop me now. If I can leave John. I'll ring you when I've made the arrangements. Oh, and I'll give Ada a ring too, she's been out of the country but she will be back soon. Thank you Patsy, thank you so much, I can't wait to see Mary." Before the call ended, Patsy heard Rosalyn call out, "John, wonderful news, we've found Mary."

The telephone in Rita's office had been on loudspeaker so Rita and Bill had been able to hear the conversation.

"Patsy, wait until it is definite before you tell Mary, you never know what might happen," Rita said wisely, and added, "Rosalyn did sound happy and very positive about coming here though."

After Rosalyn put the phone down, she spoke at length with her husband John about visiting Mary in England. True, John had developed heart problems shortly after they were married, angina attacks the doctors had said. Along with the medication, there were lifestyle changes including a healthier diet, gentle exercise and less alcohol. As a police detective it had been common practice for John to regularly join his colleagues in the local pub, and John did like his beer and whiskey.

John's illness had come as quite a shock to both Rosalyn and John. They had been blissfully happy and enjoying their retirement in the sun, indeed Rosalyn had never been happier, and she often quietly thanked Mary for introducing her to Spain.

As they sat and discussed Mary's situation, Rosalyn desperately wanted to see Mary, however she was worried about leaving John on his own.

"You go, Ros, and see your friend, I shall be fine. I'm much better now thanks to you keeping tabs on me and it's not as though you'll be gone for a long time." John reassured his wife.

Rosalyn still wasn't sure; she was torn between going to see Mary and staying with John.

"I'll go to Manchester for one week," she finally said to John. "I'll phone every day, but if you need me at home you must promise to tell me John. I am worried about leaving you."

John went off to make a call and when he returned Rosalyn was sitting on their balcony, deep in thought, still worried about leaving her husband. John took a seat opposite her; he was smiling broadly,

"I've spoken to Emma, and she is flying out on Saturday to stay with me. I've not seen her for ages and when I explained the situation with Mary, she offered to come straight away." Emma was John's daughter and they hadn't seen her since John was in hospital.

Rosalyn was delighted, "Oh John, that's marvellous and it will be good to see Emma. I can fly to Manchester Sunday or Monday." And so it was settled.

Chapter 47

Rosalyn arrived at the home the following week and introduced herself to Patsy, who gave Rosalyn a detailed history of how Mary came to be living there. Rosalyn was visibly upset,

"Mary was always so strong, so capable, and it breaks my heart to think of her living in a home. She never would have wanted that."

"Come and see her Rosalyn. I agree it is far from ideal but Mary could not care for herself any longer, and you may be surprised at just how content she is these days. Don't worry if she forgets things, that is her illness, but just talk normally, try to talk about the things you did together as friends, places, people, it all helps Mary to remember."

Patsy walked with Rosalyn to Mary's room, knocked on the door and walked in with Rosalyn. Mary was dozing in her chair; a fashion magazine was delicately balanced on her knee. "Mary," Patsy said gently, "Mary, you have a visitor."

Mary opened her eyes and looked at Rosalyn and beamed at her visitor. "My dear friend," she said and Rosalyn bent down and hugged Mary.

"Oh Mary, how lovely to see you, I've been so worried about you, I didn't know where you had disappeared to."

Rosalyn sat down and Patsy went off to get them some tea. By the time she came back with a tea tray, the two friends were in fits of laughter.

"We're talking about Eric," Rosalyn said.

Mary giggled. "Oh yes, we got him in the end," Mary said. "Shall we tell Patsy about Eric, Mary and about going to Spain?"

Patsy knew a little about Eric, but to hear the story from Rosalyn and Mary, who were very serious one minute and giggling like naughty schoolgirls the next was wonderful.

Patsy would interrupt every now and again with, "No, you didn't?" And, "Mary, you were so brave."

After only a short time Patsy had to leave, she had work to do so she had to reluctantly leave them both, still chatting away.

"I'm dying to hear more from you two ladies," she said as she left.

Much later, Patsy was getting ready to go home; thankfully the shift had been relatively quiet. Patsy noted that Rosalyn had been talking to Mary for quite some time and there were sounds of giggling still coming from Mary's room.

Just as Patsy was about to leave, Rosalyn came out of the room and went to speak to Patsy.

"Sorry, are you leaving?" she asked, but Patsy assured her that she had time for a chat. Rosalyn smiled and said how glad she was that she had seen Mary.

"Mary is so much better than I expected, I mean she couldn't remember certain things more recent events like how she came to live here but we talked and talked about all our jaunts together and she was reminding me of things that happened. Oh, and she was telling me she had found her Susan. What does she mean?"

Patsy explained about her marriage to Ed and how they had discovered that Mary was actually Ed's grandmother. Ed's mother, Susan was killed in an accident a few years ago. Rosalyn was amazed,

"I never really knew about Susan," she said. "Come to think of it though, she did mention a Susan now and again, I never paid much attention, it was all so vague. What an amazing story. Mary looks much better than when I last saw her too. She had lost weight, and she wasn't her usual smart self. I'll stay a while longer if that's OK and I'll visit every day, although I'm only here for a week."

Patsy said that Rosalyn could visit any time and she could stay and have a meal with Mary, it was no problem, and with that, Patsy said her goodbyes and went home.

Ed was already at home when Patsy walked into the flat. He was busy putting a simple meal of cold meats and salad together, frantically trying to make the food look attractive. As they ate their meal with a glass of wine, Mary told him all about Rosalyn's visit.

"The two of them were laughing like two teenagers," she told Ed.

Ed was delighted and said it was looking good for Mary, "Family and friends, how cool is that?"

Ed went on to say that he had ran into an old colleague who had told him the local television channel were looking for bright young reporters and advised him to apply. "Probably don't stand a chance, I mean they'll be looking for people with far more experience than I've got." Patsy put down her knife and fork and clasped Ed's hands in hers,

"Of course you must apply Ed, you'll never know if you don't try and I for one have every faith in my clever husband. Come on, when we've finished our dinner, I'll sort the dishes and you put your application in." And that's exactly what he did.

The next few days saw Rosalyn almost a permanent fixture at the home. She took Mary out for long walks and lunches. They looked for Mary's favourite dress shop but Mary couldn't quite remember where it was, it didn't matter though, they had a good time anyway.

Two days before Rosalyn was due to leave, Rosalyn told Patsy that Ada would visit the next day. It was a surprise for Mary. Rosalyn and Ada had booked lunch at a restaurant for the three of them and Bill was invited too.

"I can't believe Mary has such a lovely brother, but apparently they lost touch years ago. Bill said he would explain everything at lunch if, that is of course if Mary is agreeable. Did you know about that?" Patsy smiled.

"It's quite a story Rosalyn, the story of Susan and I think Mary will want you to hear it now."

Patsy was on a late shift the day of the lunch, but she came in early to help Mary get dressed up and style her hair. Mary was beaming.

"I always like going out for lunch," she said, "So civilised, and something I couldn't do when I worked."

Patsy smiled; she had heard Mary say that many times.

Rosalyn arrived arm in arm with another lady who she introduced to Patsy as Ada. Ada greeted Patsy warmly,

"Rosalyn has told me all about you and all the other staff and how good you are to Mary."

Patsy smiled, but she felt slightly embarrassed, after all this was her job, no it was so much more than a job, it was a joy to look after Mary, and she told them so.

"I can't tell you how much it means to me that we are family now. Believe me when I tell you Mary has done more for me than I have for her, she helped me change my life."

Rosalyn and Ada smiled because Mary had helped them too.

Rosalyn and Ada burst into Mary's room with shouts of "Surprise!" and soon the giggling started once again. Bill arrived shortly afterwards and the friends went out for their lunch. When they returned home, Bill told Patsy that he'd never laughed so much,

"Those three," he said, "They never stopped talking, and honestly the stories, and Rosalyn and Ada don't appear to see anything wrong with Mary. In fact, they think she is so much better. Come to think of it, she didn't seem ill at all today."

Patsy was delighted. "Did Mary agree to tell them about Susan?" she asked tentatively. Bill smiled,

"Oh yes, she did. Mary told them everything about the wedding, and the big news about finding her family. Believe me she didn't need much prompting. She didn't miss anything out. In fact, you would have thought that she was actually at the wedding of her grandson and his wife. Ada and Rosalyn were genuinely delighted for her."

Patsy thought it might be upsetting for Mary when her friends finally said their goodbyes. Ada was moving permanently back to the area and promised to visit often. Rosalyn said she would definitely be back too and that she would try and arrange her visit to coincide with Annie visiting.

Mary was surprisingly not upset. She told Patsy that it was wonderful to see her friends again, and then she asked to be taken into the lounge to see George. "He'll be missing me," she said.

"Aren't you tired Mary?" Patsy asked.

"Tired dear, not at all, I've had a wonderful time and I told them all about Susan, and your wedding, and my lovely grandchildren." Mary was still talking as Patsy wheeled her into the lounge. Mary chatted to George, telling him the news.

"Don't think badly of me George but I had a baby when I was very young, and I wasn't married."

George patted her hand,

"I could never feel badly about you 'luv'; these things happen so don't upset yourself."

Rosalyn went back to Spain feeling much better now that she had seen Mary. She realised that at some point, Mary may forget who she was, but there again she had been dreading the visit in many ways. She had been worried that Mary might not recognise her and she was worried Mary was not looked after properly. Rosalyn, like others had read about the terrible care in so many of these places. It was such a relief to know that Mary was so well, and after spending most of the week in the home with Mary, she was gratified to see the care and the kindness the staff showed to all the residents. Rosalyn had sat and talked to them all, this wasn't a depressing place, it was warm, clean and comfortable and there was always laughter.

She sat on the flight thinking about all the years she had known Mary and never a word about her long-lost daughter, Susan. Then to be reunited with her family, quite by chance, it was extraordinary but such good news. Rosalyn was looking forward to going home to see John, but she was determined that she would certainly be back to see her friend.

Rosalyn had spoken to Ada about writing an account of their friendship with Mary. Patsy had told Rosalyn how much it would help Mary to write about memories, which at some point may be lost to Mary. The two friends said they would collaborate to write down everything they could remember.

Chapter 48

Soon after, Richard came to Manchester to meet Mary. He had heard so much about this lady who Patsy helped care for. He could never have imagined that that this same lady was actually Ginny's natural mother. He thought back to the many conversations he and Ginny had about how much she would like to meet the woman who gave birth to her and he was furious with himself for not trying to find her, but life had got in the way and it never seemed to be a priority. Richard thought that he would have Ginny for many more years and one day they would start looking.

Richard arrived at Ed and Patsy's flat in the late afternoon. He was pleasantly surprised at how spacious and tasteful the flat was, and he was also pleased that it wasn't raining that day. Manchester was well known for the rain. Ed and Patsy were so excited. Firstly because he could see their home, but also he would finally meet his mother in law. They had arranged for Ed to pick Mary up from the home, and all meet in a restaurant that was within walking distance of the flat.

Ed explained to his dad, "Mary knows that we are taking her out for dinner, but she doesn't know that you are coming."

Not long afterwards, Patsy and Richard were waiting in the restaurant, when Ed came in with Mary. Richard stood and went over to help Mary into a chair. Mary looked bemused until Ed said, "Mary, meet your son in law, my dad, Richard Clinton. He couldn't wait to finally meet you and he's travelled from Devon today."

Mary was delighted; she took hold of Richard's hand. "Susan's husband, how wonderful. I'm told my Susan had a very happy life, thanks to you."

After that, it was as if Mary and Richard had known each other for years. The main topic of conversation was of course Susan/ Ginny. Every time Richard said something about Ginny, Mary would correct him. "You mean Susan dear," she would say.

Richard reminisced about how he met his wife, her talent for art, how loving and kind she was and Mary listened with pride. When they finally left the restaurant, Mary and Richard had the beginnings of becoming firm friends.

Richard spent a week in Manchester, visiting Mary every day and taking her out for walks several times. Despite his unfamiliarity with wheelchairs, he soon became an expert. With a promise of returning soon with the rest of the family, he returned home to Devon with a light heart.

It was Mary's birthday and Mary's family had arranged a trip for all the family so that they could finally all get together. Ed and Patsy found a quiet luxury hotel in the country, which was not too far for Mary to travel. Patsy asked Mary if she was happy to go. Mary smiled broadly,

"Try and stop me. That's wonderful dear; I can't wait to see everyone. When are we going?"

Patsy told her they had planned the following weekend. She smiled to herself because she instinctively knew that Mary would need a shopping trip before the following weekend, and sure enough Mary said,

"I'll definitely need a new outfit. I need to look my best. Can you take me to 'our' shop?" Patsy wanted to laugh out loud, but instead she cheekily suggested Mary wear the outfit she had bought for the wedding day, she already knew the answer.

"Oh no dear," Mary answered very seriously, "That was a wedding outfit, not suitable for a weekend away."

Mary and Patsy were back at the shop, now greeted warmly by Fiona. Several outfits later, they left with the purchases which were much more suitable according to Mary, and of course they called in for tea and cake at their usual place. Patsy and Ed arrived at the home to pick up Mary.

"She's not slept at all and insisted on getting ready this morning at 6am," the night staff told Patsy, and indeed, Mary was sat in her chair waiting with her bags packed and her coat on.

In the car, Mary suddenly said, "I do hope they like me" to which Ed replied,

"Gran, they won't like you, they will love you." Mary was pleased, if still a little apprehensive.

Waiting in the hotel reception were Richard, Ruby, Pete and little Belle. Bill was there as well with both his sons and their wives. Also present were friends, Ada Annie, Rosalyn, and John, all there for Mary. Ruby was the first to run over to Mary and hug her.

"I can't believe they have found you Mary. I feel like I have a part of my mum back now I have a grandmother. I've always wanted a grandmother."

Then, looking sheepish, she apologised for hugging Mary so tightly.

Mary tearfully hugged her back and replied that she had always wanted a granddaughter and the hug was welcome. There was no need for apologies. When all, the introductions had been made and presents from everyone given for Mary's birthday they gathered for a celebration dinner with a cake.

The mood was relaxed and happy. Patsy had booked adjoining rooms, one for Mary and the other for Patsy and Ed, so that Patsy could look after Mary. When they had unpacked, Mary couldn't wait to get back with everyone, and what followed was a wonderful weekend with much talk of Susan, Mary's shop, the escapades with Eric and many other things. Mary had a chance to catch up with her friends too. They went for long walks, taking turns to push Mary in her wheelchair and having coffee and cake at the hotel.

Mary's family had brought many photographs and some of Ginny's artwork. Mary was so proud, every photograph and painting had a story behind it and Mary felt she was at last getting to know her daughter. Richard said Mary could take the artwork if she wanted to. Mary wanted it all, but after a discussion with Patsy, she chose four paintings and she planned with Patsy where in her room it could be displayed.

As Patsy settled Mary into bed very late on their last night, Patsy asked Mary, "Are you happy, Mary?"

Mary didn't answer straight away and Patsy was beginning to think that she shouldn't have asked. Mary had found her family, which was amazing, but, she was an ill lady and the reunion could be stressful. She apologised to Mary for asking the question, but Mary did eventually answer,

"My dear friend. I have had a full and happy life, despite all the bad; there have been many happy times. The last thing I wanted was to have to move into a nursing home. When I went into that home, I was treated well, but they all saw me as just an old woman with dementia. I used to scream inside myself, wanting someone to see me as a person. You saw me dear, you didn't see a sick old woman, you saw Mary Reynolds, and you gave me hope, and a good life again. Look at me now. Thanks to you, I have a beautiful family and my friends. So the answer dear is, Yes, I am happy, but I'm tired now dear. I shall see you in the morning and thank you for helping me to get my life back."

Patsy went over and gave Mary a kiss on her cheek. "Night, Mary, see you in the morning."

That weekend was the first of many happy gatherings for Mary.

Patsy lay in bed and reflected on how her life had turned around. Yes, it was the lady in the supermarket who had started her thinking, but it had become so much more than that. The support she had had from Rita, Rosie, Rebecca and Sonia, they had all encouraged her, told her she could succeed. What would she have done without them? Oh, and of course Ed, her Ed who never doubted her and always told her that and how proud he was of her.

Mostly though, these older people who all had a story to tell had inspired Patsy. All she had to do was listen and know that behind the illness of dementia. Behind the confusion and the aggression, all they wanted was for someone to hear them and treat them as normal people. There would always be periods of forgetfulness; that was the illness. But, with the right care, Patsy also knew she had to try and change peoples' perception of what dementia is.

There was still a long road ahead on that one. It is a frightening disease and Patsy still heard fellow professionals talk about, 'senility', and senile dementia. That had to change, and Patsy would play her part in helping people to understand. She tried to remember what it was about Mary that had influenced her need to study. She somehow knew Mary was troubled by an unresolved episode in her life, Patsy could relate to that.

She knew with her new found knowledge knew she had to help Mary come to terms with what happened to her. What a wonderful thing to learn about something, which could help other people, she thought. Of course the outcome of dementia was always death, but that didn't mean that people couldn't have a good quality of life, sometimes for some years.

Patsy regained some form of relationship with her mother; she owed her that and included her in family gatherings as much as she could. Funnily enough, Ed's family didn't seem to object to Brenda's drinking and her many men friends. They just accepted her and Brenda eventually actually enjoyed meeting up with them all.

Mary, well Mary lived another five years after she had found her family, and those five years were the happiest of her life. She died peacefully at the nursing home surrounded by her friends and her beloved family, and Mary would always be remembered and talked about fondly at every family gathering.